A *New York Times* Notable Book of the Year

"*One of Us* is a delicious novel, full of understated eroticism and intellect and able to make you feel a vicarious nostalgia for a world that has been swept away."
— *New York Times*

"David Freeman's composed and engaging new novel... does not shy away from using sex as a metaphor for the imperialist structure in Egypt.... With both a rich descriptive power and an appealing reticence appropriate to the luxurious monarch and British aristocrats under scrutiny... he has splendidly re-created a fading colonial world and cleverly exposed the passions and foibles of its wealthiest and most powerful residents."
— *New York Times Book Review*

"Sometimes is takes a novelist to make things real. It doesn't matter whether the young Farouk of *One of Us* ever existed. In Freeman's hands he becomes not just a king but a country, and as such he earns our sympathy in ways the bloated exile never could."
— *Washington Post Book World*

"*One of Us* is a sly meditation on the contradictions and ironies of British colonialism. It is also a delicious comedy of sexual complications... at its best it's almost as if George Orwell's early essays on the infamies of imperialism had been rewritten by Noel Coward."
— *Cleveland Plain Dealer*

"David Freeman vividly captures the dying colonial world of pre-war Egypt when Cairo and Alexandria were the great glamour cities of the age. This is the best novel about that time and place since *The Alexandria Quartet*."
— **Beryl Bainbridge,** author of *Master Georgie*

"*One of Us* is an entrancing historical novel."
— *Orlando Sentinel*

"A grand romance like Lawrence Durrell's *Alexandria Quartet* or Olivia Manning's *Levant Trilogy, One of Us* resurrects
— *Chicago Tribune*

D0068258

"Mysterious, enticing and pulsing with life, *One of Us*... is compelling and thought-provoking historical fiction."
— *Denver Post*

"*One of Us* is a fascinating book."
— *Los Angeles Times*

"Radiant, luxuriant and written with astonishing verve, David Freeman's *One of Us* is a masterful tale of an Englishman's induction into pre-war Egypt, capturing the murky world of Alexandria, the gaudy palaces of Egyptian monarchs, the petty grand schemes of a colonial world whose every facet is caught with the splendor of T. E. Lawrence and the magic of Lawrence Durrell."
— **André Aciman, author of *Out of Egypt***

"*One of Us* is a smoothly written and evocative view of a world that no longer exists, pre-war Cairo, a place of privilege, opulence, deceit and an astonishing level of sensuality."
— *Houston Chronicle*

"*One of Us* is erotic, smoothly entertaining fiction, and a great deal of fun."
— *Detroit Free Press*

"This is handsomely crafted fiction. A stylish, startlingly inventive evocation of a pre-Nasser Egypt, with a stunning cast, all of whom are, in different ways, ultimately trapped by their appetites or willfulness. A classy, exciting entertainment."
— *Kirkus Reviews* (*starred review)

"This vibrant novel, rooted in Egypt at the time of Farouk, wonderfully captures the intrigue and passion of that chaotic age. A tour de force."
— **A.E. Hotchner, author of *Papa Hemingway***

ONE OF US

ALSO BY DAVID FREEMAN

A Hollywood Education

A Hollywood Life

The Last Days of Alfred Hitchcock

U.S. Grant in the City

Jesse and the Bandit Queen (a play)

ONE OF US

David Freeman

Carroll & Graf Publishers, Inc.
New York

First Carroll & Graf edition 1997
First Trade paperback edition 1998

Carroll & Graf Publishers, Inc.
19 West 21st St.
New York, NY 10010-6805

Library of Congress Cataloging-in-Publication Data is available.

ISBN 0-7867-0591-4

Manufactured in the United States of America

FOR OTTO PLASCHKES

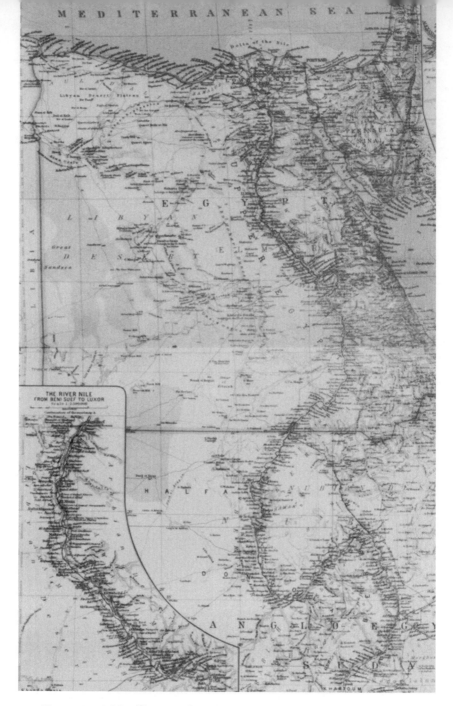

EGYPT, 1939, (ROYAL GEOGRAPHICAL SOCIETY, LONDON)

ONE OF US

MR JAMES PEEL:
Two Cities

My indulgence is memory. It's my pleasure to recall a time and a place that an ever-dwindling number know first hand. I speak of the thirties. As Auden put it, 'A low dishonest decade' though not without its inspiration. I was in Egypt where later we almost lost the war in North Africa. In Cairo, café society flourished and for a time, so did I. It is difficult for people who did not experience the war to understand that we believed, and with reason, that we would either win or perish. In the present age of exaggeration, it is futile to explain that this was not hyperbole. My patron, Sir Malcolm Cheyne, the last High Commissioner of Egypt and the Sudan, has been gone thirty years. The Commission, which was the Crown itself, is some sixty years in the past, but it was my time and one gets no other. It's clearer to me now than when the events occurred. That vivid quality of distant memory is what it means for age to look back upon youth.

I was one year out of university, back at Winchester, my old school, teaching history to bright boys who made an effort but were engaged in a ceaseless battle with their natures. I had taken the post because I hadn't known what else to do with myself, which I'm afraid was my nature. The world economy was depressed. There was not much call for a young man who had recently read history, even one with a good degree. I was fortunate to receive the Winchester offer, which in practical terms was a sinecure. My late father taught mathematics there, and I had grown up in those precincts. I rejoined the school able to identify the portraits on the walls. As Winchester dates to the fourteenth century, this was quite an array of pictures. I knew where my rooms would be before I got there and where they would likely be ten years hence. Though my family's association only dated to three generations, it was enough for me to already understand the subtleties of the Notions, the Wykehamist lexicon of hierarchy, language, and lore. New boys had to learn it, new masters hardly ever could. It was in my bones.

Like all public schools, Winchester is a kingdom of adolescence. Even the youngest master, a title for which I qualified, appears quite grown up. Still, I was more subject to serendipity than I yet knew. Soon risk, chance, and a letter from Sir Alun Reese-Jones, the Master of Trinity, my college at Cambridge, were to set my life on an adventurous course.

I was informed that the Egyptian desk of the Foreign Office required a tutor for Crown Prince Farouk. The request was for a man who might provide a measure of companionship for the Prince as well as instruction. Sir Malcolm, as High Commissioner, had made enquiries at Eton, his old school, and the request had worked its way down to me. Sir Alun had supported my decision to return to Winchester. He certainly knew the school would not be pleased at my leaving so soon. That he nonetheless proceeded was a measure of how seriously he took a request from the Foreign Office. A disruption at Winchester was not a consideration, not even for an old Wykehamist—Sir Alun had come down in '87 and was nearing retirement. He told me that as he got older, he found that the school often came back to him in dreams.

The offer to go out to Egypt made my heart leap. My feelings surprised me, shamed me really, but were undeniable. No matter what I thought I should want, no matter what I said I did want, the last thing I wanted was to know what rooms I'd be inhabiting ten years hence. I felt the excitement of impending liberation from my situation – and not for the first time. As a small boy, when my father was a master at Winchester, I developed the nasty habit of starting fires in ditches and fields. No potting shed was safe when I was in the vicinity. No doubt this was an early sign that I did not find life at the school satisfactory. I pinched wooden matches from my mother's pantry, and soon had the secret pleasure of watching blue flame stab the air. I got in all manner of trouble, certainly with my father, who despaired of my ever sorting myself out. I no longer recall how I chose which haystack or berm to lay waste, but I do know that it never occurred to me to run away. I wanted to enjoy my handiwork. I did not think of consequence, only of immediate and dramatic action. When I could feel the heat, I went light-headed and felt the few moments of satisfaction that I knew. By my troubled logic, I had discharged an obligation.

Now I thrilled to this remarkable opportunity for adventure and to help mould a king. I corresponded with Sir Malcolm, proposing that at the start I focus the lessons on large historical issues that might be of particular interest to the Prince. I would begin with the Classical period and move toward the Renaissance. We would undertake Thucydides and the Peloponnesian War, for a look at the Greeks. A little flashy, perhaps, but boys always like to hear about wars. For the Romans, Antony and the conquest of Alexandria, then perhaps on to Castiglione and *The Courtier* so the Prince might understand the political intricacies of court life in an earlier century.

I had a minor connexion to Sir Malcolm through my friendship with his niece, Miss Emma Lyttelton. A number of our friends in London assumed that Emma had played a rôle in securing my new position, but that was not so. It did not surprise Sir Malcolm that his niece and I were acquainted. Quite the opposite, it confirmed his judgement. Who better, I am sure he thought, than a friend of Emma's.

I packed my books, acquired what a functionary at the Foreign Office insisted I would require: a pith helmet, insect repellent, and Pears soap. Except for the helmet, those items proved useful, though none was in short supply in Egypt. I set out from Southampton on a four-day journey on the P&O line in a second-class cabin, bound for Alexandria by way of Gibraltar. I was to be tutor to Prince Farouk, heir apparent to the throne of Tutankhamen. He was fifteen years old. I was twenty-two.

I was young enough to assume that I would arrive in Egypt, wash my face and the Prince would be waiting for me to begin the lessons, but the Prince did not rush to his studies. I was ignored, though Sir Malcolm invited me to tea. I took the tram to Ramleh, out past the crumbling villas that belonged to European cotton brokers, to the summer Embassies. The whole of the diplomatic corps followed the King and as the summer Palace was in Ramleh, so was Sir Malcolm. There was a consulate in town, but it was a ramshackle place and Sir Malcolm was rarely there. The Embassy's chancery, the political department, was lodged at the consulate, which meant that Sir Malcolm's senior staff was always shuttling from town to Ramleh, a distance of about five kilometres. The villa became the de facto Embassy, though it seemed as much a holiday house as a working office. We were near the sea and the air had a salt tang which may have accounted for the villa's faded condition, a state I came to recognise as characteristic of Ramleh. The front walls were all but choked by red bougainvillaea which crept all round, as if it were slowly assaulting the building.

Malcolm Lyttelton Cheyne stood six-feet-six and weighed eighteen stone. His friend Noël Coward once remarked that when 'Malcolm Cheyne entered a room, heads turned, postures improved, and plans changed.' He was a mandarin of the Foreign Office, a man of Empire who believed it his duty to help Egypt find her way into the present century. He received me in the garden, sitting in a desert chair amidst silky, white frangipani that gave off a sweet intoxicating aroma which I found unsettling.

As we took our tea, he enquired about his niece, asked a question or two about Winchester, then got down to business. 'The Prince has had only Egyptian tutors. They have been less than rigorous.'

'I see. Will they resent my presence?'

'Your obligation is to your pupil. His former tutors may think what they like. What they have done to that boy is simply appalling.'

'I shall try to do better.'

'You could hardly do worse.'

At that time, Egypt was our protectorate, which meant the High Commissioner was the plenipotentiary of George V and carried independent authority. The legation was an English government within a foreign country. After King Fouad, Sir Malcolm was the most powerful man in Egypt. He had come out a year earlier, from China, where he had been Ambassador at Pekin. He was a widower with two daughters. His late wife was a Bouverie who was born and had grown up at Hysatt Hall in Oxfordshire. I felt a duty to Sir Malcolm, one that I hoped to discharge honourably.

I assumed that following my call on Sir Malcolm, I would be summoned to the Palace. That did not happen. The Prince was always occupied, and I was meant to stand by should he become available. I used the time to learn a bit about the royal family, certain it would prove useful in dealing with the Prince, should that come to pass.

His father, King Fouad, was at Montazeh Palace where he summered. No one who could manage it stayed in Cairo, which was stifling at that time of year. Montazeh was Fouad's pleasure palace. It looked out over the Mediterranean and was cooled by the zephyr winds. It appeared somewhat less than real – perhaps all palaces have a story-book quality. Montazeh was Italian neo-Baroque, though with its faded pink walls, minarets and high arched windows, it seemed a child's dream. I half expected to find Merlin or perhaps Morgan le Fay lurking within. It was the Egyptian King who was there with his cronies and his concubines, and lately with the Prince and the little Princesses, his four daughters. Queen Nazli was in Alexandria as well, but not because the King took any interest in her. The Dynasty had two important palaces there and the King saw to it that Nazli was in whichever one he was not. She and her ladies-in-waiting and her entourage of servants and dressmakers were at Ras-el-tin, fifteen kilometres away. Fouad ignored her.

A fortnight after I arrived, I was told I might observe Farouk and the King at falconry at Montazeh. I was escorted down to the water's edge, then told to stand near a sea-wall, far enough back, I suppose, that I wouldn't bother the King or the Prince. Still, I was close enough to hear much of what they said. Farouk was an appealing young man with a dark face that seemed open, even eager. I saw no cynicism there. Excepting his complexion, he might have been a fifth former at Winchester. The King, however, did not look well. Fouad was sixty-three, a thickset man with waxed moustaches and a gravel voice that sounded a bit like a dog barking. I was told his growl was the result of a gunshot wound to his throat many years ago. The bullet that had lodged in the royal gullet was from an irate husband who had not realised he was shooting at the future King of Egypt.

Fouad was middle-aged before he produced an heir, a failing in a monarch, though Farouk was born in the first year of Fouad's reign. No boy was more cosseted, no prince had more weight put upon him and his future. The Royals spoke to one another in English, the lingua franca of the Palace, though now and again they slipped into French or Italian. There were servants, called 'sufragis', and the royal bodyguard in blue and gold uniforms, as if from the chorus of an operetta, though it is likely that the operetta style derives from the Egyptian Guard and not the other way round.

The party included Rafik, the royal falconer, a small

fine-boned man whose sun-weathered face was a filigree of delicate lines. It was said of him that he could speak the language of the fierce black bird that is the ancient symbol of Egypt. The falcon soared and swooped until Rafik looked up, directing the bird with his eyes, or perhaps his mind, willing the falcon from the sky. As it homed in, expecting to perch on its master's arm, Rafik slipped a gauntlet on the Prince and said, 'Brace yourself, sir. Steady your arm.' Farouk was game, but I could see that as the bird streaked toward him, he was frightened. The King said, 'Never show fear.' When the falcon was barefaced on the Prince's wrist, Rafik covered it with a leather hood. Farouk nodded, his fright gone, accepting success without question. It was a royal response and it gave me a glimpse into the Prince's essential nature. For Farouk, falcons and much else are put on this earth for his pleasure.

I believe that my invitation to observe the falconry had been a test of sorts. I don't know what their concern was, perhaps that I would run up to the Prince and begin shouting lessons at him. Whatever it was, I seemed to have passed muster, because I was soon told to appear at the Palace.

I wore my Trinity necktie for luck and presented myself at the gate, then waited while a peculiarly Egyptian ballet of messages and permissions was enacted. Though telephones were certainly available to the guard, runners were sent back and forth to the Palace to check my bona fides.

While I was detained, I was treated not quite as a prisoner but certainly as a man under suspicion. The guards were particularly interested in my teaching supplies. I had brought books that I planned to use, as well as a jotter, a dictionary, and two propelling pencils. Perhaps the Palace was equipped in these areas and my supplies would be superfluous, but I did not wish to spend my first session chasing about for my tools. The guards looked upon my items as if they were the bombs of an anarchist.

I was shown to a small library and offered tea. After quite a wait, I was joined by Ali Neguib Mazhar Pasha, an adviser to the King, a sad-eyed man dressed as a banker. His title was First Chamberlain, though that didn't suggest the influence he was said to have. I knew Sir Malcolm often consulted him on matters concerning the royal family.

'Ah, Mr Peel,' he said. 'How good to see you here. Are you ready, then?' I must have appeared a trifle nervous, because he added, 'You mustn't be apprehensive. The Prince has been so looking forward to this.' He excused himself and went off to collect Farouk.

Mazhar Pasha was a Balliol man. His accent was closer to my own than to that of his countrymen. I believe he recognised my necktie, though he did not comment on it. He returned, preceded by the Prince. 'Your Highness,' Mazhar Pasha said, 'May I present Mr James Peel who has come from England to assist you in academic matters.'

'Did you have a pleasant journey, Mr Peel?' the Prince asked, quite amiably.

'I did, sir. Thank you.' I didn't mention that it had been concluded some three weeks earlier. Farouk looked more self-assured than at falconry. Perhaps the absence of his father gave him strength. When Mazhar Pasha took his leave, I plunged in and asked the Prince to tell me what his studies had been thus far.

'It is for you to say.'

'I thought we might take up history and political theory.'

'Yes, yes. Quite so.'

'As we are here in Alexandria, it might be of interest to begin with the Classical period.'

He assumed a look of great seriousness that all teachers know masks a profound indifference. A more experienced man might have found a prompt way out of that morass, but I was still uncertain of myself. 'Do you know, sir, that the Palace across the harbour at Ras-el-tin is where Menelaus, brother to Agamemnon and unhappy husband to Helen of Troy, came ashore some three thousand years ago.'

'Yes, yes,' he said. 'Ras-el-tin. It means Cape of Figs. The Queen is fond of it.'

Feeling encouraged, I added, 'To the Greeks, Menelaus was the first visitor to Egypt. It is an example of how limited the view of the ancients could be. To the Greeks, if they had not been there, then a place did not exist.'

'Marvellous, Mr Peel. Quite fascinating.'

Perhaps I had misread the Prince. He was listening, he was participating. I was optimistic as I launched my discussion of Thucydides, allowing my voice to rise and fall, hoping with my oratory to impart some of the excitement that other boys had felt. 'Though Herodotus was the predecessor, and a man much interested in Egypt, his *History* now seems more a retailing of myth than an accurate record of the past. Thucydides's account of the Peloponnesian War is the beginning of written history in the modern sense. As we consider Thucydides, we take our place in a chain of men who wish to know the past.'

'How marvellous,' he said. 'Most exciting.'

'I have brought an edition in the Crawley translation.'

'Thank you so much,' he said, accepting the book and opening it, eagerly.

'I would like for you to read aloud in the first section. Then we will discuss it.'

'I have a question for you. Tell me, Mr Peel, if you can, what is the difference between an Indian elephant and an African elephant?'

'I don't quite follow, sir.'

'About three thousand kilometres! A lovely lesson, Mr Peel. You're off to a splendid start.' Then he was up and out the door.

I stayed in the library for quite some time replaying in my mind what had happened. When Mazhar Pasha came to collect me, he seemed to think the tutorial had gone quite well.

'I thought it rather abruptly concluded,' I told him.

'Not at all, Mr Peel. The Prince has many demands on his time. He seemed quite pleased.' Mazhar Pasha could see that I was still confused, so he arranged for me to look in on another of the Prince's activities that he said 'might offer something in the way of clarification'.

Later that day, he took me to the Palace mosque, just before prayers. I stood in an arch that led to where Farouk was taking instruction in theology from an Imam, an older gentleman with a distinguished white beard. Mazhar Pasha translated. 'Why is God great?' the Imam asked. Farouk offered no opinion and eventually the Imam said, 'Yes. No man can know the mystery. Excellent.' I took Mazhar Pasha's point. In the Palace if Farouk were to say red was green, someone would no doubt praise his wonderful imagination.

There was an exception to this in the form of Mrs Edna Parsons, a formidable Englishwoman who had once been the Prince's nanny and now served as proctor, supervising his behaviour. She was about fifty and true to her quondam profession, she could be quite strict. Farouk was adept at giving her the slip. Running off from her was sport for him. She would often make him sit stock still in a chair in the garden for one hour. If he were to move or speak, she began the clock again.

I came to see that Farouk was quick with a bright natural intelligence but had no discipline, despite Mrs Parsons's attempts. He was best at bluffing. He believed it was a legitimate response to any question. If he could spin out an argument on a topic of which he knew little, he had by his standard achieved an intellectual victory. He never had playmates or friends as such. His sisters, the four little Princesses, were his usual companions. In the evenings Farouk and his sisters often went to a cinema in the nursery to watch Shirley Temple movies. When he began inviting me to join them, I was glad for the diversion. I had assumed they watched different Shirley Temple movies, but they had only the one in which Shirley sings 'The Good Ship Lollipop'. They always had the engineer stop the film and show that part again. They liked to sing along.

The girls had a serenity absent in their brother. They understood that Luky, as he was called in the family, was Crown Prince and that someday they would depend on him for everything. Passivity had been bred into them. They had an entire wing of rooms in the harem, near their mother's apartments. They were irresistible, usually dressed alike, often in little black pinafores with satin bows in their hair and white cotton socks, as if they were mismatched quadruplets. The oldest, next in age to Farouk, was Fawzia, called Wuzzy, beautiful even as a child. Years later she married the Shah of Iran. It was a dynastic marriage and when she gave him no sons, he divorced her. Fathia, the youngest, called Atty, wound up in Los Angeles where she was shot dead by her husband. Faiza and Faika did not have such dramatic lives, and each found a measure of happiness.

The cult of the letter 'F' was the result of a fortune teller's counsel. A royal astrologer told Fouad that if each child he sired had a forename beginning with 'F' good fortune would come to the Dynasty.

I prepared for my subsequent sessions with Farouk determined to teach and not be derailed. Soon after we next began, the Prince announced that he was engaged in several scientific endeavours. He asked if I was familiar with the theory of relativity.

'Do you mean the Einstein, sir?'

'Just so. Good man, I'm sure. I don't believe he's got it all sorted out. We'll have him to tea. I've a few questions for him.'

'I think it might be useful if we discussed our purposes and goals. I believe it would behove you to take part in what I might call English-style tutorials.'

'Yes, yes. Quite good.'

'It will be more productive, sir, if you allow me to establish the subject matter and the reading.'

'Absolutely right. I have also been examining the American Civil War. Do you know it?'

'I think perhaps a bit, sir.'

'Good for you. I don't think the historians have got that one quite right.'

'Perhaps later we can read in that area. We shall learn about it together. I would like to try again with Thucydides and his account of the Peloponnesian War. You will recall that Thucydides was the first historian. I should think that would be particularly significant to you, sir. Your place in history, the King's place, and in fact the place of the Dynasty will be established by historians. You would do well to know their ways.'

'Quite fascinating. I'd like a look at that. It was the Crawley translation, I believe.'

'It is, though for centuries there was only the Hobbes.' I handed him the volume once again and watched him make a fuss about examining the pages.

'Quite impressive. I am grateful to you for pointing it out to me. Now, Mr Peel, please tell me what is black and white and yet red all over.'

I can't say why I didn't just give the answer in the hope that we might then move on, or why I didn't reject the wretched question out of hand and insist on returning to Thucydides. All I managed was a plaintive 'Please, sir.' Perhaps it was because he had settled down to watch me as if I were a music hall act imported to amuse him, someone on the lines of Mr Data, the man with all manner of useless information at his fingertips.

'The newspaper, Mr Peel. The newspaper,' he said, answering his riddle, positively crowing in triumph. Then he insisted on explaining it.

The novelty of my presence soon wore off. The Prince might arrive for our session, or he might not. He might listen to me go on about Antony's battle for Alexandria or my disquisition on Castiglione and *The Courtier*. He might simply get up and leave while I was in mid-sentence, saying 'Thank you so much. Most interesting.' I don't believe he was aware that he growled such remarks, in imitation of his father, though his youthful voice lacked the low, dark quality that distinguished the King. The Prince was a puppy trying to bark like an old dog.

Farouk would not sit still save for Mrs Parsons. I asked

to see her, and she invited me to tea. Her apartments in the nursery of the harem had been turned into a version of a London house of some years earlier. She too had brought a bit of England with her, but her version seemed to centre on tins of Marmite and grey frocks. She was intelligent, though more in a practical sense than any other. She would have looked at home with a pram in a London square. I explained my position and asked, 'How do you get him to obey you?'

'I don't really know. It's his task, don't you see. As your task is to instruct him, his is to learn.' As she spoke, saying little of useful value, I realised that I was sitting upright in my chair, stiff as a shop mannequin. It was the answer to at least part of my question. Everyone obeyed a nanny, certainly not excluding me. 'More tea, Mr Peel?' she asked. I wasn't about to risk exposing my table manners any further, so I thanked Mrs Parsons for her consideration, made certain my elbows were not on any firm surface, and took my leave.

When the Prince failed to appear for our next tutorial, I felt annoyance. When he missed the following session, I felt irritation. The third time, I wondered if coming out to Egypt had been a terrible blunder. I made an appointment with Sir Malcolm prepared to resign and return to England. This was not an easy decision. Sir Malcolm had made it clear that he expected me to deal with whatever problem might arise. Now I had to confess that after a few pitiful lessons, I had failed.

He invited me to luncheon at the villa. The more gracious he was to me, the more I feared our encounter. I had no doubt that Sir Malcolm would not accept failure easily. I had great respect for him. This was at a time when young men had heroes. He was one of mine, and the thought that I could not fulfil my obligation to him caused me dread.

We sat on the terrace, shaded by the palms and ate shrimp from the Red Sea with a Chablis Premier Cru that was the Embassy's vin ordinaire. I summoned my courage and said, 'Perhaps I am not the man for this after all. I fear the Prince is unteachable in the usual sense.'

'Mazhar Pasha tells me the Prince is quite taken with your tutorials.'

'I believe something may have been lost in the telling.' I explained my position, slighting neither Einstein, the American Civil War, nor the riddles.

'Attention is not always a royal quality,' Sir Malcolm said. 'It does not follow that the lessons are without value.'

'I am unable to teach him anything.'

'The issue here is character, Mr Peel. What is required is for you, as a young Englishman, to serve as a model. If he fails to grasp the significance of Thucydides, he will nonetheless learn that Englishmen take the matter seriously. You see the distinction, I am sure.'

'I believe the Prince would be happier with a nanny or a royal keeper.'

'You are not expected to make a scholar of him. Teach him to behave as a boy his age in England would do. He should learn not to lose his temper at tennis. You understand, I am sure.' At that, Sir Malcolm put down his fork and pushed back his plate, a clear sign that he was cross and that our luncheon was concluded.

My discussion with Sir Malcolm marked a change in my behaviour. I found myself giving less effort to my preparations. I turned up, played chess with Farouk, and if the subject happened to arise, discussed history, much the way one might in a London pub, albeit quite a luxurious one. Once I accepted that Farouk was beyond instruction, and that Sir Malcolm didn't much care, I began to relax. Farouk certainly was pleased. He had won. As a tutor I was a failure, but as a paid companion I was doing well enough.

As I now had a great deal of time on my hands, I was free to walk in the wide streets, breathing the sea air, absorbing the smell of jasmine that was everywhere. It put me in an easy, receptive mood and encouraged my exploration. In the souk near the Cairo Station, I saw a young boy weaving flowers into a garland for the girl at his side. She was dark and plump in the way Egyptians favour. He draped his garland round her neck and she smiled shyly, averting her eyes. They had such a sweet innocence about them that when they walked on, aware only of each other, I found myself wandering after them, enjoying the simple purity of their romance.

They stopped in a dusty street in front of a two-storey house, larger than its neighbours, with walls covered in flowering vines. The gate was open and a dozen men were gathered in the courtyard. The lovers glanced in, but then hurried on, no longer holding hands. Perhaps I felt ridiculous following them, or was drawn to the sweet aroma of the vines, but I stepped inside the gate.

I believe that the men gathered there were merchants from the souk. Two of them had pushed a woman up against the house and were holding her there. She wasn't struggling, though she was obviously frightened. She was about my age with large dark eyes, rimmed with kohl and her feet and fingers were marked with circles and stripes of henna. I stepped deeper into the courtyard, not knowing if I would be set upon myself (I was the only European), until I was close enough to the prisoner, if that's what she was, to realise that she gave off a rank odour – urine, probably – a sign of fear. Her smell mingled uneasily with the delicate scent of the vines. She asked, I believe, for mercy, but the crowd was unforgiving. Her robe had been torn – had she been chased? Beaten perhaps? When I was closer, I saw that stones had been placed beneath her feet and she was balanced precariously. One of the men pushed her head back against the wall, his palm stretched over her face, while the other produced a hammer, and to my horror, set about pounding a nail through each of her ears. With a few quick strikes, he anchored her to the wall. I am sure I was the only one in the courtyard who was put in mind of Christian iconography by this display. Her tormentors stepped aside, showing their handiwork to the others. Then the fellow with the hammer kicked the stones out from under her feet, causing her to dangle there. She stretched her toes, trying to make her feet bear some of the weight. She grazed the ground but it brought her no comfort. The self-righteousness in the air suggested a romantic transgression of some sort. I suppose she was an adulteress, or a would-be adulteress. The men laughed until her stoicism melted into tears and she begged for relief, for mercy. It made the crowd jeer her more. I do not know how long she was meant to dangle there, but when she went silent, resigned to her punishment, I could bear no more and turned away.

I had been under the impression that my lodgings at the Hôtel Minerva, near the Place Mohammed Ali, had been arranged by the Embassy. Then I learned that the Palace had taken charge of that aspect of my employment. The

Minerva was near the British Consulate, so it had probably seemed practical to someone at the Palace to put me there. That Sir Malcolm was usually at the villa in Ramleh was of no interest to the Palace. The misunderstanding taught a good lesson for future Egyptian life: Make your own accommodation.

The Minerva was a six-storey brick pile which always seemed on the brink of utter collapse. My rooms, which had violet wallpaper, featured rotting lace and a looking glass so decrepit that it reflected only shadows. There was a balcony off the bedroom, though it would take a man braver or far lighter than I to use it. The Minerva had intermittent electricity and was considered luxe though I found the rats in the corridors unsettling. The proprietors didn't seem to notice or perhaps considered them house pets. There was also a colourful array of strange insects creeping about, some large as my thumb. The repellent that the FO had urged upon me seemed unlikely to do much more than provoke these creatures. I decided to sleep under netting and hoped to establish an entente cordiale with nature by day.

The Minerva's lobby was a dusty arena with withered palms, cane chairs and lazy overhead fans. It might have once possessed a faded splendour, but was now decidedly shabby. The lobby was a gathering place for any number of talkative intellectuals, most of them failed. I'm sure I fit in more readily than I knew. There were religious men, political zealots, language instructors, guides, fortune tellers, and a rheumy-eyed European who worked in the Cotton Exchange. I made an attempt to learn the Arabic language. My tutor was a man called Aziz, one of the denizens of the Minerva lobby. His instruction had a political cast to it. On a good day, I might learn that

'Istiqal el tam' was the demand for independence. In turn, Aziz wanted to learn to say, 'The English are running dogs' and 'King George is a jackal.' As I grew weary of 'Istiqal el tam', I taught Aziz to say, 'The English are running water' and 'King Timahoe is a bumblebee.'

The European gentleman from the Exchange, a Mr Giddoes, read Arabic poetry and spoke of jinni and spirits or Sufi mystics. He was in his forties with a dark, dreamy face. He wore soiled white suits, or perhaps it was one suit, and often a fez. He was pleasant enough, but his passion for all things Arabic seemed excessive. Just where on the continent Giddoes was from was unclear, though I believe he would have preferred to be Egyptian. There is of course nothing wrong in that. It was hardly my business. What put me off was that he emulated a poor Egyptian, going about as if he were penniless.

The lobby was presided over by a Mr Kheirallah, a plump, satisfied fellow who was the Minerva's boab, a job that fell somewhere between concierge and dictator. Kheirallah determined who might sit all day in the lobby, who might be offered tea, and who would be told to leave for infractions unspecified. He usually lounged in a dilapidated Morris chair, wreathed in the smoke of Turkish cigarettes. When I asked Kheirallah about the rats, Giddoes responded with a question:

'Have you ever been round them before?'

'Not in such numbers.'

'"It is new, therefore a pleasure,"' he said, then explained that this was a line of verse from Al-Hutay'a.

'I am not familiar with him,' I said.

'He was a poet of bitterness. He has been with Allah for fourteen hundred years.'

'Is he still bitter, do you think?' I asked, perhaps rudely.

'Only Allah can answer such a question and only He may ask it.'

I thought I would just make my peace with the rats, but the next day, Kheirallah, with Giddoes in tow, turned up at my door, saying, 'I have brought you a rat-catcher.' He offered a pistol as if it were a little-known device. The degree of inappropriate seriousness that Kheirallah affected was an indication of how large a tip he felt he deserved. He saw the gun as a potential bonanza. When I hesitated, Giddoes said, 'It is the only way.'

I wasn't sure just how Giddoes fit into this scheme, but the three of us went up to the roof because Kheirallah insisted that rats were plentiful there. I was dubious but when we arrived atop the building, I saw there were shanties that must have been home to someone, though Kheirallah's presence had sent them into hiding. Each shack had an enormous mound of rubbish next to it. At least I thought it was rubbish, perhaps the tenants thought it valuable. As I was looking out at the rooftops and the minarets and the mosques, gaining a new sense of this dreamy city, Kheirallah began firing. He wasn't much of a shot, but the noise stirred up the rats and there were so many that he was able to hit a few. Giddoes encouraged him, but he wasn't offered the gun. He managed a look which suggested that having been denied the weapon, he was now on the side of the rats.

Kheirallah insisted I take a turn. 'You must learn how to do it. I won't always be here' he said – an argument I found unassailable. I wasn't any better a shot, but I was no worse. As I sent the rats skidding about the roof to their death, I began to see the appeal of handguns. I might not be able to get anywhere with Farouk, but when I shot a rat, mine was the last word.

When we had used all the bullets and destroyed a dozen of the filthy things, Kheirallah picked up the remains, twirled them about by the tail, and flung them off the roof, down to the nameless – but not uninhabited – alley below. The tip I gave him was adequate, though Kheirallah looked at the Egyptian pound notes sadly, as if I had offered so tiny a sum for such a large service that he had no choice but to weep. He was no better an actor than he was a marksman.

There was a kitchen of sorts at the Minerva, but I took my meals at Pastroudis in the rue Fouad, one of the better cafés that catered to Europeans. It was decorated in ebony and chrome and might have been in Paris, the sort of gathering place where people knew one another, or assumed they might. The food was Greek and good enough. As I was having my evening meal, Giddoes came in and looked about as if he were there to join someone. That seemed unlikely, as I had never seen him with anyone other than Kheirallah. When he approached, as I knew he would, I asked him to join me. He salaamed in thanks and I knew I was host for the evening.

Giddoes's Egyptian manners appeared real enough to me, though I saw that the waiters found him risible. As a matter of course, Pastroudis set out a plate of mezze – olives, dates, and some Greek cheese. Giddoes began sampling it with his fingers, working his way through the olives, then the feta. The man lived in the Minerva and worked in the Bourse at the Cotton Exchange, yet he always appeared slightly desperate and usually broke.

I was drinking retsina and I called for a glass for him. 'Have you seen much of Alex?' he asked, managing to suggest that if I had, I had probably done it ineptly and it was a good thing he was now here to set me right. That was very Egyptian, as self-appointed guides often presented themselves in public places, offering their services.

'I just wander,' I said.

'If you will accept my company,' he said, 'I would be honoured to show you something of the city.'

'Perhaps we could. I'd like that.'

'Now you must have your dinner.' As he had finished the mezze, I suggested that he join me. 'Oh, no,' he said, 'I rarely eat in the evening.'

'I was going to have the mousaka. Why don't you try it?'

'I am intruding. I'll take my leave.'

'Please join me. I'd enjoy the conversation.'

'To keep you company, then,' he said, looking as if he were about to tuck into my plate before his own arrived.

It was the longest conversation I had yet had with him and as I listened, I realised that no matter how Egyptian his manners were, his voice had a bit of England in it and he was educated. Mr Giddoes was a seeker, though of just what I wasn't sure. He spoke readily of cotton, saying, 'The best customers are from the mills in Manchester. Your good English clothing is almost certainly made of soft cotton from the Delta.'

'Are you a broker?' I asked, regretting the question as soon as it was in the air.

'Nothing so grand as that. I came out a few years ago to learn the trade, but I'm afraid I'm not much good for it. I keep the ledgers.' It was an uncomfortable topic for him, and he soon said, 'May I ask what it is you teach the Prince?'

'I see little of him. That's why I have so much time to wander.' It didn't surprise me that he knew about my position. There was so much gossip in the lobby, that if he hadn't known, it would've been remarkable.

'It is my dream to meet the King,' he said.

'I'm afraid I can't be much help there. I rarely see him.'

He shrugged this off in a manner Egyptian enough to be worthy of the Palace. 'You will someday be known as the man who speaks to the King.'

Did he think I could arrange for him to be presented at Abdin? I said nothing and he shrugged again and sighed. Then he attacked his mousaka.

The next day when I had wandered the city, looking at more mosques and monuments than I could possibly recall, I stopped in the Place Mohammed Ali where I saw European cotton brokers in white silk suits and Italian straw hats, sitting in the Square, taking the sun. I often listened to their talk in Pastroudis. They usually spoke of arrangements and commerce, and always, always of money. My dinner with Giddoes, or perhaps it was that glimpse of those dazzling suits, of which Giddoes's was a poor step-cousin, prompted me to go into the Bourse to have a look round the Exchange, which had been built as a house for a Greek Counsel-General, done in the Hellenic style with columns in front that someone must have thought evoked the Parthenon. I found a chair at the back of the Exchange's selling floor and watched the chaotic activity. The buyers, Europeans in grey dusters, shouted madly and all at once. The sellers stood on a raised platform, and waved their arms in a code that was plain to everyone but me. A man from the Exchange stood on a ladder marking the ever-changing prices on a slate. I couldn't imagine how Giddoes fit into it.

Each time one of the shouting buyers concluded a purchase he sent a runner to record it. And there was Giddoes, at a wooden table surrounded by runners who were invariably rude. The menial nature of his task had not been clear to me.

That evening, he turned up at Pastroudis and once again we performed the gavotte of an accidental meeting. If Giddoes knew I had been in the Exchange earlier, he didn't say. After I paid the bill he was ready to show me something of Alex.

We set off in the direction of the rue Attarine, which Giddoes called Sharia Orabi. He began talking about the Minerva, passing on idle gossip of our fellow tenants. I nodded and allowed him to ramble while I enjoyed the evening air. He asked what had I seen of Alex thus far. I mentioned a few of the guidebook attractions and he remarked 'We have a fondness for moral failing here. It's the antidote to all the religious fervour.' The relevance of this eluded me.

He led me through a maze of streets, one giving on to the next, many without English names, a labyrinth of dusty lanes without drainage or electricity. 'I think you will find this of interest,' Giddoes said, when we were in an unfamiliar alley, stopped at what appeared to be a private house. Like so much of Alex, it was in urgent need of repair. We entered a modest courtyard with one scraggly palm. The door to the house was carved with a few Arabic words. Giddoes read them out, and translated: 'Opener of portals and Allah is His name.'

A sufragi brought us inside to a dark reception hall. As my eyes adjusted to the dim light, Giddoes asked, in a most casual way, 'Have you taken the pipe?'

I had seen an opium den in a film once. It was set in Macao, I believe, and the participants lay on harsh wooden benches and smoked themselves silly while a sloe-eyed Oriental temptress skulked about stealing their money.

There were no benches or temptresses here, though soon enough a European gentleman appeared. Giddoes introduced me only as his colleague, as if to pronounce my name would put me at risk. I felt no need to correct him. The proprietor was called Kasparian, a short muscular fellow with dark hooded eyes. He and Giddoes spoke in what I now realised was Armenian. If that was Giddoes's nationality, he was surely the first of his countrymen to be entirely impractical. Kasparian, on the other hand, seemed the very embodiment of a businessman. He referred to his establishment as an opium house and asked if I would care to settle the bill before we proceeded. I paid the equivalent of three pounds sterling. No wonder Giddoes never had any money.

Kasparian took us to a drawing-room, where I was offered the most comfortable of several chairs. I confess to some trepidation and the odd thought that if I actually went through with this, I would not turn into an opium-eater but into Giddoes, who could sense my doubt, I am sure.

'The great poet of the city wrote about hesitation,' he said. 'Did you know that?'

'Do you mean Cavafy?'

'"For some people the day comes when they have to declare the great Yes or the great No." Perhaps this is your time.'

He had a point, or Cavafy did, though I was still unsettled at the prospect of opium and too embarrassed to acknowledge my fear.

He prodded me a bit, saying, 'Why come to Alexandria and treat it like Kensington?'

'I'm not quite used to the idea, that's all,' I said, as

casually as I was able. The truth was, I found the idea of opium nerve-rattling.

'Certain things are inevitable,' he said mysteriously. 'Alexandria knows what you want even if you yourself do not.'

'Opium, do you mean?' I asked, dreading the mystical mumbo-jumbo I could sense he was about to deliver.

'I mean Allah's will.'

'Does Allah's will concern itself with the opium experiments of one Englishman?'

'May I tell you a story about the winding path of His will?'

'Yes. Please do.' I settled in for whatever would come. Kasparian rang a bell and a sufragi with a blue sash, which meant he was the chief servant, brought us tea and two long stemmed pipes with silver decoration and copper bowls. The amber mouthpiece was draped in coloured fringe. Kasparian made a little show of removing the fringe, as if it were a curtain, revealing grains of black opium which he called afiyoon. The servant gave the first pipe to Giddoes and lighted it with a wooden match like the ones I once nicked from my mother's pantry. The second pipe was for me. I signalled that the fellow should wait before he lighted it as I was still not quite convinced that I wished to proceed, Allah's will notwithstanding.

'The story is from the Sufi masters,' Giddoes said, his voice taking on Arabic rhythms. 'It is for this House of Answered Prayer.'

'Answered?' I asked, smiling.

'For some.'

'For me?'

'Allah alone can say, but when you know there will be no doubt.'

I accepted this answer and settled in with my tea if not yet my pipe, to hear him out. As he spoke, his voice took on authority. The pipe, or perhaps the story, was transforming bumbling Giddoes into a teller of tales.

'One night in Old Cairo, and not so long ago, a thief climbed through a window to enter a house, but the sash was weak and it broke under his weight. The thief tumbled into the house, falling across a copper trunk. He felt a jab of bone and he knew his leg was broken at the knee. He was in pain, but he was also indignant that such a grand house could cause him harm. He had entered many such houses before and nothing of this sort had ever happened to him. The thief went to the court and pleaded for justice. The gentleman of the house was sorry for the thief's misfortune, but he said, "Sue the carpenter. He is at fault." The carpenter was found and he said, "The sash was weak as all can plainly see, but the glassmaker is at fault." When the glassmaker was called, he said, "As I worked, I was distracted by a beautiful woman who walked back and forth under the moonlight, tempting my eye. Her ivory skin and fiery eyes quite overwhelmed me." The beautiful woman was brought forth and she said, "It's true, I walked there, near the glassmaker, but I am not a beautiful woman. I do not cause such disturbances as men cannot do their tasks." The judge listened and agreed that though the woman was not without charms, she was not such a beauty as the glassmaker described. The judge asked, "If you did not distract the glassmaker with your allure, how then did this happen?" The woman said, "On that

*night I wore a beautiful gown, cunningly dyed in shim-
mering stripes that moved about me as I walked and
attracted the eye of all men." The judge said, "Now we
have the author of this crime. Call the man who dyed
the gown. He is responsible for the harm done to the leg
of the thief." The judge did not have to look far, because
the dyer was already in his court. He was the beautiful
woman's husband and his leg was broken at the knee,
for the dyer was the thief.'*

When the tale was finished and Giddoes had fallen
silent, it occurred to me that Sir Malcolm would have dismissed the parable or whatever it was as so much balder-
dash, but it put me in a contemplative mood, thinking
about Allah's complicated path to justice. Kasparian lit
my pipe, set it in my mouth, then withdrew. The fumes
from the smoke that I exhaled were quite appealing, delicate and warm. I drew more into my lungs. Giddoes
seemed to have fallen into a trance. I was certainly aware
that I was in an opium establishment in Alexandria, and
yet I was also far away. A radiance came over me and I
went light-headed. It was not unpleasant and I did not
feel at all unhinged. Quite the opposite. I was serene. I
was escaping the judicious and temperate in favour of
heightened sensations. My mind and body were one, a
union much sought but rarely achieved. My forehead felt
oddly tight, while my mind felt unbound. It was a con-
tradiction that made complete sense to me. I experienced
a pleasant sensation of melting colours and patterns,
which I found entirely absorbing. I had no sense of the
passage of time. As a boy I had been told that dogs had
no notion of time – which used to puzzle me. Now I was
timeless for several hours, though like the dogs, I hardly

knew it. I hadn't lost the ability to determine the hour, it was rather more that I had no interest in the matter. Time had less significance to me than the floating pictures.

My pipe was refilled and I continued to smoke in a most casual way. The colours and patterns gave way to more literal pictures. I saw Emma's face and form in front of me. She was unclothed and yet the moment was not lubricious. I felt no impulse to reach for her. Emma's shadow soon changed into a similar picture of a house-maid at Winchester when I was a fifth former. She was called Ruby and she was the source of considerable ado-lescent anguish in hundreds of young Wykehamists, 'La belle dame sans merci', though I now realise she was sure-ly frightened by so many lustful glances. She was a deli-cious creature that I had fancied but had never found the courage to speak to directly. With opium my heated imaginings of poor Ruby gave me pleasure rather than the endless feeling of being denied that I had once known. It was a mixture of eroticism and memory, not the experience itself, but a distillation of it, intense and moving.

The next day, I woke rather later than usual, feeling quite peckish. I had Turkish coffee and flat bread sent round. As I did not feel an overwhelming desire for the pipe, I assumed I had not become an afiyooni – an opium-eater. I did find myself considering Giddoes's sit-uation. He was an odd brew of the European and the Oriental. Those sometimes contradictory qualities weren't layered one over the other, perhaps by travel, but seemed permanent cornerstones of his character. I took him at his word that he had come out for the cotton trade, though I could now see why he stayed on.

· · ·

I continued to walk about Alexandria, though by myself. Giddoes asked once or twice if he might accompany me again. I thought he was going to pester me about it, until I demurred using the wonderful Egyptian compliment of refusal, 'May Allah prosper you tenfold.' I became neither Giddoes nor an habitué of opium houses, though there was a change in the way I viewed Alexandria, perhaps brought on by the opium, but more likely induced by the spirit of the city. Earlier, when I had walked the streets, I felt like a tourist, and not a very imaginative one. Now I seemed to sprout antennae. Instead of earnestly looking at monuments and mosques, I felt meaning in simple things – the laundry that hangs like flags outside tenement-house windows and the tea and cakes at the cafés. A sense of elusive metaphor concentrated my mind and made me aware I was in a place that is a factory for memory. Even newly minted memories feel old here. As I walked about, I knew I was in the present with its clatter of modern, mechanical sounds, but at the same time, I felt a part of the mythological city. Alexandria keeps her secrets, but she tells them, too, enscribing ancient answers on anyone who cares to ask.

Before my opium experiment, I hadn't thought to seek out pleasures of the sort Alex is well known for. In my new spirit of adventure, I found myself wandering in Sister Street, down by the harbour, where brothels are common as tea shops in London. One didn't need an introduction or even an address. It was sufficient that I was European and looking about. There were nods and soft calls and soon enough my sensual proclivities were revealed. I might have been hesitant before indulging in Giddoes's House of Answered Prayer, but in Sister Street, I did not hold back. In airless rooms with windows that

admitted no light, there were dark girls from desert villages or up from the Sudan. Their degradation enflamed
me and told me of desires that could not be denied even
if they couldn't always be named. I gorged on unknow-
able companions. There was a fierce satisfaction of the
flesh, if not the spirit. There wasn't much subtlety to it. I
soon saw that I wanted anonymity and compliance and
both were on offer in Sister Street. I revelled in the coarse-
ness of those foetid rooms.

Perhaps it was the vision of poor lost Ruby, of an
opportunity sacrificed to the uncertainty of youth, or perhaps it was simply that the Egyptian girls were there waiting. I sprawled amidst cushions and cotton sheets as two
or even three of them swarmed over me, their sweaty bodies, their abundance, at my command. I wallowed in a sea
of flesh taking every thing female that had ever been
denied me. They would pull and push, rub and lick, shaping my flesh as if it were clay. Their ears had been pierced
and decorated with tiny blue beads to ward off the evil
eye. One dark shining girl wore only long strands of
coloured beads that wrapped round her breasts and then
hung low, drawn between her legs and bound tight round
her thighs. She would spread the beads apart and make a
portal for me. It never failed to put me in a frenzy.

We had no common language save for my desire. They
were to do as I wanted without my so much as saying
what that might be. Their task was to know what it was
even if I did not. I can't say what they thought – I hardly
knew what I thought. Perhaps they felt they were taking
something too, beyond money that is. When I spent my
time with merely one, she might whisper a few words that
I believe were meant to be endearments. When there was
more than one, they said nothing, each working to satisfy

me in a separate way. There was rarely so much as a sigh. It felt charged of course, even delirious, and when a gramophone was playing, usually some tinny circus melody, I felt as if I were in a silent film.

My new haunts catered to Egyptians which meant that they offered the services of both sexes. There were Englishmen who came for the Arab boys. I never developed a taste for my own sex, though in those days I left nothing untried. It was the women who called to me. I wanted to linger in their corruption, and perhaps find my own. Those young girls, their minds numbed by opium and their tasks, were my princesses of anarchy. If they thought at all in a European way, did they know they were agents of change in me? Would they have cared? The girls of Sister Street had loosened something in me and I could no more stop its bursting forth than the King could stop the dust storms in the desert. It was a show of excess that had no relation to my romance with Emma. How could she know what Alex was doing to me? I would spend my nights in Sister Street and then the next day, write a letter to Emma in which I told her many facts but nothing of the truth. The more debauched the night before, the more coolly reasoned the letter that followed, as if Emma were going to give me a mark instead of her soul.

Dearest Emma,

I may not be making much progress with the Prince, and your uncle may have some doubts, though Alex is a wonder. I've been walking endlessly. It's a city of Gods — spiritual but also venal. There are four aristocracies and they manage to exist together because each is venerable enough to believe in its own distinction: British, Greek,

Egyptian and Sephardic. Moslems are the majority, but
there are Coptic Christians, Sephardic Jews, Anglicans,
Greek Orthodox, Sufis, Gnostics, Hindus, animists –
crocodile worship is not unknown, perhaps we can try it
– and God (any God) knows what else.

   It's like Rome, but less organised, or Jerusalem with a
secular side. There are God-besotted mystics who see
divinity everywhere and are as likely to pray to palm
trees as to Yahweh or Allah. A number of them believe
religious personages of the past reside in them. They go
about preaching not just the gospel of, say, John, but as
if they were John. The whole business puts me in mind
of the drawings in Punch about lunatics who think
they're Napoleon. All that zeal gives off a very
Alexandrian musk, thick with intrigue and secrets and
fervour. Over it all, the voice of the muezzin comes from
the mosques, five times a day. It lifts the spirit with its
music. It's readily translated. They have sweet, piercing
voices. It echoes from the towers which are set against the
sky which looks like your mother's Wedgwood plates.

        The perfection of God, the Desired, the
        Existing, the Single, the Supreme: the
        perfection of God, the One, the Sole . . .

   I am in the great puzzle of cities, built on phantoms
and echoes. Imperial in the days of Antony, it is now frag-
mented and hollow in the time of Fouad. It is a city that
has forgotten nothing. Nothing fades. All the anger, the
love, even the loss of the great library which means memory itself, remains and lives in every citizen, though not
the King and not the Prince. Like the Bourbons, they
remember nothing and forget nothing. Do I sound com-

pletely mad? I hope not, perhaps excited. I want to show it you.

With my love, J.

Rather than finding a way to suggest I was in turmoil, we calmly discussed her coming out – would she stay a month? Six weeks? What was the P&O's schedule at this time of year? We descended comfortably into an exchange of the particulars of travel. Emma and I had been closest following my graduation from Cambridge. We were both in London then and our romance blossomed. She visited me at Winchester from time to time and I went down to London when I was able. For the most part we wrote letters. If she had not been Sir Malcolm's niece it would have been simpler. I would either have invited her or not. She would have accepted or not. Now it became rather confused with a family errand, complicated by the fact that I was leading a life that would be unimaginable to her and one that I doubt she would forgive. I did not have the sense to say, Come because I long to see you, or Stay away, because I am in the midst of a soul-changing adventure. She did not have the skill to put me at ease over such a momentous issue. Young women didn't easily show their serious side to their suitors, lest we be frightened off. Emma worked at being easygoing, but in fact was a very determined young woman. When it was finally established that she was coming out, she decided she required a travelling companion. That meant she was not coming expressly to decide if she should marry me. Emma and her friends saw these matters with a subtlety that I, and most men of my generation, pretended we did not grasp, though we saw it plainly enough. Emma's journey was still some months off, but she had already selected her great friend Vera Napier to be the companion. I had known Vera in London. Her father, Sir Hugh Empson Napier, had been King's Counsel and was now a judge in the High Courts of Justice in the Strand. It was a puzzling choice, as Vera always left a trail of discarded admirers. I suppose it was a measure of Emma's certainty of my devotion that she chose her. There was no way Emma could know that Vera was not the threat to our alliance.

Dearest Emma,

I so want to show you the evenings here. The entire city comes out to watch the sun disappear. The twilight doesn't last long and is changeable, sometimes the colour of lilacs, other times a deep orange. It can make one giddy. I sometimes think it isn't so at all, that the colours are no different to any other, but that I am so determined to have a memorable time that I'm imagining it, or perhaps exaggerating, making it a memory worthy of the place: part experienced and remembered, but also part invented, a fever dream of geography and history.

It's not all mystical dreaming of the ancients. I have become acquainted with the Prince's former nanny, a Mrs Parsons whose duties now include monitoring the Prince's behaviour, an uphill task. I can just imagine your thoughts. Mrs Parsons is more than twice my age and looks like Mary Poppins's mother. But she is English. I turned to her for help in understanding the Prince. She wasn't much good at that, but she did tell me a bit about his daily life.

Farouk begins his day awakened by a military band. The soldier-musicians, led by an officer in a red tarboosh, gather outside his window, playing the Egyptian

anthem. One storey above, in the Prince's bedchamber,
Nubian sufragis bring tea and toast with marmalade.
One servant runs the bath while another warms the
lavatory seat with hot towels. It is an honour to minister
directly to the Prince, and the servants charged with that
duty have medals attesting to their station.

The Prince's horses, two red roans, are brought each
morning. They stand with the musicians until Farouk
has sipped his tea. At the window he calls out, 'Good
morning, Sammy. Good morning, Silvertail.' Those are
his first words of the day, because he never addresses the
servants at all.

With my love, J.

Now that I had stopped fussing about Thucydides, I
believe Sir Malcolm found my services more valuable.
Farouk was tabula rasa, and in that there was opportunity. Sir Malcolm set out to write history with and upon the
Prince. Thucydides or no, I was a part of that scheme.
Fouad would not likely live to an old age. Farouk could
be on the throne for a long time. If he could be taught to
see the world through Sir Malcolm's eyes, England would
profit. The nub was Suez, which meant access to the sub-
continent and the oil fields of Arabia. Sir Malcolm saw it
fully. That's why he pursued the Prince with such single-
mindedness.

For a time, Sir Malcolm's campaign for Farouk centred
on motor-cars. He would sometimes tell me about his
efforts, just as I told him of mine, when we were having
tea or cocktails at the villa.

Fouad owned dozens of motor-cars, mostly German
and Italian, including an Isotta-Fraschini, an opulent
land yacht with thick sloping wings and wire-spoke

wheels, as much sculpture as motor-car. He had one English vehicle, an Aston-Martin, an open drop-head coupe, that Farouk was permitted to drive within the Palace grounds. His sisters were usually his passengers. It was one of the reasons Farouk liked Montazeh. In Cairo, at Abdin, a city palace, he had fewer opportunities to drive. In Alexandria the Prince would load his sisters into the Aston and drive over the lawns and flower beds, occasionally getting stuck in the sand when he took it in his head to drive down the footpath to the water's edge.

The Embassy motor-car was a Rolls with crystal flower vases and a burled mahogany fascia panel. Sir Malcolm would come to the Palace, dismiss his driver and invite the Prince to take the wheel. They would go for a spin in that great, humourless English beast that seemed to be pulling all of the Empire.

The Rolls was considerably larger than the Aston and Farouk had a tendency to pop the clutch and lose control. Despite that, as he manoeuvred, he said, 'Not a bad machine at all.'

'The Rolls is a particularly British undertaking,' Sir Malcolm told him. 'One needn't be an Englishman to build them, but it helps to think like one.'

'Which is better, Rolls or Benz?'

'Different machines entirely. Your Highness ought to know both. You really ought to know all sorts.'

Farouk thought about that and said, 'It's acceptable.'

'We like them,' Sir Malcolm replied, with a dryness that eluded the Prince.

The idea of friendship was not in Farouk. Everyone he spoke to, excepting his parents and sisters, were in his employ. Occasionally, well-to-do Egyptian children, the offspring of a Palace official or of one of the King's mis-

tresses, would join Farouk and his sisters to watch the
Shirley Temple movie or for an afternoon at the King's
seaside. There was never any of the squabbling that
required adult intervention which usually marked the
activities of the nursery. The children all deferred to
Farouk. They too knew he would one day be King.

When he was a small boy, the Prince took an interest
in electric trains. A room at Abdin was given over to them
and Farouk amused himself sending the carriages through
little Alpine villages and across trestle bridges. Unusual
engines and accoutrements were shipped in from round
the world. The trains were often broken, because when
the Prince was unhappy with their speed, he was known
to pick them up and throw them to their destination.
They were repaired by Abdin's chief electrician, one Luigi
Catania, a Sicilian who had spent his life in the employ
of the royal family. Chief electrician was quite a significant position at the Palace, more like superintendent than
odd jobs man. Catania specialised in schemes and devi-
ous plans. He always looked shiny to me, like a tango-
dancer's patent leather shoes.

Farouk liked nothing better than to seek out Catania at
the Palace garage where the two of them could hunker
down over some question of mechanics. The Prince
enjoyed putting a motor-car on the hoist and then standing beneath while Catania pointed out the various parts.
When they weren't talking about the steering relay or the
clutch bearing, Catania informed the Prince of the fine
points of seduction and about the techniques of amour to
be found in different national groups. Farouk spent a
considerable part of his adolescence hearing about the
words of passion uttered by French, Italian, Greek,
English, and American women. Catania believed that

Catholic women of all countries tended to shout, 'My God!' at intimate moments, while Protestant women always said, 'Oh, shit!' Farouk spent more time in Catania's company than with anyone else, certainly more than he spent with his English tutor.

To go to Montazeh or the villa from the Minerva, I took the tram which I boarded near the government hospital, where there was always an unruly group of local women waiting for a corpse to be brought out. They were professional mourners, draped in black scarves and carrying tambourines. When they thought there might be custom, they would rise up as one and begin keening, praising the qualities of the departed, whoever he might be. The bereaved families would select the few they thought most genuine or most dramatic or perhaps simply loudest. There was always a negotiation that followed, a ritual no less exact than the funeral itself. The fees didn't vary much, but it was unthinkable to both sides that the haggling not occur. After I had seen it many times I thought that the bargaining served to comfort the bereaved as much as the funeral. The best wailing-women had real feeling for their work. I often wondered what it did to them to assume deep grief again and again, all day long.

Occasionally when Sir Malcolm was in town he would offer me a ride to Montazeh. He might be on his way to take tea with the Prince or just to walk in the gardens with him. Farouk understood that Sir Malcolm was selling England to him. Sir Malcolm never pretended otherwise. He believed in the rightness of the cause and was convinced that if Farouk would only listen, he would see it too. I am not entirely certain why Sir Malcolm described these sessions to me. Perhaps he thought it might prove useful in my attempts to instruct the Prince.

It may have been, more simply, that I was the only other person who found it amusing.

To a visitor they might have looked like a father and son as they strolled through Montazeh's marble colonnades.

'The modern view is that a future King ought to be exposed to something beyond his palace walls,' Sir Malcolm told the Prince, keeping his tone conversational, trying not to lecture. 'Military study would be useful.'

'My father did that. In Italy.'

'I shouldn't think Italy is the likeliest prospect for a military education. You will one day command the military, sir.'

'Did you?'

'I was at Eton.'

'You want me to be English.'

'I want you to see England. You will be a better man and eventually a better ruler for it.'

'I've seen pictures of it.'

'You have an extraordinary opportunity. I want you to make the most of it.'

'You want it for England.'

'For England, for Egypt, and for you.' Sir Malcolm could dissemble to an adult, but I do not think he could lie to a boy. And he liked Farouk, or at least he wanted to like him. For the Prince's part, he had no experience of this sort. Adults either fawned, or as in the case of his own father, paid little attention. Farouk got a sample of a traditional English parent, and for Sir Malcolm, it was a chance to have a son. No matter what Sir Malcolm's original motive might have been, the many hours he spent with Farouk helped to forge a bond between them. That is not to say that they got on perfectly. Farouk ignored anything that didn't capture his fancy; Sir Malcolm believed in duty. Still, in a way that was new to both of them, a closeness began to grow.

Sir Malcolm had led a predictable life. He had gone into the Foreign Service instead of university, which was not unusual for a man of his class. The Cheynes were old stock, though Sir Malcolm was not himself a moneyed man in any significant way. Lady Cheyne left her husband with their two daughters and funds sufficient for the upkeep of Broughton House, a Victorian mansion in Scotland that had been in the Cheyne family for several generations. It was Sir Malcolm's most valuable asset.

There were certain traditional diplomatic chores involved in running an embassy, and Sir Malcolm had had a lifetime of cable protocol, trade policy, chancery politics, treaties, and junior ministers, though it often seemed his principal occupations were games and elaborate luncheons. He loved to shoot and ride. He took flying lessons and if there were a mountain in the vicinity, he would make a point of climbing it.

Sir Malcolm believed in the diplomatic uses of luncheon parties. He did much of the legation's work at table. Invitations to the villa were sought. The lists were made out by Mr Edward Forbes, the First Secretary, usually with the help of his wife, then vetted by Sir Malcolm. Forbes was a career man with the Embassy. He expected to stay in Egypt for the duration of his service. The Forbes's had three children and they provided a certain domestic stability. What all the hostesses of Alexandria, and later of Cairo and of London, agreed upon was that Sir Malcolm Cheyne needed a wife.

Alice Cheyne had been by all accounts a formidable woman. She had the grace and the personal fortune to run large houses. She knew how to give a luncheon for sixty, followed by a reception for two hundred, three hours later. Those skills are no longer held in high regard, but at the time there was no shortage of candidates for the position of the next Lady Cheyne. Sir Malcolm was just what all those hostesses were looking for. He was a handsome man, if a trifle large, of high position and normal habits. No one doubted he would marry again. The question was when and to whom.

The last person Sir Malcolm saw at night was his valet, Old Chu, who had been brought out from China where his family had served the Cheyne family. There were Chinese in Egypt, certainly in Alexandria, but they were businessmen. I believe Sir Malcolm took Old Chu with him because he felt he could not manage the journey untended. He was grieving the loss of his wife. His daughters were fragile. Now that Old Chu was here, in a land with far more servants than could ever be employed, Sir Malcolm was never quite sure what to do with the fellow. He simply ignored the situation. Old Chu, who spoke only Chinese, was quite alone. He had a queue and he dressed in a black silk tunic with braided clasps. When in repose, he had the Chinese habit of appearing to shake hands with himself. The sufragis the Commission employed gave Old Chu a wide berth, believing that he was meant to spy on them. The best measure I know of the distance between Malcolm Cheyne and the Embassy servants is that they presumed the High Commissioner thought about them at all.

At night Old Chu helped Sir Malcolm off with his clothes, held his pyjamas and dressing gown, then turned down the bed having already delivered the brandy tray, with a few Huntley & Palmer biscuits. Old Chu lingered for a moment then let himself out, permitting Sir Malcolm to extinguish the light when he was ready.

Old Chu was the first person Sir Malcolm saw in the morning. He let himself in at seven-thirty, opened the curtains, replaced the brandy tray with the tea tray, and while Sir Malcolm performed his private ablutions, Old Chu laid out the clothes for the day. If Sir Malcolm was going to the Palace on diplomatic business, he wore a morning coat and topper. If there was a ceremonial occasion, Old Chu laid out the full dress that Sir Malcolm had had cut at Gieves before he had gone out to China: a blue coatee with a stiff collar and a great deal of oak-leaf and fuss on the shoulders and cuffs – the epaulettes and aiguilettes – and best of all, a majestic cocked hat with ostrich plumes. It made him quite formidable at the Palace. The first time I saw him in the full fig, I all but applauded. Part of it, I'm sure, was his great height. In full dress, he looked alarmingly like a battleship, HMS Albion, perhaps. For ordinary days at the villa or in town, he wore a city suit. Sir Malcolm was partial to spotted bow ties and they became an emblem of his office.

When Sir Malcolm was finished with his tea, Old Chu escorted Mr Robert Dugdale, the ADC, to the bedchamber. Dugdale carried the scarlet despatch-box with the royal crest, containing the overnight cable traffic and the day's schedule. Dugdale was a capable man who had not yet decided if he would try to make a life for himself in the Foreign Service. As ADC he had something of a personal relationship with Sir Malcolm. It was Dugdale who reminded Sir Malcolm of his appointments, with whom he was to take his meals, what transport would be required and when his language lesson was to be held.

Sir Malcolm had engaged a tutor to give him a daily dose of Arabic. He concentrated on useful phrases and vocabulary rather than grammar and to English ears seemed quite adept. The Egyptians seemed impressed by his skills, though the more I watched, the clearer it became that they couldn't follow much of what he said. They were pleased to meet an Englishman who was trying to learn their language. They didn't understand that Sir Malcolm was not doing it for their benefit, but so he might let it be known at the FO that he spoke Arabic.

At nine o'clock, Old Chu would return to help Sir Malcolm dress, buttoning the collar, knotting the tie, giving the boots a final brush. Then the High Commissioner would come down to the morning room where senior staff, and sometimes myself, would be assembled. 'Good morning, gentlemen,' he would say with a crispness and an assurance rarely heard outside the British diplomatic corps. Then the day would begin.

The Embassy was preparing a luncheon in honour of a visiting nabob, a representative of de Havilland, the aeroplane manufacturers, who were suppliers to the Egyptian military. He was a Mr Pennymore, who was knowledgeable about aeroplanes, one of Sir Malcolm's interests. I thought the plan excessive for a chap who was after all a salesman – even though the encouragement of government trade with English companies was one of the Commission's obligations.

Mr Pennymore's luncheon was held in the garden at the villa, under a white marquee that took twenty men four hours to put up and two more to take down. The guests were drawn largely from Alexandria's commercial circles. Before they were seated, everyone was lined up so

Sir Malcolm might make his entrance. He shook the hand of each guest. The ladies made a demi-curtsy and the men bowed. At such ceremonial moments, Sir Malcolm's need for a wife at his side was plain.

Sir Malcolm called for The Northumberland Fusiliers and arranged them in front of the big veranda where they played marching music. It was very impressive, even if Mr Pennymore didn't realise that on other occasions more than one band was turned out. Still, there were glasses for champagne and claret as well as a great sea of silver, crystal, and linen. There were almost as many sufragis as guests. They were like slaves, dark and silent, in their white gallabeiahs. How could one not see it that way? Until one had been in Egypt for a long while, it was difficult not to think that at any time all the sufragis might rise up and slice off our heads, make sashes from our hair, beads from our teeth, and feed our blood to their animals.

Pennymore was a pleasant enough fellow, about forty, thickening in the middle, and given to grave pronouncements about the state of aeroplane manufacturing. Sir Malcolm offered a toast that concluded, 'Due to the good skills of the de Havilland company, the Egyptian Air Force soars high and protects the nation.' The guests nodded, but Sir Malcolm, who never gave much thought to the Egyptian Air Force, scowled at the banality of his own toast. He had probably glanced at the speech without quite reading the end. The junior who had prepared the remarks had worked hard to please his boss, but putting words in Sir Malcolm's mouth was a hopeless undertaking.

A week later, a de Havilland silver Dragon Rapide with tapered wings was made available to Sir Malcolm. Pennymore saw to the maintenance and every year until the war he replaced it with a new model. Sir Malcolm kept it at an aerodrome in Heliopolis, outside Cairo, and flew about whenever he liked, occasionally buzzing the villa as a greeting to his daughters.

In the days preceding Mr Pennymore's visit, I had been in a bit of a state. Not over the luncheon – my few months in Egypt had already made me a veteran of such affairs – but because Emma, accompanied by Vera Napier, had arrived. I went down to the harbour to meet them, bouquet in hand and no little trepidation in my heart. Emma looked smashing, which was a relief but not a surprise. Happily, the Lyttelton side of Sir Malcolm's family did not run to such large sizes as the Cheynes. Emma's thick chestnut hair and pink English complexion was not unusual in London, but stood out here as if she were waving the Union Jack. She wore light brown culottes, had a red-covered Baedeker in her pocket, and a pith helmet tied round her neck. It gave her a vaguely military air that was quite fetching. I didn't ask if she had brought insect repellent and Pears soap.

It was Vera, as always, who attracted attention. She had perfectly shaped features and a figure that was at once slim and yet quite full. She managed to look both aloof and approachable at the same time. That was because her smile had a slight downward curl, as if she were saying – all at once – I don't approve of you but come over here right this minute. Vera had the quality of assurance that great beauties are born to. The debarking passengers – the men at least – were watching her with admiration and regret. Emma looked about, trying to get a sense of where she was and where I might be, a perfectly sensible response to the situation. Vera simply stood there as if she were saying, I am here, certain that would be sufficient.

I was a bit nervous of how we might conduct ourselves. I was so used to being different to most of the people I saw outside the Embassy that it was pleasant to be with someone who understood all that I said and who looked more like me than not. Still, it wasn't easy. It really did come down to what Emma referred to as intimacy. Though she was certainly curious about the Minerva, Emma was not comfortable there. In the brief time she spent in my rooms, she always seemed to have an eye out for rats.

She and Vera stayed at the villa. I took the two of them on excursions round Alexandria. Sometimes we were able to use an Embassy car and driver. When it was just Emma and me, we took the tram. It was great fun to see my familiar route through Emma's eyes, and to point out to her the bare-footed conductor, which she never found quite as interesting as I did. Once, as we were returning from town to the Embassy, we watched a spectacular Alexandrian sunset. We were in the open section of the upper deck and Emma unpinned her hair and the sea breeze blew it all about. The sky was streaked with red and then for a fleeting moment, before darkness fell, it was washed in yellow light. It made Emma swoon and I kissed her with a passion and a tenderness that I hadn't felt toward her since England.

When we walked in the city in the hot afternoons, I saw that Emma had a gait more brisk than I had recalled. She looked at things as if she were checking off items in the Baedeker, or perhaps my letters, making certain that she was getting full measure. It was efficient enough, but a bit more organised than my usual pace. When a merchant in the souk pursued us calling, 'Gorge. You, sir, Gorge,' I held up my hand and said, 'Ma'alesh,' which simply means, 'Never mind.' Emma was quite taken with such mastery of Arabic, but wanted to know why he had called me Gorge.

'He's saying "George. George V." He means to honour us. In the bazaar, we're all disciples of Gorge.'

'Cheeky, aren't they? Your Arabic is quite impressive.'

'My skills are hardly sufficient to understand what's said on the wireless.'

'That's a good way to learn more, I should think.'

'Local wireless is useful for listening to very long religious commentary at all hours.'

'Ma'alesh, Ma'alesh,' she said and then she kissed me.

As we wandered through a bleak little Midan, near a Moslem cemetery, Emma stopped to watch some ragged boys playing with trained hares. They had rigged a ground level ring, measured out with bricks. I was always glad when something interested Emma without a build-up from me.

I knew at a glance that these were no fuzzy creatures from Beatrix Potter, but desert hares with sharpened fangs. The boys, city urchins, were gambling on these near rabid animals.

'How can they be so vicious?' Emma asked.

I wasn't sure if she meant the boys or the hares, though the one answer I knew might apply to either. 'They feed them a desert weed that works on them in a horrible way. They eat it naturally in the desert. Here, they're fed an excess of it. Do you see?' She nodded but I don't believe she yet understood.

The hares stayed in the ring, shredding one another with their fangs. Hare's blood spurted across the boys. Only people putting down wagers had ringside positions, so we were spared the splashing blood. As the fight concluded, the victor pounced on the corpse of its opponent, ripped off a hind leg, and began running in a mad circle with the furry stump between its teeth until it too fell dead. The boys found that great fun. Emma had seen enough, and so had I.

Later, as we were drifting past the alleys and court-yards, pungent with human odours and cooking smells, places where crowded conditions caused a closeness for the residents that lacked even the simplest privacy, Emma said, 'When I imagined this journey, I had rather pictured us walking at seaside in moonlight. More like the sunset we saw from the tram.'

'Then that's exactly what we'll do.'

'What I mean is, the part that you fancy most is not that at all. You've developed a sort of nostalgie de la boue.'

'I suppose I have. Does it bother you?'

'No,' she said, meaning I am sure, yes. Emma had sensed something of the truth, though she didn't know the half of it. Then she changed the topic back to our friends in London. It seemed far away. I had to work at summoning any interest at all in who had married and who had not. The plain truth of it is, I never quite heard the ends of Emma's sentences. By the time she got to the predicate, my mind had wandered.

Emma was one way in her correspondence and another in her person. I could hardly complain on that front, and I suppose we all are, but it took some getting used to. If she had found Alexandria more compelling, it might have been easier. As it was, we seemed always to be taking the temperature of our friendship.

Vera Napier, on the other hand, had already cut a wide swath through the Embassy staff. Dugdale had taken a shine to her and was mooning about. I have never been much good at assessing the appeal of my contemporaries

to women. At an Embassy luncheon at the villa, I asked
Emma about it. She assured me that Dugdale was considered handsome, then said, 'Do you mean you haven't
noticed?'

'Well, yes. That's why I ask. He acts like a puppy.'

'Not Dugdale,' she said with exasperation at what she
took to be my obtuseness. 'My uncle.' Vera had managed
to be seated next to Sir Malcolm and they were deep in
conversation. Vera was gazing at him with a reverence
that seemed to say, You are what I have always needed but
never before realised. With you, I can be complete. Sir
Malcolm saw it, how could he not? He found it appropriate, I am sure, and concurred without argument.

Emma had seen what I had not. The women at the
luncheon could talk of little else. At that time, one didn't
know the ages of females beyond about sixteen, but I certainly knew that Vera Napier was a good thirty years
younger than Sir Malcolm Cheyne. She was Vera
Cansello Napier, her late mother, Anna Cansello, was
Italian. Vera had large charcoal eyes, her mother's tem-
perament and her father's English colouring. She had
been born in Florence and grown up in Rome and
London. Being in an exotic capital was less daunting for
Vera than for Emma.

In defence of my not noticing anything, I pointed out
that Vera always flirted. It was her way of marking terri-
tory, I suppose. In any room she would decide who was
the most attractive or most powerful man and then seek
his attention. It meant no more than that, though no less.
'This is different,' Emma said. 'My uncle never flirts. He
doesn't know how.'

'Well, he seems to have picked up the rudiments.'

'He is looking at her with far more interest than you

have been looking at me.' I believe I blushed, which made
Emma laugh. Vera had a receptive face. If a man looked
at her, she responded with her eyes. Her glance was bold,
but it never seemed that way. She managed to suggest
that the man's interest was helping her to see more clearly. Hers was an unstoppable reaction to the wonderful
cleverness of the fool who had been grinning her way.

When Sir Malcolm was not gazing back at Vera and
her saucer-eyes, he was conducting business, having a
chat with Ali Neguib Mazhar Pasha. Sir Malcolm was
wary of Mazhar Pasha's Englishness. He knew full well
that such men owe their allegiance to their own King and
no other. Still, he was valuable as a conduit. I had been
grateful for Mazhar Pasha's help with the Prince, but I
had been far too tense to take much real notice of him.
He had a long mournful face that seemed to collapse into
its own chin. Sir Malcolm attributed his doleful appearance to a longing for England. When I heard that, it was
all I could do not to laugh. It said more about Malcolm
Cheyne than anything else. The English quality in
Mazhar Pasha's voice that I had noted at the Palace made
what he said sound true, at least to the English. No matter how precise an Egyptian's diction or how upstanding
his character, the English never believed him. What we
never quite understood was that it worked both ways.
Egyptians took for lies what my countrymen thought of
as their own good manners.

Vera Napier was Sir Malcolm's guest for an evening at
Montazeh. I escorted Emma, and our party was filled out
with Sir Malcolm's young daughters, Sarah and Elizabeth,
and their nanny, Miss Sutton, who seemed a less severe
version of Mrs Parsons. The children were coltish English

schoolgirls, sweet and unaffected. They had, of course, recently lost their mother. The older girl, Sarah, kept her eye on Vera looking for signs of romance. It meant little to Elizabeth, who I guessed was about eleven years of age. Mazhar Pasha had arranged the invitations, saying only that it would be 'quite a little beano'. Emma had told me earlier that Vera had been thrilled when Sir Malcolm asked her to accompany him. She had spent hours, according to Emma, trying on various frocks looking for the right effect. She settled on a silky thing that billowed gently in the evening breeze. In deference to Moslem sensibilities she wore a shawl, but when she saw that the women of Alexandria, Moslem or not, wore what was most becoming, she showed off her milky shoulders. For Vera, there was an audience of one, and she measured her success by his reaction.

Sir Malcolm, a man known for playing his cards close, famously cool in any negotiation, was looking only at Vera. Now that it had been pointed out, I could watch little else. It seemed that Sir Malcolm had to make an effort to look at Vera's face and not at her shoulders or even her bosom. When boys are old enough, at least in England, their fathers are meant to explain that when they speak to young girls they are to look them in the eye and nowhere else. Compliance can prove difficult, but by the age of about thirteen one is expected to have learned it.

Watching the two of them provided amusement for Emma and me, and gave us something other from ourselves to discuss. 'She will sit there and smile,' Emma said, 'until he turns entirely to marmalade.' I laughed, though I could see that Emma was right and whether or not Sir Malcolm knew it, he was Vera Napier's prisoner.

The party was an outdoor affair near the Palace, where

a pond with a little island had been put down in the sand, under a voluptuous moon. The guests, tout Alexandria, were seated at low tables at the edge of the pond. The tables had Bohemian crystal candelabra with tall shades of Turkish glass that gave off a soft flattering light. It made flesh glow and put everyone in a dreamy, romantic mood. As always at Montazeh, there was a grand feast: Turkeys that had been turned on a spit, brown rice with sultanas, rolled vine leaves, and stuffed pigeon, though nothing to drink but for fruit juice and the ubiquitous bottles of soda water. It was said that the only thing the King ever drank was the sweet water from the sacred spring at Mecca. If it was in evidence tonight, it was not offered at our table.

On a platform a few metres above the tables, a viewing station had been erected for the royal family. It was a peaked tent, of a sort called a sewan, made of coloured squares of a quilted fabric, draped over poles in the desert manner. Sir Malcolm told us that it housed Fouad and a few of his cronies, Mazhar Pasha among them.

'Where's the Queen?' Elizabeth asked, perhaps concerned for mothers in general.

'I'm afraid you won't see much of her,' Sir Malcolm said. 'It's a different sort of royal marriage.'

I wasn't sure if entertainment was planned or if there was a purpose to the evening beyond the food and the soft light. I asked Sir Malcolm about it and he lifted an eyebrow slightly, as if to say, 'Something will happen, sooner or later.' Not long after, without announcement, the light dimmed on the island and a strange guttural shouting, part prayer I believe, as I heard a good bit about 'Allah Mowlana', which means 'Allah is our Lord'. For the most part, it seemed agonised screams. As the light came up on the little island we saw assembled there about twenty men in a loose circle. They were dressed in an assortment of kaftans, some without sleeves. A few were bare-headed, others wore white skull-caps. They were all yelling individually with no attempt at unity. The girls were frightened by the display and held on to their father.

'Dervishes, I should think,' Sir Malcolm said.

As that gave his daughters little comfort, I added, 'Sufi holy men. Itinerant beggars.' That too had little effect on them, but as the shouting had lessened, they appeared to accept the explanations.

The dervishes had tambourines and a drum, but until the discordant shouting had eased, none of us had heard the music at all. They were leaping about, assuming strange postures, as if they had lost control of their limbs. They seemed quite mad until they began spinning about like drunken toy tops, engaged in the activity for which they are best known. This was not done in a particularly theatrical manner, as many of them had wandered into corners, or had turned their backs to us. They were transfixed and unaware of anything beyond their own movement. The speed with which they whirled was breath-taking and seemed inhuman. As I thought this could get no odder, one of the dervishes came forward. A small brazier with red coals was presented to him and the fellow extracted a live coal with his fingers. This caused Emma and Vera to gasp. Sir Malcolm appeared relaxed, but he stole glances at his daughters, to see how they were faring. The dervish transferred the coal to his mouth, which he opened wide so we might see into it. As the others continued to whirl at their dizzying speed, the coal-eater added more of the hot lumps to his mouth and began to chew, as if he too were dining on the King's feast. With his fingers, he offered live coals to the others who popped them in their mouths like sweets. When the coals were all consumed, the whirling eased and the dervishes were concluded. There were no bows, no encores. They simply stopped and walked off. It fell between a music hall presentation and a demonstration of religious ecstasy.

The light dimmed once more and we prepared for Act Two, which turned out to be a tableau vivant. Young women in diaphanous gowns were posed round a rapacious looking Colonel Blimp. It did not require the Prince's tutor to explain to Sir Malcolm's daughters that the women were meant to be Egypt and the gent, England. Sarah, who was astonished at the scanty costumes, said, 'They didn't have this in China.'

'Try not to gape, darling,' Sir Malcolm said.

The tableau changed to muscular young men in falcon head-dress attempting to assume the classic Egyptian pose of antiquity: head in profile, shoulders twisted to the front. They were menacing the Englishman who was portrayed by an overweight and sallow Egyptian. He was groping at one of the maidens who was about to lose her frock.

'It's time for the girls to go on now,' Sir Malcolm said to Miss Sutton who herself looked shocked. They got a reprieve when Mazhar Pasha came to our table and announced that the King awaited our party.

As we paraded past the tables, I could sense the other guests watching us, telling one another just who that large Englishman was. Vera took his arm, which seemed to frighten Sarah.

The royal enclosure was decorated with a bead curtain and carpets and lighted with candles. It had a Bedouin air about it, in keeping with the exterior. It surprised me, as

His Majesty rarely showed interest in anything beyond the European. The King was reclining on a chaise longue. Farouk was next to him, in a desert chair. Fouad nodded as we entered, but Farouk had to be prompted with a glance before he acknowledged us.

'Have you enjoyed our fantasia?' the King asked.

'Illuminating, Your Majesty,' Sir Malcolm said with a wry smile. He had an extraordinary ability to defuse potentially difficult circumstances. Another man might not have been able to keep politics out of such a response. Sir Malcolm managed to suggest that he had been enchanted by the King's own wit. As the King and Sir Malcolm were speaking, Farouk said, 'Good evening, Excellency.' Sir Malcolm bowed his head slightly to Farouk, acknowledging his greeting, but not interrupting the King. It was the second demonstration of his diplomatic skill in less than two minutes. I glanced at Emma to see if she was aware. She was looking at Vera, who was glowing.

'And these are your daughters?' the King asked. Sarah, who was a large girl, built along her father's lines, was at an awkward stage of life. Any public display of herself was an ordeal. Elizabeth had not yet endured a burst of growth and was still untouched by adolescence.

Sir Malcolm said, 'Your Majesty, may I present Miss Sarah Cheyne, Miss Elizabeth Cheyne.' The girls curtsied to the King, who was looking them over as if he were about to make an offer. Sir Malcolm saw that too, and simply moved on, presenting Emma, Vera, and me. I felt uneasy in Fouad's presence. People are often that way with royalty, though not Sir Malcolm. I don't know if it's possible, in a social sense, to be superior to a king, but if anyone was, it was Malcolm Cheyne. Farouk was staring at Vera. 'Do you like motor-cars?' he asked.

'Very much, sir,' she answered as if that question had been long on her mind.

'I might give you a ride.'

'Miss Napier is visiting Alexandria,' Sir Malcolm said.

'It can be her welcome.' The Prince continued to examine Vera with his eyes. His look was one that I had come to recognise. It always put me in mind of the cock who believed that the sun rose each morning to hear him crow.

In the fall, Fouad moved from Montazeh and the seaside of Alexandria back to Cairo, a journey of three hours. All the family, the retainers, the sufragis who were not permanently a part of Montazeh, and others, including myself, who had managed to attach themselves to the King, boarded the royal train. The Prince's horses, Sammy and Silvertail, had their own carriage in the event the Prince felt the need of their company. On the adjacent track, there was a second royal train for the Queen and her entourage.

I sat with Farouk for the journey. We were talking companionably enough and thus far he had not posed any of his riddles, when a short, beefy Englishman with a red face and an almost comically large nose appeared making a fuss about tea, though as yet none had been provided. I knew this fellow to be Titterington, the King's dispenser, though I had not yet met him. 'Titters!' the Prince said in greeting. 'What have you to report today?'

'Begging your pardon, sir,' Titterington answered, all but tugging at his forelock, 'I'll ask you not to take your tea till we've had a look. I've said as much to His Majesty.'

'Trouble, is there?' the Prince said, hoping for a conspiracy, I am sure.

'It's the trains, now isn't it? Don't quite have the controls.'

'Rascals in the galley?' the Prince asked.

'Palace staff only, sir. It's a train now, isn't it? Doors are open and shut all the time and who's to say? Better safe than sorry, sir.'

'No tea, then. We'll rough it. What do you say, Mr Peel?'

'I'll try to make the best of things.'

Titters, as I would now and ever more think of him, cast his eye upon me. He seemed to be considering the possibility that I was planning to lace the Prince's tea, should it ever arrive, with arsenic. Titters wasn't the King's dispenser at all. He was the royal taster, and a more suspicious looking fellow I had never encountered. I don't know that Titters actually tasted all the food before the King or the Prince ate, but I was told that his duties included inspecting the royal stool, pere et fils, which may have accounted for the blue veins that stood out so vividly on his heroic nose.

The carriage had red walls and a domed ceiling. The windows were covered with curtains of a darker red. The seats were wonderfully plush and draped with Oriental carpets. To the English, certainly to me, it seemed overdone, a little ridiculous. The Egyptians were taught to believe that whatever the royal family had was therefore luxurious. If the King were to appear on a velocipede, they would believe velocipedes next to God. For us it was the opposite. We had what I can only characterise as an ill-judged belief that whatever was Egyptian was a tad vulgar. We believed that without question. Egyptians have an ingrained respect for authority – used wisely or not. They accepted our collective view of them. It was how they maintained equanimity in the face of what we regarded as their inferiority. For us it was how we believed in what we thought of as our superiority. That was the social order and those beliefs were the engine that drove the country.

We were not long out of Alexandria when Mazhar Pasha, who had been with the King, joined us. 'Do you mind, sir?' he asked Farouk and drew the curtain without waiting for a reply. As the bright light poured in, it jolted me as if I had been struck on the head with a hammer. The Prince simply turned and looked out at the desert. He began to wave, a slow, slightly mechanical roll of his hand, modelled on a gesture his father often used. Farouk was greeting an astonishing number of fellahin who stood by the railway tracks waiting for a glimpse of the royal train. They stood in the dust, in their gallabeiahs, with their children, watching and waiting. I wondered if they had been assembled by the Palace in a sort of Potemkin Village demonstration of fealty or if in fact they had come of their own accord. I asked Mazhar Pasha how long they had been there. With a world-weary Egyptian smile, he said, 'They have always been there, Mr Peel.'

In addition to the crowds along the track, the royal train was accompanied by a procession of Embassy motor-cars, each legation bearing its national flag. The Embassy Rolls, followed by the German Ambassador in a Mercedes-Benz, then the French Embassy, the Italian, the Scandinavian nations, the Russians and the Asian countries. The Europeans were accompanied by motor-cycle escort. The motor-cars had all been fitted out with wide desert tyres for the journey, because though the road followed the railway track, it was occasionally overwhelmed by sand. The pageantry struck me as wonderfully quaint. All these national shadows chasing the King of Egypt who was bliss-

fully indifferent to them. I doubt that the fellahin understood much of it. I suppose some of them knew that the
motor-cars represented other nations. That those nations
should be less than the Egyptian royal train must have
seemed proper to them. They had Allah five times a day,
but in the here and now there was the King. His Majesty
may not have been beloved, but he was necessary to the fellahin conception of life. To them, the King was no less central than water or air. Without him, there was nothing.

Emma had gone back to London, which had been our
plan, though there was tension between us, which hadn't
been anyone's plan. Vera, however, had decided to stay
on, and was now making the journey to Cairo with Sir
Malcolm in the aeroplane that Mr Pennymore had so
generously left in his care. Farouk had heard about this
adventure and was quite impressed that Sir Malcolm was
a pilot. I could see that it offered another area for discussion. No doubt, Sir Malcolm would manage to suggest
that only in Britain could a young man learn to fly an
aeroplane properly. The Prince and I watched the sky for
a silver Dragon Rapide. Farouk claimed he saw it, though
I'm sure he did not. I imagined Sir Malcolm finding the
Nile, then simply following it to Cairo and Vera telling
him how clever that was. Vera's staying on had been
unsettling for Emma. I was in awe of it. Vera and Sir
Malcolm were certainly the subject of gossip, though they
didn't care what anyone said. They were two people with
feeling for one another. I respected them both for it, but
it had driven a wedge between Emma and me. I wanted
to swallow Egypt whole, to make myself a part of something that was different to its ancient core than steak and
kidney pie or Winchester's rituals. For Emma, Alex had
been an interlude that she might talk about in future with

her friends. It reminded me of the way I once thought I might stay at Winchester permanently. It seemed right, until I saw more. I didn't like to think of Emma that way, but I did.

As our train moved south, we headed into one of the sudden sandstorms that can blow throughout the country. I thought perhaps because of the swirls of dust it was an out of season khamsin or perhaps the red harmattan. The Egyptians have as many names for desert storms as Eskimos have for snow, though I seemed the only one with an interest in nomenclature. Perhaps it was the secret wind whose name was erased from the earth and can never be spoken. Whatever its name might be, the fellahin kept to their station along the track, though they could see little through the swirl. Surely they could not speak in the screaming wind, which was now the only voice. The motor-cars stopped to wait out the weather. Farouk continued his mechanical wave, though he could no longer see the road. The sand rose up through the floor-boards and came in under the windows. There was grit in my nostrils and my eyes. A helmet of crust settled on my hair and my throat went raw. I thought I'd choke. As I looked out, I couldn't tell what was solid ground and what was not. I lost all sense of the train's movement, though I knew we were hurtling forward. Farouk simply kept up his rolling wave until Mazhar Pasha came by and closed the curtain, murmuring, 'The people are grateful, Your Highness.'

We sat together in silence. The waving had put him in a sort of trance from which he either didn't care to return, or was unable to. When the storm lifted, and the sand in the carriage retreated to the floor, sufragis opened the curtains again and I saw that we were in the farm land of the

Delta, near where the Nile forks, which meant Cairo was near. Where there had been countless fellahin only moments before, now there were cotton fields, the source of Mr Giddoes's employment. Occasional flashes of vivid colour were provided by ibises, kingfishers, and brilliant feathered creatures that surely had names, but were unknown to me. They were a rich contrast to the pale flat terrain. The chess-board squares carved out of the sand, divided by irrigation ditches, were an affront to the desert and a triumph over it. I looked out at the green fields dotted with the occasional black buffalo and thought surely a country with such resources should never be hungry. Still, the hordes of fellahin that had so recently been standing along the track seemed untouched by the Delta's bounty. No matter the fellahin's fate, nor the cotton grown in the desert, the royal trains kept moving south into Cairo, to the principal seat of the Mohammed Ali Dynasty: Abdin Palace.

By way of amends for the accommodation in Alexandria, Sir Malcolm offered me rooms in the Residency, as the Embassy in Cairo is known. It's an imposing Victorian house, large and angular, that serves as home and office to the High Commissioner. It's painted colonial white and stone lions mark the portico. The old Queen's cypher is entwined in the gate. Sir Malcolm's apartments look over lawns that are made for garden parties and that run all the way down to the River Nile, which provides the water that keeps the grass (re-sown every year with English seed) so brilliantly green. A grove of scarlet flame trees along the embankment marks the end of England's careful property. On the chancery side of the Residency, where the work of the Embassy is done, the lawns stretch to Sharia al-Waldah, a desperate little street of alleys and rickety houses that runs outside the Residency gate, a last native enclave amidst the posh precincts of Garden City. The Arabic name – Waldah means 'mother' – is used because neither we nor the French ever gave it another.

It was autumn when I arrived to continue the task I sometimes regarded as a fool's errand. The city was still hot and close, smelling of wood smoke, unwashed clothing, and animal leavings, all sweetened a bit by the pungent aroma of cooking spices that seemed to float in little pockets of the air. In Alex, I met local people frequently. I knew Egyptians of several classes. Less so here, where the Europeans do not so much mesh and blend as show off. Despite the easy Egyptian charm, the relaxed smiles, there is a rage that is never far from the surface. It is a breeding ground for rancour that threatens to consume this desert bedlam of a city. Though Cairo is built on the Nile, unless there are winds from the sea, the city remains lost in its own dust, in a state of daytime torpor well into October.

As my life settled into an easy routine, I saw there was something beyond generosity in Sir Malcolm's gesture. He also installed Vera in the Residency. My presence there served to suggest that putting up young people who were vaguely attached to the legation wasn't unusual. I'd take my morning meal in the Residency, often with the family and Vera, occasionally with Dugdale or Forbes who had come from their offices in the chancery for morning meetings with Sir Malcolm. The girls were meant to be at school in London, but they were often in Cairo on holiday or simply because their father missed them. He would bring them out for a few weeks, whenever he fancied. At first he thought I might give them instruction. Perhaps that's what he suggested to their school. This wasn't likely of course, as Vera had told him. Vera had a strong realistic streak. Her goal was to demonstrate to Sir Malcolm that she was capable. She did this with a combination of coquettishness and practicality.

Vera's energies were concentrated on Sir Malcolm. Still, whether she meant to be or not, she was a model for the girls, particularly Sarah, who was looking for guidance. Both were a lovely café au lait colour from the sun. Englishwomen usually went about in sun hats and long skirts in the belief that they could retain their pale skin. Not Vera, though. And as a result, not Sarah.

I saw them together once, sitting on the Residency lawn. Vera was in a white cane fan-tail chair, brushing Sarah's hair. Beyond the portico was the striving city, but here, within, the world stood still in privileged serenity. It was the final quarter-hour of the day and the last of the pale yellow sunlight lay easily in a pool at their feet. In that hovering light that comes just before darkness, everyone, even a High Commissioner's mistress and daughter, seems more vivid, more alive. They were drinking lemonade and the aroma of sliced ripe lemons drifted toward me.

'One hundred strokes, every day,' Vera said, as she pulled the brush along Sarah's straight auburn hair.

'Then what?' Sarah asked, basking in the attention.

'Then your hair will shine. And so will you.' I could see by the care Vera was taking that she understood how confusing her presence was for Sarah. Vera's behaviour was calculated, though her goal was generous, not venal. Sir Malcolm loved his daughters, but he could hardly help them in matters such as hair-brushing technique.

An Embassy motor-car would take me to Abdin each day for my teaching duties. Abdin is a city palace, rougher than Montazeh, a place of business, thick with intrigue, with spies, sycophants and royal whores. It's about seventy-five years old. For Egypt, that is a span that hardly mattered, but it was time enough for the Palace to have grown a bit creaky. There are Oriental-style rooms and receiving halls, banquet rooms, a mosque, and a theatre. The Prince and I met in the library, a more elaborate version of the one at Montazeh, though equally unused. To get to it, one went through the Byzantine Hall, the main public chamber of the Palace, a striking room that could contain several hundred chairs when the occasion required. Palace officials often said that the Byzantine Hall was 'the most beautiful room in the Orient', as if that were an official designation handed down perhaps by an international commission on interiors. Still, it was a lovely place, with a high gilded ceiling, mosaics, and gold candelabra. It was vast enough so that though one could walk from one end to the other, it might be advisable to take along a light lunch. The Hall itself gives out onto several smaller rooms – the Suez Canal Room, the Diplomatic Room, and finally the library, which was filled with handsomely bound volumes in several languages. While I waited for Farouk, a frequent occurrence, I examined the shelves, half-expecting false bindings, as in a stage set. The books were real enough, though their pages were uncut. Often, rather than lessons, the Prince would insist on playing chess, the royal game. He took pride in his knowledge of the history of the many chess sets at Abdin, some in gold and silver. He knew the general procedures and some of the more famous ploys. For the most part he just moved the pieces about indiscriminately until he eventually called out 'Checkmate', which was the end of the matter.

When we did have more traditional lessons, Farouk showed interest in royal history, particularly that of his forebears in the Mohammed Ali Dynasty, and in diplomacy. This last was down to the influence of Sir Malcolm, and I took it as a positive development. He asked how often did the High Commissioner communicate with the King. I thought he meant Fouad.

'The King of England. How often?' he said.

'Not often, I shouldn't think, sir. Sir Malcolm sends despatches to the Foreign Office on matters of concern. Those are often shown to the King, but many of them are technical.'

Farouk took that to mean that Sir Malcolm didn't know the King at all. I explained that he certainly did and that he had an audience whenever it was appropriate, but that cables came into the Foreign Office from all parts of the Empire every day. Sorting through despatches was hardly a task for His Majesty.

'What does he say in the despatches?'

'I believe at present the Commission is working on P.E. printings. Political evaluations of the parties here.'

'The Wafd? Moslem Brothers?'

'Most probably. And the others.'

'And His Excellency does that?'

'One of the juniors does it. The High Commissioner will approve it and it will go out over his signature.'

'Very good. The English have been up to this sort of thing for a long time.'

'We have had diplomats round the world for some five hundred years, sir.'

'Oh, that's very good. Quite long, then. How old is Egypt? Do you know?'

'Six thousand years, I should think, sir.'

'Just right. Very good. Now, Mr Peel, we shall turn to other matters. What did the wall say to the floor?'

'I'm afraid I don't know, sir.'

'Meet you at the corner. Good day, Mr Peel. Well done.'

And then, as always, he left the library. When he was on his own at the Palace, he often walked about the corridors, sometimes trying to see his father and sometimes going to the harem to visit his mother. The problem for him there were the eunuchs who controlled the corridors. They were great hulking Sudanese. It was said they had been castrated at an early age and groomed for their positions.

The Queen was meant to stay in the harem, and as long as Fouad was there, she did. When he would leave Cairo, for another palace or a trip abroad, she did as she pleased, going about the Palace with her children. Also in the harem, though far from Nazli's apartments, were Fouad's concubines. The number wasn't known, but probably five or six at any one time. The King had a fondness for young Circassian girls with their fair skin and blue eyes. They would be brought to his bedchamber at night, by Ahmed, the Sudanese eunuch who was Fouad's valet and doorkeeper. Ahmed thought nothing of turning away the Prince if he felt the King was 'otherwise engaged'.

The harem wasn't quite what it sounded like to us. The Queen, who was about forty, lived in great luxury there attended by her ladies-in-waiting, who were social figures in their own right and who lived outside the Palace, though they also retained apartments in the harem. They came and went bringing rumour and gossip. The first, Madame Zulficar, was of Nazli's class and the mother of a young daughter often mentioned as a possible wife for Farouk. The other was Miriam Rolo, who was married to a businessman who was a financial adviser to the King. The Rolos were Sephardic Jews, pillars of the haute Juiverie. Miriam had been in Alexandria with the Queen at Ras-el-tin while I was at Montazeh, though I didn't meet her until

Abdin. She was a tall, elegant woman with olive skin that
appeared Egyptian but was, in fact, Spanish colouring. She
had a high forehead and eyebrows that were more drawn
than grown. It gave her a theatrical quality that held great
interest for me.

Miriam was related to most of the old Sephardic families. She was of Egypt, certainly, but at least to me, her
eyes remembered Spain and reflected five hundred years
of exile. She had inherited the Sephardic sadness of those
centuries and yet retained – against all experience – an
optimism I came to see was a belief in the redemptive
power of physical passion. In the act of love, her exile fell
away and Miriam entered her own true country.

It was a heady time for me. I found myself more and
more in Miriam's company. Emma and I wrote occasionally, but as a romance that was over. I had never been
involved in an affair with a married woman, nor for that
matter with one older to myself. I do not mean to suggest
that I thought our affair wicked or sinful, but merely that
I had never before had the opportunity. One needn't have
been a member of the secret police to assume that Miriam
had been asked to keep an eye on Farouk's tutor. Mazhar
Pasha most likely put her up to it.

There were rules about who could be in the harem and
it was certain that the Prince's English tutor was not on
the lists. *The Abdin Protocols* was a volume that had accumulated over many years and was meant to account for
every imaginable set of circumstances. Most of it concerned who took precedence in seating arrangements for
state dinners and what sort of uniforms were to be worn.
It was also clear about who could go where in the Palace.
Miriam's apartments were held at Nazli's sufferance,
though they violated the protocols, as did the presence of

her occasional visitor. Should someone of high position wish to get rid of Miriam, it would be said she had violated the protocols and so, sadly, must be dismissed. At Abdin, rules were swords above everyone's head.

Once, in those rooms in the harem, when our mood was apres-amour, when Miriam was stretched out like the odalisques for whom this part of the Palace had been designed, I asked if she was meant to spy on me, to write daily reports perhaps. She laughed and said, 'Well, of course, darling. We don't call it that.'

'What do you call it?'

'I was asked to see what it is you are teaching the Prince. That's all.'

'And this?' I asked, running my hand along the undulating line of her hip, then tracing a finger round her black, liquid eyes.

'Would you rather I interview you with a little book, as if I were from *The Times*?'

'This is much better, thank you.'

'You are so English. Now I suppose you'll tell me you want to fight a duel with my husband.'

'It's Austrians who do that. We just suffer in silence.'

She purred, a sound she often made and one that always caused me to shiver in anticipation as she again rolled into my arms. She was my Sephardic cat and she accepted intrigue as the normal order of things, not unlike the weather. Perhaps Farouk was right. To Hell with Thucydides, to Hell with history. This was why young men leave home. I was in Egypt, in a languid sun-drenched room in the harem of the Palace, in the arms of a woman who knew more about love than I did.

Ours was a life of afternoons. I would be with Farouk for an hour or so in the library, hearing his riddles and telling him what little I might about the past, and then I would go to the harem where the present was all that mattered. I was drunk on the hedonism of it.

When we lay in her bed, which was made of bentwood and curved at the foot like the prow of a boat, I sometimes felt myself floating up to the whitewashed ceiling and watching the two of us wrapped together below. It was a sort of vertigo that I knew wasn't real, but was still every bit as vivid as the lovemaking itself, the reality of which I did not question. Miriam knew it, perhaps even caused it. To signal her awareness of my airy state, she might touch me gently or let her hair, which moments earlier had been pinned in a chignon, graze across my face. The personality I had brought to Egypt was breaking off in little chunks, like melting ice. This wasn't in the manner of the dark girls in Alex, where there was great physical sensation, but also a fundamental anonymity. Miriam and I sailed together on her boat of a bed, though I launched into the air quite alone. Later, when we were sated, she would look at me with sad eyes and say, 'Je suis désolé.' I knew it was time for me to go.

Miriam regarded the activities of the English, certainly Sir Malcolm, as a kind of theatrical diversion that existed on the fringe of Egyptian life, which for her meant Abdin. 'He is too much there,' she said of the High Commissioner. 'Always fussing about his plans for the Prince. It is presumptuous.'

In the evenings, I would go with Sir Malcolm and Vera, and occasionally other guests, to the clubs and cafés. We might stop for a cocktail at the Long Bar at Shepheard's, where the barman would see Sir Malcolm approaching and start mixing his famous Suffering Bastards. Dinner might be at the Mohammed Ali Club, which was largely

Egyptian but had a good kitchen, and then onto the Royal Automobile Club for chemin de fer or to the Scarabée where there was usually a band from the continent playing American swing on saxophones and slide trombones. The evenings were enjoyable, but I was often uncomfortable because when I was with the two of them, Vera and I looked like a pair and Sir Malcolm like our chaperone. It made me self-conscious and, I suspect, not always the best company. Sir Malcolm towered above everyone and had long since put self-consciousness of any sort behind him. He either didn't notice my discomfort or didn't care.

Vera and I acted as if we were brother and sister, or perhaps great friends. She was beautiful, near my age, and we were both English. The plain fact of it was I was attracted to her, though I did not allow myself to dwell on it. Vera was so absorbed in her campaign for Sir Malcolm's affections, that I'm certain she was unaware of any feeling I might have had for her. To diminish the likelihood that someone might assume that she and I were together, Vera began to invite other young women to come along. This made things simpler, and several of the women were quite pleasant and I saw them again, on my own. Miriam knew all about it of course, and always expected a full report. If there was one that I particularly fancied, she insisted on making suggestions for how I might woo her. It was all too much for me, and I asked her wouldn't she please at least pretend a little pique, if not jealousy. Instead, at a Palace reception she introduced me to her husband. He was charming and may well have known all about his wife and me. Miriam said he was not faithful to his mistress, let alone to her. As she said it, she laughed a musical little laugh that meant, Don't bother about such matters and come to bed.

With Emma, I always had the feeling that she was considering what we should call our first-born, or whether
we would live in town or in the country. When she heard
about the evenings that Vera had arranged, Emma took it
as disloyalty, a breach, on Vera's part. She felt badly used.
I explained my position in a letter, which only exacerbat-
ed matters. I was not trying to defend myself to Emma.
Our romance was over by mutual consent. It was that
whatever else I felt about Vera, I was also protective of her
and did not want to see her damaged in Emma's eyes.
Neither woman knew about Miriam of course. I doubt
that Sir Malcolm was aware of the turmoil.

Sometimes after those evenings, when we'd been to a
string of clubs and restaurants, danced to the orchestras
and eaten continental food cooked by Egyptians who
would have preferred couscous or ful but who dutifully
prepared veal Orloff – which Sir Malcolm delighted in
identifying as water buffalo Orloff – we would go to a coffee house near the Mediaeval Gate in the old city. We
called it simply Ali's, which may or may not have been the
name of the fellow who always made a great fuss over the
arrival of the High Commissioner. It was a dimly lighted
place with dripping candles on brass tables. The padrone,
or 'perhaps-Ali', as Vera had taken to speaking of him,
served our coffee himself, using an ibriq, a small copper
jug on a long wooden handle. He held it high above the
tiny cups and without so much as a splash, poured out a
long, cooling stream of the thick black liquid.

Later, over an arak, that anise-flavoured Egyptian
liqueur that with a little water turns milky as Pernod, I saw
a side of Sir Malcolm that was more relaxed. The discussion often turned to Farouk and his future. Sir Malcolm
rarely said anything harsh about the Prince. He didn't have

to. His views were well known to me and certainly to Vera. When he did speak frankly, I could sense that in his mind he was trying to look into the future. He spoke Shelley's lines about the Egyptian monarch, 'whose frown and wrinkled lip, and sneer of cold command' did not quite fit the Prince.

'He's not yet King though, is he?' I said.

'He will always be more sensual than military,' Sir Malcolm said, 'until I can make him face that martial side of himself.' I could see that Sir Malcolm, a man not much acquainted with self-doubt, had qualms about his ability to develop anything like a 'sneer of cold command' in Farouk, though he seemed certain he could turn the Prince into a man of value, both for Egypt and for England. He had been corresponding with the Royal Military Academy at Woolwich. 'I believe it is the best school for him,' he said. 'Forbes was there. That speaks well of the place.'

Sir Malcolm had first thought of his own school, but because of my difficulty instructing the Prince, gave it up as impractical. 'It is not Sandhurst, but it will do,' he said of Woolwich, by which he meant that an idiot prince would not be entirely out of place.

Perhaps thinking that he had been too harsh in Vera's presence, he turned the conversation to the political in a way that he made personal. He talked of his affection for Egypt, and he meant it. As with so many of our countrymen, he liked the idea of Egypt more than he cared for Egyptians. In one breath, he could speak with awe of the history of the country, of the accomplishments over the millennia and of the influence the nation had on the world, so far out of proportion to its size. Then, in the next, he'd speak of the fellahin as little more than dust of the desert, no more educable than house-pets, of the country's political leaders as poseurs and shams and of the royal family as accidental. 'The country may have ancient roots, but this lot is three generations out of Albania,' he said.

Sir Malcolm was not a man one easily disputed, but this after all was the end of a long casual evening and I said, I hope not in an argumentative tone, that even if the Dynasty's tenure had been brief, still Egypt had a thriving complex civilisation when England was nothing more than warlords in animal skins. It surprised him – not the assertion, which was not in dispute – but that I had made it. He thought for a moment, then said, 'On the very next occasion England requires pyramids or perhaps instruction in the funereal arts, I shall recommend that we seek Egyptian counsel.'

We must have been the stuff of gossip. The other tables had students and poets, dark, with fiery desperate faces, smoking kheef, arguing about the Kabbalah or the intricacies of Arab poetry. And there was Malcolm Lyttelton Cheyne in evening clothes, quite possibly the largest, certainly the most vivid, white man they had ever seen. Watching him there, in that dank coffee house in the light of flickering candles, I saw that he was right to so fully identify with England. He was the Empire, and just as our country had colonialised Egypt, he personally was determined to colonialise Farouk.

It was only with Vera that he wasn't calculating. I could see it in the way he looked at her, with a surprised adoration. He didn't think about loving Vera, he simply did it. He courted her five thousand feet up in the air. They managed their own nocturnal retreat at the Residency, where the only one who had to know the details was Old

Chu. Privacy during the day was difficult for the High Commissioner. His duties required being in public and for romance to thrive lovers must have time alone. So Sir Malcolm would call for the Dragon Rapide, escort Vera to the second seat, push her earplugs into place, put a blue beret on her head and take her up, thrilling her with flight over the city, then out over the western desert to show her the endless sand – the desert, so brown and distant with its high conical dunes that seemed carved out of time itself. Then back to the Nile so he could follow it into Upper Egypt, swooping down over the feluccas with their white sails and the mud villages on the banks, flying into the gaudy pink sunset.

There is a shooting lodge in the desert sixty kilometres south of Cairo, at Qarun in the Fayoum, that the King enjoyed. It's stocked with plump Sudanese doves, kept in pens when citizen hunters are there, and sent into the air to be fired upon only by a royal party. It is an arrangement that would not work in England, but seems practical to the Egyptians. Sir Malcolm, through Mazhar Pasha, had arranged for a small group from the Palace and the Residency to go there for shooting. The party consisted of the Prince, who had been fitted out in plus four tweeds and a flat shooting cap, Sir Malcolm, Mazhar Pasha, Forbes, and myself. We motored down, followed by a lorry filled with servants, who would function as loaders, dog handlers, and general factotums. The Fayoum is well staffed, and we could easily have utilised the resident servants. They were at leisure because the presence of the Prince meant no one else would be admitted, no matter who they were or how long-standing their arrangements. We set out on our excursion the way royalty so often do: extravagantly equipped and with an inflated sense of purpose.

The Fayoum is an oasis in the arid desert, fertile and green, with scattered villages made of whitewashed clay boxes. The lodge is quite posh, built round a lush spring, though the shooting butts are no different to more modest enterprises. It didn't matter as our purpose was to cram Woolwich down the royal throat. I had never questioned the legitimacy of Sir Malcolm's campaign to turn Farouk to the West. When I had thought about it, it was as a matter of tactics: What would be the most efficient way to proceed. I have no doubt that my afternoons with Miriam were the reason I now questioned the whole business. Perhaps that had been the larger plan all along. If Sir Malcolm could try to make Farouk an Englishman, then Miriam might well try to turn me to the East. If Mazhar Pasha had engineered all that, then he was an ex-officio double agent. It sounded possible, because it sounded very Egyptian.

We crouched in the reeds, behind barrels moored in the marshes. The loaders handed us our twelve-bore shotguns, the beaters sent the doves into the air in front of us. There's a certain music to the twelve-bore, especially when several are fired at once. A satisfying thunder is created and with it the counterpoint of birds falling from the sky and splashing into the water. As the dogs waded out to retrieve the kill, each man announced his bag.

'Four,' from Sir Malcolm.

'Three,' from Mazhar Pasha.

'Two,' from Forbes.

'Two,' from me.

'Sixteen,' said the Prince.

'I believe, sir, that some of your bag may have fallen into the brush,' Mazhar Pasha said. It struck me as a remark made by a man who had been on other shooting expeditions with the Prince. By then, Farouk had already forgotten. He was inspecting Sir Malcolm's shotguns. 'Have you seen my Purdeys, Excellency?' he asked.

'Good weapons, indeed,' Sir Malcolm told him.

Farouk showed the rest of us his shotguns which were hand-crafted, the stocks polished to a soft gleam. 'You really should shoot Purdeys, Excellency.'

'Perhaps someday I shall,' Sir Malcolm said, with a smile that implied the Prince had made a marvellous suggestion.

'Mazhar Pasha shoots Purdeys,' the Prince answered, unwilling to let the topic rest.

'Yes sir. I got them when I lived in London,' Mazhar Pasha said, then straight away asked, 'Did you learn to shoot at Woolwich, Mr Forbes?'

'I spent happy years there, sir. The Shop, we call it,' Forbes said, with what he may have thought was a nostalgic note in his voice. So far, the charade seemed glaringly obvious in its intent, but the Prince seemed interested.

'How long does it take?' he asked.

'The course is two years, sir,' Forbes said.

That seemed rather a long time to Farouk. We stood about waiting for his response. When none seemed forthcoming, Mazhar Pasha said, 'You've already mastered what Egypt has to teach. It's time to think about going abroad.' That made good sense to Farouk. Sir Malcolm agreed and then suggested that he and the Prince retire to the spa for a lemon squash, leaving the rest of us to shoot yet more of the King's Sudanese doves. Sir Malcolm was going to try to seal the arrangement. Mazhar Pasha and I, having no more interest in birds, stationed ourselves not far from Sir Malcolm and Farouk, both hoping to listen without any mention of it.

They sat on the veranda while Sir Malcolm pressed his case. 'Part of being the Prince is that everyone wants something from you.' Farouk certainly understood that. He also understood that Sir Malcolm was trying to promote Woolwich. 'You do well at shutting out what you don't want, sir. You could stand some improvement in accepting good counsel.'

In the odd way that Farouk knew things, he knew not only that Sir Malcolm was right, but that the issue was the crux of the royal dilemma. 'How am I to know which is which?'

'You must develop an instinct for just how much to compromise under pressure without collapsing.'

'That's worse than ever!'

'I'll help you learn to assess motive and judgement. That's the standard that endures.'

Farouk knew that was right, or at least a valid point. Instead of taking advantage of the wisdom or simply saying thank you, it made him retreat a bit. 'Woolwich, Woolwich,' he said, feeling cornered. 'Bring it here.'

'I don't quite follow, sir,' Sir Malcolm said, hoping there was an opening.

'To Egypt. Woolwich.'

'It works best in its own place,' Sir Malcolm said. 'It's been there since the eighteenth century.' Farouk shrugged, indifferent to the argument. Sir Malcolm let it rest, believing he had accomplished at least part of what he had attempted.

. . .

After our return from the Fayoum, the Prince cancelled my tutorials for a few days. Sir Malcolm thought he might be considering the Woolwich question. Perhaps he was, though I could not imagine Farouk considering anything at length. It meant I was at the Residency more than usual and I saw that Vera was making her presence felt. I saw her inspecting the carpets in the ball-room. They were of peculiar sizes and all similar – cloud formations with backgrounds of blue and deep yellow. Alice Cheyne had collected them in China. There were few signs of Alice in the Residency, excepting her daughters, of course. Vera was looking at Alice's carpets as if she might be preparing to light a fire. I understood the impulse. She didn't look up, but she called out, 'Don't skulk about.'

'Sorry,' I said as I entered. 'I didn't know if I was disturbing you.'

'What do you think should be done with this room?' she asked.

'Bit out of my department.'

'There are rather too many of these carpets. They have odd shapes.'

'Yes. I see.' She was right, they were oddly shaped, though I knew that had little to do with her concern.

'They're quite wrong here. The ceiling is too high.'

'I'm sure you're right.'

'I'll tell Malcolm that you said so.'

'Best to leave my views out of it,' I said rather too quickly. 'I have no eye for this sort of thing.'

'Of course you do. Everyone does.'

I could see that she now had the advantage of me. She might not exercise it about the carpets, but there would come a time when she would use it.

Because I was not at Abdin, I did not see Miriam. She called me at the Residency, which was unusual as she believed that the telephones were not private. She told me that Farouk had visited the harem on the evening he returned from the shooting expedition. Miriam hadn't seen it all herself, but she'd had no trouble finding out the details.

As he often did, Farouk wandered the corridors of the Palace. There were guards, of course, though they had little to do, as almost nothing irregular ever happened in the bowels of Abdin. The Prince's occasional presence was the closest thing to an unexpected event. He would just walk up and down, a young boy adrift in the seemingly endless chambers. Abdin was five hundred and fifty rooms. Not even a young man who was heir to it could remember it all. He walked from his rooms in the Belgian wing to the harem, and approached his mother's apartments. Like any visitor, royal or no, Farouk was stopped by Murgan, the formidable keeper of the harem, who towered over him though not as much as Sir Malcolm did. Murgan was Sudanese, with skin the colour of claret. He dressed in striped trousers and a morning coat, like an English government minister, and carried a walking stick with an ivory falcon on the head. It was said that Murgan never left the harem, ever. 'Good evening, Your Highness,' he said, drawing out the words, filling each syllable with caution.

'I want to see the Queen.' Farouk rarely had trouble sounding imperious. It was a skill he was born to, though Murgan alone among all the people Farouk met, gave him pause.

'Am I in error, Your Highness? We were not expecting you.' Two lesser eunuchs, also Sudanese in striped trousers, came out of the Queen's chamber and bowed to Farouk. It emboldened him and he pushed on. 'Please inform the Queen that I am here.'

'I am so sorry, Your Highness.'

As Murgan was preparing to stare down the Prince, the Queen herself appeared, having heard the activity in the corridor. That she had opened her own door seemed a scandal to Murgan. He knew his power was gone for the moment. He looked severely at the eunuchs, who hurried to hold the door for the Queen. 'Luky! Come here, darling,' she said, unaware of any other drama.

Nazli, in early middle-age, still retained some of the harsh beauty that one could see in her children. The King had not married her for that, but for her blood-lines. She was haute bourgeoisie, descended from the French officer who became Suleiman Pasha. The King was the latest generation in a line of Ottoman conquerors. Fouad knew that the Dynasty had to be made more Egyptian. Nazli was also a part of the haute Musulmane, and she had produced Farouk. Fouad's ministers would have preferred a few brothers – an heir and a spare as they put it, in the English manner – but they were relieved to get what they had. Nazli knew that as long as the Prince thrived, her position was safe.

She was with Miriam and Madame Zulficar in her drawing-room. They often stayed with her into the evening, spending the night if the Queen was restless. Nazli's furniture was French, and quite smart if one had been asleep for fifteen years. She seemed unaware that the Parisian style of the moment was Art Déco and not the swirling line of Art Nouveau with which she lived. On the occasions her son had been beyond the drawing-room, he had seen that his mother slept in a gold bed. As

Farouk sauntered in, the Queen hugged him and caressed his face. 'I haven't seen you all day. You're more handsome than yesterday.' Farouk basked in his mother's praise, accepted a cup of tea from Miriam, and then forgot why he had come.

Madame Zulficar took advantage of the moment to say to the Prince, 'Fafette's at home now. She asked me to send you her greetings.' Farouk had no idea who she was talking about. It was her daughter, who was two years younger than the Prince. Madame Zulficar devoted a great deal of energy to arranging a match. Nazli did not object and Fouad had shown no interest in the matter. Farouk certainly knew he would one day name a Queen, though the issue seemed remote. The thought was enough to remind the Prince that he had come for his mother's view of the Woolwich question. She knew that the High Commissioner was pushing the idea of sending Farouk away to school. Fouad hadn't informed her, he rarely spoke to her at all, but Miriam had, in her capacity as go-between from me to the Palace. The Queen's answer was ready. 'Two years is too much. What could they possibly teach you that would take so long?'

'About war,' Farouk answered.

'Your father has an army. Let them teach you.'

'What about Fafette?' Madame Zulficar asked, concerned that the Prince might well meet other girls if he left the Palace for so long. Farouk looked at her blankly, trying to recall Fafette. 'Safinaz,' she said. 'My daughter.'

'You like her, Luky,' Nazli said, putting her imprimatur on the Fafette question, but also putting the question aside. 'England is a terrible place, darling,' she said. 'I assure you, the people worth knowing there will not be at this Woolwich.'

'I don't want to go,' he said, swept up in his mother's view. 'I already know how to review troops and I'm an expert marksman.'

'Yes, dear. Certainly.'

'I'm going to tell my father.' Then he was gone. His mind had moved on and he was no longer aware of his mother and her coterie. When Miriam told me this, I assumed that she would not have any information about what might have happened in the King's quarters. I had underestimated Miriam Rolo. She assured me that if anything happened in the harem, she knew about it. Nazli required information and Miriam was the person to get it for her. My occasional presence in the harem was testament to that. Miriam spoke to the servants and the servants knew everything. It was quite possible that she spoke to the King's concubines. They were young girls, cut off from the outside. If Miriam had insisted, Murgan would have arranged a discreet interview. She also assured me she had been inside the King's bedchamber. She said it in a way that did not invite discussion. It made me smile. Fouad claimed any woman he wanted. That certainly did not exclude the Queen's ladies-in-waiting.

Farouk walked the corridor that led to the King, ready to face his father. In that echoing hall, there is an erotic mural that features a bearded potentate, an ancestor of Farouk's perhaps, with several concubines ministering to him. One of them has insinuated her fingers into her master's anatomy in a manner not much considered in England. There is a gymnastic quality to the poses of the ladies. It is realistic, specific, one might say, yet still Victorian in its pale colours and declarative style. As the Prince lingered to look at it, Ahmed, the King's valet, approached and told him that it was not possible to see the King just then.

Perhaps he was still basking in his own decisiveness, or perhaps Ahmed was not as imposing as Murgan, or simply because he was a little older than the last time he had come here, Farouk moved the valet aside and banged his fist on the high door to Fouad's bedchamber. 'Please, sir. It is not possible,' Ahmed said, worried that he might be held responsible for this interruption. Farouk was feeling powerful and continued to knock until his father appeared, wearing a yellow silk dressing gown, made for him at Sulka, the royal crest embroidered on the pocket. Farouk said, 'I would like to talk to you. Please.' Fouad stepped aside allowing his son to enter. Farouk had been in this room very few times, and his eyes fastened on the enormous mahogany bed. It featured a silk canopy with curtained sides, a chamber within a chamber. No boy can fully grasp the reality of his father's sexuality, but Fouad's erotic life was the stuff of legends and word of it had reached Farouk's ears. His eyes darted about, trying to parse the mysteries. A concubine, a girl only a few years older than Farouk, stood waiting in the shadows. Her fair skin had been rubbed with salves and oils that had first been used for the pleasure of the Pharaohs. She wore a soft, revealing costume and waited patiently for her instruction. Farouk watched her, unable to look away, as he spoke to his father. 'What is this Woolwich?' he asked.

'Do you object to it?'

'Why, though?'

'You will have to deal with the English. They are a fact of your life.'

'I already know about that.'

'Woolwich will be a help. Not for the reasons the English think, but to see them as they are.'

'Can't I learn here?'

'We cannot make you older, nor Us younger. You will
be Farouk of Egypt, in your time.' The Prince was hyp-
notised by the Circassian concubine's beauty and was no
longer listening to his father. 'Does she interest you?' the
King asked. Farouk could only stammer as his father
beckoned to her. She stepped forward and turned about,
showing herself to the Prince. Farouk tried not to trem-
ble. His father saw that, too. 'Never show fear,' he said.

'I know,' Farouk answered, gaining control of himself.

'Are you old enough?'

'Yes,' Farouk said. 'I am.'

Fouad nodded to the girl and left the bedchamber. The
concubine, who knew her duty, introduced the Prince to
her flesh. She considered it an honour and did for Farouk
all that the King had taught her.

The Prince sailed to England from Alexandria, off for the
life of a student soldier. Sir Malcolm had arranged for the
British cruiser Devonshire to carry Farouk to England. By
that act he meant to tell Fouad that the Commission considered this expedition of the highest importance. It
seemed excessive to me and I was able to ask Sir Malcolm
about it, with what diplomacy I could muster. He told
me, 'I want to put the boy in agreeable British surround-
ings. Suitable circles. I see no reason not to start immediately.' Farouk was accompanied by an entourage of some
twenty retainers. Mazhar Pasha, who had manoeuvred for
the opportunity, was the senior figure. He alone was happily anticipating England. The group included Titters and
Luigi Catania, as well as a fencing and combat tutor, a
military tutor, a professor of Arabic, a cook, a valet and
servants. Mazhar Pasha had wanted me to accompany the
Prince as well. I demurred, insisting that my work was

now done. I might return to England for a visit, but I would do so on my own. My plan was to try to spend some time in Alex, unencumbered by the Prince. I went to the dock with Sir Malcolm and Vera to see Farouk off. Sir Malcolm was feeling triumphant. As he watched the Devonshire raise anchor, he said, 'Woolwich will make the boy one of us.'

The Prince stood on the deck, waved, and held up two fingers, for the years he would be away. He seemed forlorn, though I didn't know whether that was because he didn't want to leave his own country or because neither of his parents was at the dock to see him off.

MISS VERA NAPIER:

The Year of Three Kings

Jimmy Peel was in love with me, you know. He was. He pursued me in London and in Egypt. I tried to hand him off to Emma Lyttelton, my late husband's niece. Jimmy got mixed up with some ghastly woman at the Palace, one of the old Queen's pals. God only knows what that was all about. He thought it a great secret, I'm sure. Everyone knew about it except Malcolm. He liked Jimmy so much, and if he had heard that after the tutoring with Farouk, Jimmy stayed on for more lessons, he would have been appalled. Not at the romance, but because surely those characters at the Palace were using Jimmy in their own way.

Jimmy's been dining out on our Egyptian experiences for years. I suppose it sounds dreadful for me to say it, but I'm older now than I ever could have imagined possible. Frankly, I don't care. I may have led him on a bit. I was thought of as flirtatious. It had a different meaning then. I liked him. He's a patriot. It doesn't matter that he was such a Nosey Parker or unpleasant to Emma Lyttelton.

He stood up when it mattered. The thing about Jimmy is his mind is stuck in the thirties because being with us was the most exciting thing that ever happened to him. He's a schoolmaster, really. For a while he was at the centre of what my late husband once termed, 'the world's moment'. Jimmy was never near the centre of anything after that. If he was in love with me it's because I led him on, I am sure. He was quite taken with titles. He used them whenever he possibly could. Malcolm walked away from titles. He said they were only good for impressing clerks and shop assistants. Of course, later they gave him the peerage. Everyone said our marriage wouldn't last, that I had bewitched him. Well, I did. We bewitched one another for thirty-five years, and in all that time our marriage was tested only once.

When the Prince came to England to attend Woolwich, Malcolm followed him. He wanted to keep an eye on things, to make certain that Woolwich was working. Malcolm was also in London for the Foreign Office to work on the Anglo-Egyptian treaty.

I knew so many Foreign Office wives in those days. The successful ones knew a lot about diplomacy. I understood that treaty, not so well as Malcolm and the men who negotiated it, but well enough to hold my own in discussions at the very highest level, right up to the Foreign Secretary, Sir Walter Greville, who was in theory Malcolm's boss – though no one, except the King, and I mean George V, was Malcolm Cheyne's boss. Sir Walter would put his hand on mine or on my knee to make a point, usually something to do with agricultural policy. The point was made, but the hand remained. Because I could question him intelligently and knowledgeably about the treaty, the matter was contained and not without its amusing aspect. Now I've gone off there. I'm alone now. I live too much in my own mind. My children tell me I can't focus on anything long enough to complete it. They don't put it that way, but that's what they mean.

Malcolm's great achievement was the Anglo-Egyptian Friendship Treaty of 1936. The heart of it was, we removed Egypt from being our Protectorate, part of the Empire. In exchange, Egypt guaranteed us the Canal and the right to station troops there. It meant Malcolm could no longer be High Commissioner, primus inter pares, but simply Ambassador Cheyne. He did that for the benefit of the country. The brilliance of the treaty is quite obvious now, though when Malcolm proposed the outlines of it, no one was yet talking about war in Europe. Malcolm saw into the future. He protected the nation based on what he foresaw. It is a significant achievement and why he may be thought of as a great man.

I spent as much of my time with Malcolm as I possibly could. Farouk was at Woolwich pretending to take his studies seriously, though he spent his time in town. He had uniforms cut in Savile Row and he absolutely hoovered up everything at Asprey's. He'd go up and down the aisles pointing at all those gold birds and bric-a-brac, saying, 'That, that, that, not that.' His henchmen, Luigi Catania and that crowd, would trot along behind. A vulgar little mob gathered outside and stared in the window. They had to be shooed away.

Farouk went every night to a brothel in Shepherd's Market. Ran up quite some charges, I am sure. Jimmy Peel went with him on more than one occasion. Mazhar Pasha had tried to get Jimmy to come out to Woolwich and get Farouk to concentrate, but Jimmy was no more successful than he'd been at Abdin. Now instead of play-

ing chess with Farouk rather than working, Jimmy went
to Mayfair with him. To hear Jimmy tell it, they might
have all gone to the brothel, but all he did was wait in the
road.

Lady Russell gave a dinner supposedly for Farouk but
really so she could introduce Malcolm to a few of her
wretched widows. It was at her house in Belgrave Square.
The house is an embassy now for Yemen or Nepal. One
of those countries that one can never quite get a handle
on. There were cut flowers set out in Meissen bowls and
some exquisite French statuary. The furniture was old,
though it attracted no attention. Lady Russell thought Sir
Malcolm would arrive with the Prince and a detective and
one other guest. I don't know who she was expecting but
I was that guest.

Lady Russell had Farouk on her right. He looked at her
with great seriousness and started posing riddles. Lady
Russell was about seventy at the time. She had iron-grey
curls and for private occasions such as this, she wore her
diamonds. She was the Dowager Lady Russell. I would be
called dowager now too, if anyone still used that term.
She could be lovely, and later I got to know her, but she
was imperious. She and her late husband had been regulars at Buckingham Palace. Now here is this boy saying,
'Tell me, Lady Russell, do you know why the fool
climbed to the roof of the pub?'

'I do not,' she said.

'Because he heard ale was on the house.'

A woman like that can't be upset at a dinner party, her
own or anyone else's. She simply turned the conversation
and began talking to the old coot she had on the other
side who was intent on telling her the true history of
some great financial crisis the nation had lately endured.

I was seated next to Lord Bullen. He had a son about Farouk's age who was there that night. They made a plan for a shooting weekend in Scotland. I suppose he wanted his son to be friends with the Prince. Lord Bullen kept me engaged that evening. It irritated his wife, but I would have been at sea without an interesting man to talk to. The more Lord Bullen drank, the more he kept wanting to see me later. He was dear, really. I was trying to listen to Malcolm's conversation with the widow that Lady Russell had selected for him. To hear them, I had to move a bit toward Lord Bullen. He took that as encouragement and was really quite naughty. The widow, Alice Chadwicke, who was my mother's age and gone all silvery, was saying, 'You see, Sir Malcolm, if one believes in heaven, then one must account for the little creatures.'

'Yes. Quite.' When Malcolm said 'Yes. Quite,' it meant he was bored stiff. It was his diplomat's tone. The more I leaned in to listen the more Lord Bullen thought I was leaning toward him. I had to keep removing his hands.

'One should very much hope to be reunited with pets as well as anyone else,' the silver widow was saying. 'I'm so looking forward to seeing Fluffy again.'

'Recently gone, is she?'

'Oh, no. Fluffy passed on when I was a girl. A dear thing.'

'I'm sure.'

I had heard enough to know that at least this widow would not offer competition.

London would be the test of our alliance. It was one thing in Egypt, where we could escape in his aeroplane or where we were under the same roof. Now there would be his friends and no doubt more silvery widows with fortunes, as well as people from the Foreign Office. I wasn't worried that I wouldn't know what to say, or wouldn't measure up to some impossible standard that was in Lady Russell's mind, though I hoped not in Malcolm's. My concern was simpler and well founded. I didn't want his friends poisoning him about me because they felt someone older would be more suitable. If that were to happen, then what was so important to me would become just a passing romance, a fling after the death of his first wife before he settled down with his second. I wasn't after his money, which is what some people thought. Malcolm didn't have all that much and he was too extravagant for what he did have to last very long. Most of his first wife's fortune was in trust for the girls. Malcolm had been taken care of, thank you, but if it had been money I was after, I would have looked elsewhere. There were plenty of Lord Bullenses about. I loved Malcolm. I fell in love with him in Egypt and I stayed in love with him. I don't see that I have to defend or explain that any further to anyone.

It wasn't as easy for us to have privacy as it had been in Cairo. I was answerable to my father, not in a Victorian way, but I could hardly stay out all night. And Malcolm was not likely to go creeping about in hôtels. The FO kept a suite at Claridge's and Malcolm had the use of it. It was awkward though, because his daughters were there. I can see how someone might say I made myself purposely unavailable so that it might encourage him to propose. I can imagine Jimmy Peel's view of this, but in my defence, if that's what I was doing, I wasn't aware of it. Sometime after Lady Russell's dinner, Malcolm and I were dining at the Savoy. We had been drinking champagne and laughing about the silver widow and the Prince and his riddles. It was such a sparkling time for us. Courtship can be just the headiest thing. Malcolm said of the Prince, 'I never quite know what to expect. Puts me off a bit.'

'It's working though. English school. Shooting week-ends or whatever that was with Lord Bullen.'

'Lord Bullen seemed to take quite a fancy to you.'

'I shall call him Lord Hands.'

'Oh, I see.'

'Lord Hands was no more successful with me than the silver widow was with you. Lord Hands didn't want to discuss theology, which seemed to be your topic. Let us not mention either of them again. Now. The Prince.'

'I can't ever seem to speak with him. I believe if I could, I might be able to modify his behaviour somewhat.'

'He will confide in you if you talk to him, not just deliver him to dinner parties. Tell him what you feel.' Malcolm knew I was right, but he wasn't comfortable with the idea. I didn't mean he should turn into an agony aunt to Farouk. Malcolm had such a pained look. 'It's not a punishment you know. It's good to say how you feel sometimes.' He knew just what I meant.

'I want to see you. I miss our privacy. Can't we be alone again? Here in London?'

'Oh, Malcolm. Just when I forget about our ages, you say something positively antediluvian.'

'So sorry. I mean to say that I long to be alone with you. I ache for it.'

'Much better, indeed,' I said, not hiding my pleasure and giving him the most lascivious glance I could man-age.

'You understand, my dear, after Alice's death . . .' He stopped speaking in mid-sentence. He had never before so much as spoken her name in my presence. I had been at a loss of how I might bring it up. It was a barrier between us that I could not be the first to broach. His silence had now gone on so long that I was concerned he had lost his train of thought.

'What is it?' I asked, as gently as I could.

'It is that I believed my romantic life, if I may put it that way, was concluded. I am aware that there have been any number of women who did not agree with that. Still, I had assumed I would devote myself to my work and my daughters. Do you see?'

'I think I understand. I admire your loyalty, but I can assure you, your romantic life is quite vigorous.' I do not believe any woman in Malcolm's experience had ever made such an unambiguous reference to that particular department. I certainly had his attention.

'Does my age bother you?' he asked, which I took to mean that perhaps I'd been a bit too bold.

'What bothers me is not seeing you.'

'I believe I was happiest in Cairo. With you.'

'It was wonderful.'

'I worry, my darling. You know about what.'

'Not my age again.'

'No. Mine.'

'I want to ignore the whole question. I know people won't. Do you care?'

'I worry that I'll be too old too soon.'

'That should be my concern. And I don't care. I wish to be perfectly clear about something. I am twenty-three. You do know that, don't you?'

'It is very much on my mind. You're old beyond your years in so many ways, though I believe to understand what it is to be fifty-four, one must be fifty-four.'

'Is it so horrible?'

'Not at all. In my own mind, I'm no age at all. Or still

at Eton, perhaps. One does slow down a bit, though.'

'Then I'll join you in your mind where age doesn't matter.' We reached across the white linen of the Savoy's table, entwined our arms and each drank champagne from the other's glass. He took my hand, held it for a moment, then kissed the palm. I thought I might melt.

My friendship with Emma Lyttelton had proven difficult after Alexandria. Her visit to Egypt had not turned out as she had planned. It was her own fault, really. Jimmy Peel was quite malleable at that time. If she had gone about it with any cleverness at all, they would now be married. Men are not all that difficult. If you tell them they're wonderful and do as they want, with just a bit of resistance, they'll do what you want, certainly English ones will. Malcolm often invited Emma to FO receptions. He wasn't match-making – Malcolm didn't think like that – he simply thought she might enjoy it. There were always lots of men about at those things. I had a good talk with her at a party for the Ambassador from Brazil, who had been recalled. Everyone felt sorry for him, having to leave London for whatever the capital of Brazil was. Emma looked lovely that evening. A party at the Foreign Office should have been perfect for her. What with the Exchequer to one side and No. 10 to the other, the FO men all get so puffed up. It never fails to put single men in the proper mood. Several eligible ones were quite ready to go all silly over her, not that she had the sense to do anything about it.

We went off to a little sitting room where the walls were absolutely covered with pictures of dogs, so we could talk. She was my oldest friend, though I knew that in some way she couldn't identify, she felt I had behaved badly by taking up with Malcolm as she herself was breaking it off with Jimmy. She wanted to know how he was, which really meant was he suffering or had he found a new girl. 'He's staying at the Residency, now,' I said.

'I know. I had a letter. It has to be better for him than that horrible hôtel in Alex.'

'Do you miss him?' I asked, hoping it wasn't the wrong question.

'Oh, I don't even know,' she said with both sadness and exasperation in her voice. 'It's ever so much nicer if you have a man waiting.'

'Yes, but then others don't call, do they. Best to have one in the vicinity.'

'Oh, I know. I suppose I made a hash of it in Alex. He seemed so different. Perhaps if we'd had more privacy.' She was quite upset. She didn't like being envious, but I suppose she was. 'You're happy, aren't you?'

'Very.'

'Our family talks of little else, you know.'

'I'm not surprised. I'm glad you're there to defend me,' I said, wondering if she did. 'You'll meet someone, Emma. I know you will.'

'I just hate being unsettled like this. I feel as if I've a sign on me: Available. Enquire within. I could just throttle Jimmy. I could.'

She was about to cry. I put my arms round her and held her, trying to comfort her. I wish I could say my motives were entirely generous, but I was thinking, I'd better be nice, lest she find a way to harm my relations with her family. I wanted her to be happy, but not nearly so much as I wanted Malcolm for myself without complication. I let her cry on my shoulder, but I knew I wouldn't be seeing much of Emma after this evening.

· · ·

Malcolm kept getting reports from Woolwich about the Prince. Much of the time he didn't show up or he would be outrageously late. He ignored all the assignments. The only thing he did much about were the drills. He had taken a fancy to putting on puttees and marching about. He wasn't even a real student there. He was supposed to be cramming for admission proper while Mazhar Pasha had worked out an arrangement that had him taking the classes. It really was difficult to know what was true and what was just propaganda from Kenry House, a grand old mansion near the school that Farouk had taken for his stay.

Malcolm decided to pay a visit. I assumed he was going to have the conversation that I had urged. Perhaps that was his intention but then he asked me to accompany him. The idea that a man who regularly stood up to Prime Ministers and was at home with kings was having second thoughts about talking to a boy was unnerving. We were to observe something called Cannon Day at Woolwich, which turned out to be a pleasant and leafy place, even if it appeared a tad too drab for Malcolm's taste.

The GC's, which was the Woolwich term for Gentlemen Cadets, were turned out in their dress uniforms, all quite smart. Farouk, dressed as the others in a tight white tunic and dark grey breeches with a red stripe, stood at attention on the parade ground. Well, perhaps attention is too strong a term. The others were at attention, Farouk was waving to us. Accompanied by Mazhar Pasha, we had joined the other visitors who were for the most part parents of the GC's and old boys come back to watch. That low character, Luigi Catania of Abdin, was there as coat-holder for Farouk. Malcolm, standing on the edge of the parade ground, was wonderfully imposing. Had he chosen, Malcolm could have gone into the army. He would have made quite a general. The Prince broke ranks and came over to greet us. 'So good of you to come down,' he said to Malcolm, though he was looking at me all the while. He began greeting the other visitors as well until the instructor, a spit and polish veteran of battles on several continents, came to collect him.

The Academy's military equipment at the time was rather dated. Malcolm identified the artillery as Boer War vintage. The point of it all was that the GC's were to get some practical experience in firing the weapons. Haystacks had been piled up as targets. The instructor called for the first GC and told him, 'Enter your co-ordinates and fire two hundred metres.' The cannon went off with a grand boom though it fell short of the target. We applauded anyway. Farouk was watching, but Malcolm said he wouldn't stay on the sidelines if there were explosions to be had. He waited through the next GC who fired two hundred fifty metres and put the ordnance on the mark, setting the haystack aflame. As a squad of snookers, the students who weren't yet GC's, ran to douse it with buckets of water, Farouk jumped to the head of the queue. 'I'll have a go,' he said. Then, as he was fiddling with the co-ordinates, watching the barrel lift into position, he addressed the visitors, saying, 'I fired one of these in Luxor. A military tutor of mine was fond of it.' The instructor stepped forward to see what the Prince was doing, but before he could, and certainly before he gave approval, Farouk fired. The ordnance made an orange flash that for a moment was lost against the bright sun. It went sailing over everything, then spread out in an unruly puff that fell into the Academy's old open-back lorry which was parked in the road. It hit dead on and blew the thing up in a great fiery explosion. It was empty at the time, a blessing. The GC's gasped, then cheered and called out, 'Hip, hip, the Prince!' The water brigade of snookers looked stupefied. The only person unaffected was Farouk. 'Too much punch, I suppose, but we did the job and that's the thing. Thank you.' Then he walked off. Mazhar Pasha and Luigi Catania trotted after, leaving Malcolm and me behind.

One story that later got to Malcolm caused some alarm. As I understood it, in addition to artillery, the Prince had taken some minor interest in boxing. Malcolm thought the sport would be beneficial. 'Pugilism is pain not felt as pain,' he said. 'Until later, when one counts the bruises.'

Farouk had been given a match with another cadet and punched the poor boy silly. It later developed that the loser accused the dread Catania of bribing him to take a dive as Malcolm insisted on calling it. It was never proven, and one way or another, the whole thing was hushed up. I wouldn't doubt it though. That incident and my urging Malcolm to chat up Farouk in a more friend-ly way than he had ever done, or possibly anyone had ever done, was enough to convince Malcolm to pay a second visit to Woolwich, this time by himself.

Persuading him to tell me the whole business of what went on was like extracting teeth. He said I should have been a news-hen, one of those girl reporters who go about asking people impertinent questions. I told him I was capable only of getting information out of him.

The two of them went for a stroll on the lawns so that Malcolm might speak frankly, telling the Prince what was

on his own mind, as I had suggested. Malcolm was anticipating an ordeal.

'Well, what do you make of it?' Malcolm asked him.

'The Shop?' Farouk had picked up that term and now
used it to distraction. 'I'm going to get down to the studies. I've a plan of approach worked out. Good lads, every
one. I'll make friends, be with me always.'

'Do you miss Cairo?'

'No. No. Quite pleasant here.'

'I do a bit. I must say.' That was the most personal
thing Malcolm had ever said to him. It made Farouk
think for a moment.

'I miss my sisters sometimes. Atty writes me good letters.'

'Do you reply?'

'I'm getting stationery and that sort of thing organised.'
It was another fabrication of course and Malcolm knew it,
but he also knew they were indeed talking. They sat at an
open bungalow and looked out over the green lawns.

'It can be a hard thing to go away,' Malcolm said.
'When I went, my family was in Scotland.'

'You went to Eton. The King was at the Turin Military
Academy,' Farouk said, trying out the names.

'They're proud to have had him there. I'm sure
Woolwich will one day feel that way about you. Do you
have photographs of your sisters?' Of course he didn't.
Farouk was fond of his sisters. They were the children he
knew best. 'Why don't we see to it,' Malcolm said. 'It
would give you comfort.'

'Very good, then.'

'You know, sir, I am in London to work on the treaty.'

'Oh, yes. How is it?'

'If we are successful, both countries will benefit.'

'The King is for it.'

'Two Kings. And someday a third,' Malcolm said. 'The treaty will be my legacy to both nations.'

'Then you'll go somewhere else.'

Malcolm was getting more than he bargained for. He thought speaking with Farouk would be about school matters or family pictures. He hadn't counted on the Prince asking questions. Malcolm was committed to having a personal conversation, so he pushed on, no matter how unlikely it seemed. 'I had once thought I might be interested in India. It is a great challenge. I don't think about it much, really.'

'India. Quite large, isn't it?'

'Greater than England and Egypt together. I was thinking the other day that I am an Englishman and I believe a patriot, but I have feeling for Egypt, as well.'

'You can't be two kinds of patriot.'

'I think you can. I think it is the modern way. More feeling for one's own country, certainly, but that doesn't preclude a sense of duty to another.'

'It is like ladies, I think.' That absolutely astonished Malcolm. He wasn't a prude at all, but it offended him that Farouk would say a thing like that. The Prince just kept right on. 'I can only be Egypt. But you can have as many as you fancy. India and ladies. It is very good.'

'We are not speaking of mistresses in Mayfair.'

'Do you go there? Great fun.'

What irritated Malcolm was that it was all so casual. Farouk never had the slightest sense of his effect on another person. 'I am speaking of how you deepen your Egyptian patriotism by your feeling for England.'

'It's the same. Two countries, two mistresses. Three countries – '

'It is not worthy of you to trivialise patriotism with such an analogy.'

'Quite so. I have enjoyed our talk. That is all.'

'Not quite. Before His Majesty's accession, he believed it fundamentally important that he show the very best of manners to the people round him. Exquisite manners. Royal manners.' Malcolm was angry and allowing it to show. No one had ever spoken to Farouk in that tone. Malcolm was just getting started. 'You must train yourself to treat others with grace. If a commoner falls, he does not fall far. If a prince or a king falls, it is a serious matter.'

'I didn't mean anything.'

'You must accept that your words have power beyond what you may intend. You must learn to be judicious. You must not ever equate your nocturnal errands with the two countries that require your service.'

'I'm sorry.'

'I accept your apology.'

Malcolm arranged for Mrs Parsons to send out photographs of Farouk's sisters. He put them in Kenry House and I'm sure Farouk found a measure of satisfaction in them. It would be lovely to say that Malcolm's visit to Woolwich changed the Prince's behaviour, though nothing changed Farouk. He was always making new plans in his head, and I'm sure that while Malcolm was there he intended to mend his ways. Then he went back to Kenry House where if he said the world was flat they would all applaud and declare a holiday. It did make a difference in Malcolm, one that was important to me. After his conversation with Farouk, Malcolm invited my father to join him for a drink at Brooks's.

My father, Sir Hugh Napier, had spent his life in service of the law. When I was a girl he was a KC and I recall thinking it glamourous. When he became a judge, I realised that he's also very wise. I took pride in that, and still do and I have told him so. He has always had the most wonderful salt and pepper hair. There are lots of reasons to wish he would never grow old. For me, it's so that his lovely hair might never change. His only interests beyond the law, so far as I ever knew, were Italy, my late mother, and me. My Florentine mother used to say that the reason I am such a flirt is that at an early age I was competing with the Uffizi Gallery for my father's attention. My father has shown no inclination to remarry and as a result, I am sure, we are quite close. My father knew all about Malcolm and me. Well, perhaps not all, but he knew enough. I wanted desperately to be a fly on the wall at Brooks's. That of course was impossible. If it was difficult to get Malcolm to tell me what had happened with Farouk at Woolwich, it was nothing compared to getting him to say what he and my father discussed. I certainly knew the subject, but I wanted the very words. I grilled both of them relentlessly, trying to piece it all together.

They met in the Great Subscription Room, quite the grandest place in Brooks's. It is unchanged since the eighteenth century. I'd visited there as a girl. They began over gin and bitters for Malcolm and whisky soda for my father. Malcolm said, 'I am in your debt, Sir Hugh. I find this easier than I had imagined.'

'I always pictured a conversation of this sort. I hadn't expected the chap to be quite so distinguished, shall we say.'

'Older than yourself, I'm sure you mean.' My father was two years younger than Malcolm. It was the single part of this that gave me pause. Not that I cared, but I knew they both would.

'My regret is you'll be taking her so far away. I'm sure you understand.'

'I hope you will visit often and for as long as you are able.'

'I'm afraid the felons and riffraff of London keep me chained in High Court.'

'Bring them along! They'll be easily at home in Cairo.' I think at that point my father, who was certainly skilled in matters of argument, simply ran out of objections that might put off the inevitable. He knew that my mind was made up and there was no point forcing a breach. Both of them knew there was only one outcome to this and that they had best make it as easy as possible. 'If we do not quite have your blessing, Sir Hugh, may we at least count on your goodwill?'

'So be it.'

As far as I was concerned, the whole point of Malcolm's time in London was to court me. Now that my father had agreed, albeit reluctantly, I saw no reason to wait to be married. Malcolm was in endless meetings in Whitehall negotiating his treaty. The big sticking point was the mixed tribunals. It amounted to British citizens in Egypt not being bound to Egyptian laws, but rather to English ones. From a modern viewpoint that sounds quite pukka I am sure. At the time there was concern that if we were meant to obey Egyptian regulations even when they conflicted with English law, then every Bimbashi in the Egyptian police would treat us like camel drivers. It is amusing now that such a debate could have been the obstacle to a momentous treaty. Malcolm pushed it through with a few minor concessions, not because he believed their niggling changes were proper but because without them, there would have been no treaty at all. The first signing ceremony was at Abdin. Malcolm flew out and spent a week there. I missed him terribly and resented that he could be in Cairo without me. There was a second ceremony at the Foreign Office. Signing for us were Prime Minister Baldwin, Foreign Secretary Sir Walter Greville, and Malcolm as High Commissioner. A whole slew of Egyptians signed, though Fouad and the PM had already done so in Cairo. Farouk was brought down from Woolwich to lend his presence.

As Mr Baldwin was affixing his signature, Farouk realised he was meant to be merely a spectator. He marched up to the big mahogany table, and as Mr Baldwin was about to hand off the pen to Malcolm, Farouk just snatched it up and said, 'I'll make this official.' He scrawled 'Farouk' across the page, paying no attention to where the other signatures were. His letters were so large that he blocked out the part where Malcolm was meant to sign. Malcolm said there was some good in it because now the PM and Sir Walter knew first-hand what he had to contend with.

One of the reasons Farouk was so bold was the difficulty we'd been having with our own royal family. The old King, George V, had been succeeded by Edward VIII who didn't last the year. His American divorcée made a fuss about not wishing to harm the royal family as she went about all but dismantling it. Edward was later replaced by George VI. It made the country dizzy! Nineteen thirty-six became known as the Year of Three Kings. The newspapers and the BBC had long since agreed not to discuss the foibles of royalty. The reason for that, though now largely forgotten, is that by the iron rule of etiquette, royalty is forbidden to reply. Mr Baldwin had taken a strong stand against the marriage.

There was definitely mixed opinion about Mrs Simpson, though there was enormous sympathy for the King. I remember a dinner party in Holland Park at the height of it, where the toast offered was, 'God save the King from Mr Baldwin.'

It was particularly difficult for Malcolm in regard to Farouk. Here was Malcolm going to great lengths to assure the Prince that using the English as a model for himself would benefit Egypt. The Prince had no trouble making the connexion. He was heard to say that as we couldn't seem to settle on a monarch, perhaps it would be just as well if he used Egyptian royalty as his standard. Malcolm would never complain about it, but it was a burden for him.

We were married in Chelsea Old Church by Dean Maurice Thwaite of St Swithun's Cathedral in Kent. Dean Thwaite, who was a friend of my father, had christened me. I had already been christened once in Florence, but Dean Thwaite, who I believe was a vicar then, had insisted on doing the honours in our own church, as well. Now that my battle was concluded happily, of course I asked Emma Lyttelton to be bridesmaid. I had to plead with her a bit, but as I did not want even the appearance of difficulty, I was convincing. She arrived with Jimmy Peel! The two of them hardly knew if they were fighting or if they had made it up. Emma was nice to Jimmy, though I could see from one look at him their romance would not be rekindled. Poor Emma. She had no instinct for dealing with men, even the easy ones. I determined to find someone for her, though not just yet. My father gave me away and Sir Walter was best man. It was quite a bash, with Mr Baldwin and a batch of Royals. We invited Farouk, of course, and to Malcolm's immense pleasure he came turned out in his Woolwich dress uniform. He looked quite dashing. My father asked me to wear my mother's wedding gown and Malcolm was in full dress with white plumes and sword. After the ceremony, the Prince shook Malcolm's hand, then said to me, 'May I be the first to call you Lady Cheyne.' He kissed my hand and said, 'Charming, utterly charming.' It was the dearest he had ever been. Malcolm was beaming.

When we came out of the church, the sun shone on the gold oak-leaf braid on Malcolm's uniform. It made him radiant. What with all the Royals and the government people and then Farouk, a crowd had gathered. The pictures kept cropping up in magazines for months. The press office from the FO made a scrap-book of all the cuttings. On cold evenings I still look at it.

Our wedding trip was to Paris. Malcolm wanted to fly us there himself. He had made arrangements with de Havilland for an aeroplane but Sir Walter got wind of it and said absolutely not. It was amusing to think of Malcolm as the wild boy of the air, but next to Sir Walter he was just that. I assumed we would take the ferry across the channel, then pick up a motor-car. Malcolm certainly knew there was a ferry. He referred to it as public transport. He said that if Sir Walter was putting the kibosh on the aeroplane, then he could jolly well sort out an appropriate substitute. He believed that if the government could send the Devonshire to bring Farouk out of Egypt, they could send her to Southampton to deliver us to France. A driver from the Embassy in Paris met us at Le Havre and whisked us off to the Crillon. We had just settled in when Malcolm got the cable that changed everything. Fouad was dead.

2

The abrupt end of our honeymoon was the least of the problems that the King's death created. Malcolm had always said it would take two years in England to make Farouk one of us. He had been in London six months. Now he was going home to be King. Egyptian law required that he be eighteen, counting from conception, before he could be crowned. That meant a regency until three months past his seventeenth birthday. Malcolm said that it wouldn't be an insurmountable problem, because the Palace would take the entire time till the Prince was of age arguing about who the regents should be. 'My darling,' he said as we were flying back to Cairo, 'if you think Prince Farouk could be difficult, I assure you, we have seen nothing compared to what will come our way with King Farouk.' The title made me blink. It was so new, it sounded strange.

Fouad was interred at Al-Rifa'i, the mosque of the Dynasty, where his forebears rest. An enormous cortège marched from Abdin, down the Sharia Mohammed Ali,

past the night-clubs and restaurants, all closed for this
solemn day. The staffs, in their uniforms, were standing
in the street, many of them weeping. Fouad's bier was
covered in gold cloth and Farouk walked behind, watching with a face that showed no emotion. What was he
thinking, I wondered? There was no way to know, of
course. Farouk was born a public figure and on an occasion such as this his royal mask was in place. Following
the Prince were the members of the government and the
ambassadors of the other nations, of whom Malcolm was
the first. At the Mosque, which is in front of the Citadel,
seven tethered bull oxen waited. When the procession
arrived, the throats of the bulls were cut and their blood
spilled on the King's remains. It also splashed on his son.
In the odd way that one can react to significant events, I
found myself concerned with the disposition of those
slaughtered bulls. I was relieved to learn that as a matter
of custom, the meat is given to the poor.

Malcolm and I were taken into Al-Rifa'i but kept
behind a wooden barrier, in what I suppose was a side
chapel. We had a plain view of the King's body which had
been laid out on a marble bier. Farouk knelt and prayed
before it. He looked up at us and nodded to Malcolm.
When Farouk looked to me I could feel his eyes linger.
This was a solemn Moslem occasion. I was covered
appropriately. Still, it was an appraisal and not of a sacred
nature.

Malcolm was right about the regency. They finally
managed to come up with three regents. One of them was
Farouk's uncle, the old Prince Mohammed Ali. He was
next in line for the throne until Farouk produced an heir.
He carried the name of the Dynasty, but he was an
Anglophile. Had he been King, England wouldn't have

had much to worry about. He was unknown to the common Egyptians, and they loved Farouk. They already thought of him as their King. Farouk didn't pay any attention to the regents. He went on holiday trips to the continent and ignored Malcolm's attempts to convince him to finish his schooling in England until he was of age.

Cairo looked different to me now. I had never complained about it of course, but it had always seemed a harsh place, not nearly so pleasant as Alex. It's a sand-coloured city, best at night when silvery moonlight lay over the buildings and flickered, like fire-light. It could be wildly romantic. On the night of Fouad's funeral, when my husband and I embraced, Malcolm whispered that I was his 'nymph of the downward smile and sidelong glance'. I hadn't thought I had a 'downward smile' but as at that moment we were as close as a man and woman can be, I saw no purpose in disputing him.

On Sundays it was Malcolm's custom to go to Gezira for the races. It was great fun for me as everyone there fussed over us. Malcolm never seemed to enjoy it particularly, or even notice it, but I know he did, as he rarely missed a Sunday. Before our marriage, people at Gezira regarded me as some sort of femme fatale, which I of course adored. As Lady Cheyne I may have lost some of my mystery, but I had another concern: Sarah and Elizabeth. I got on well with them though I knew better than anyone that our relations were fragile.

As I was showing Malcolm the picture hat I planned to wear on Sunday next, I asked, 'Would the girls enjoy the races, do you suppose?'

'They well might,' he said.

'Why don't you ask them?'

'Good idea. You do it.'

'Of course. What do you think of this hat?' I asked. It was trimmed with cabbage roses and I thought it absolutely smashing. I had brought it out from London. I turned about like a mannequin, showing it off.

'It's lovely. Can you arrange something similar for the girls?'

Malcolm wouldn't deny the girls anything, it's just that he never thought about taking them to Gezira. I imagine that if he thought about it at all he would have concluded that had they wanted to go, they would have said so. As a result, they had never been. They were pleased at the prospect of the expedition, though not as excited as with their new hats. We got them at Cicurel's, the department store in Kasra al Nil Street, that Cairenes invariably call the Bond Street of Cairo. It was the only shop that could accommodate a request for wide-brim picture hats. Malcolm had no idea how difficult finding simple items could be.

The racecourse is at the Sporting Club on an island in the Nile. It gets rather confusing as Gezira is the name of both the Club and the word for island. It is a green oasis where the air is sweeter than the rest of the city. I believe Sarah and Elizabeth thought it glamourous, because when we arrived they stopped adjusting their hats and just gazed out the window of the Rolls. Each time I came to Gezira I wished (though I never said it) that we might live in one of the lovely houses here rather than the draughty Residency. I suspect the girls were having similar thoughts.

As we walked across the great central lawn, most everyone nodded to Malcolm and smiled admiringly at me and the girls. They might have come out for the racecourse or the links, but it was seeing Malcolm, en famille, that they would remember. As one entered the club, there were terraces on either side. The one on the left was for ladies. The girls and I stopped there to sort ourselves out before we joined Malcolm who had gone on ahead to the paddock. He was in the habit of inspecting the horses before the races.

It was a time for him to see and talk to any interested parties in an unofficial way. It is not a custom he would have followed in England, but it was useful here. I don't mean that he was a Sultan dispensing favours to desperate supplicants, but simply that while we admired the horses and had a word or two with the jockeys, someone might greet us and speak a few pleasantries, perhaps informing Malcolm of a situation that did not warrant an official call. It was going smoothly until a Major Rand all but waylaid us. The Major was a part of an organisation called the Community Council, an association of Englishmen resident in Cairo, who take an interest in civic affairs. The Major is elderly and goes about with a parrot on his shoulder, a habit Malcolm detests. The girls thought it enchanting. Before the Major could monopolise Malcolm, with his view of the Mixed Tribunals, a topic of limited appeal, Sarah and Elizabeth crowded round him to see the parrot, who was called Charger.

'Can he speak?' Sarah asked.

'Let's ask him, shall we?' the Major said. 'Ladies, may I present Charger. Now, Charger, you are in the presence of the Misses Cheyne. What do you say?'

To our delight, the bird answered, saying, 'Cheyne, Cheyne. Hello.'

'May I touch him?' Sarah asked.

'Certainly, my dear.' The Major stroked the white feathers on Charger's breast to show how it was done.

Each girl did the same, with a greater reverence than I would have expected. Charger seemed to like it, as he cooed contentedly. I caught Malcolm's eye just then, and I knew he was thinking that for once the Major didn't seem quite such a bore.

After we had seen the paddock and the Major had moved on, as we were going to our seats for the first race, the club orchestra played 'God Save the King'. The English, which was almost everyone, stood. Malcolm acknowledged them with a tip of his hat and a gracious nod of his lion's head. Sarah and Elizabeth were watching me to see what they should do. I had done this before, of course, but never as a model for the girls. I smiled at my husband, then turned my head slightly to smile at the people. I kept my gesture smaller than Malcolm's and I was careful not to do more than he did. The girls, bless them both, simply followed my lead. Cheyne blood showed when as a matter of instinct, and not instruction, the girls kept their nods and smiles slightly less than mine. They understood the nature of the exercise perfectly. I know Malcolm saw it all because he was in a good mood all the rest of the day. I knew then what my marital challenge would be. I must conduct myself appropriately to public life and I must see that the girls do the same. I had managed part of it in that the girls already looked to me as a model, though they didn't realise they were doing so. The larger step, of developing real feeling among the three of us, had yet to be accomplished.

After the last race, we took them to the dining terrace, quite the nicest place in the club. It looks out on the polo ground and the links. I wanted them to see the main table, where the evening's buffet was laid on in a manner that never failed to make Malcolm and me smile. Each item of food had been reconstructed after it was cooked. On this day, six pheasant had been put back together, including the feathers, and spread out in a circle, surrounded by fish, presumably cooked, with fins and scales in place. The girls found it as amusing as we did, though they refused to eat any of it.

'As it owes as much to taxidermy as cuisine, you are excused,' Malcolm said with a grin.

'What happens to it?' Sarah asked.

'Whatever is left is given to the servants,' Malcolm explained.

I could see that pleased Sarah. I didn't explain that it wasn't done out of generosity but rather that the club would never serve yesterday's food. When we were seated at a table under a comforting acacia, the girls were amused by the sparrows who came near, picking crumbs from the ground. Then a rude black-tailed kite came swooping down, coming straight for us at an alarming speed, its wicked little beak stretched wide. Sarah grabbed my arm as that screaming feathered scavenger plucked a slice of buttered toast directly from our table and flew off with it. It had happened before, many times I'm sure, but not to the girls. They were caught between fright and fascination.

The most irksome difficulty in my new life at the Residency was with Alice Cheyne's wretched Chinese carpets. Malcolm had put them in the ball-room because he hadn't known what else to do with them. They were a barrier for me and I longed to resolve the dilemma. Jimmy Peel had once seen me looking at them. He hadn't quite been spying, but he had been lurking about watching me. He understood my problem, not that he was willing to help me with it. Jimmy saw everything, but never could bring himself to act on any of it. I all but begged him for help and he pretended it was simply a matter of décor. Perhaps if I had been older I would have been able to ask my husband to remove the carpets that were associated with my predecessor. I didn't want to bring up her name if I didn't absolutely have to. The idea that Malcolm would have brought carpets to Egypt always struck me as faintly ridiculous. This country doesn't have much, but it certainly has carpets. The ball-room is the Residency's most famous feature. There are handsome reception rooms and galleries, but every visitor asks for a look at the ball-room, so despite the fact that the walls are hung in silk damask and the ceiling is quite high, the conversation inevitably turns to Alice's carpets. I made short work of similar problems. There was a collection of furniture that had accumulated since the last century. Much of it was in need of repair. I either had it set right or I removed the markings and gave the lot of it to the servants. I suppose they sold it in the bazaar. The carpets alone made me cross. I didn't think much about Farouk because excepting the thorn of Alice's Chinese carpets, I was happy in my life.

Emma and I wrote regularly during that time. She and Jimmy were talking again. I don't think she knew anything about his friend at the Palace, though that seemed to have cooled a bit. I told Emma she was well out of it. He'd never marry her. Jimmy had been having a high old time. He was a great dinner guest and a good fellow to go to night-clubs, but not a husband for Emma.

In one of her letters she asked, wasn't it difficult to run the Residency? It wasn't, really. For one thing, there's a competent staff and they do most of it. When I was a girl we had spent a great deal of time in the British Embassy in Rome. The Ambassador was a friend of my parents. I lived there the entire summer I was Elizabeth's age.

My problem wasn't menus or diplomatic receptions. What I longed to know was how did I measure up to Alice. Malcolm and I were quite happy in our private life. Still, I wondered about Alice. Had she done a better job in China with the Embassy than I was now doing? Had she done it differently? Malcolm wouldn't entertain questions of that sort. He would have thought it disloyal. I wasn't fishing for compliments. I wanted to know.

When Noël Coward was in Cairo and staying with us, I thought I might learn something. He had also been a guest in Pekin. In one of his rare comments about his former life, Malcolm said that Noël had adored Alice. Malcolm and Noël weren't close friends – Malcolm didn't have close friends – but he admired Noël enormously and enjoyed his company. Noël was immune to my flirting, of course. There was always some unpleasant remark or another from someone about him. Malcolm wouldn't permit that sort of talk. He really did fancy night-clubs and entertainment and he was hardly going to limit his pleasure based on what certain persons of an artistic nature did in private. Nöel must have known that Malcolm had defended him, though they never spoke of it. To have Nöel at the piano after dinner was a treat given to very few. He sat at the Residency's old Bechstein and sang:

> At *twelve noon*
> *The natives swoon*
> *And no further work is done.*
> *But mad dogs and Englishmen*
> *Go out in the mid-day sun.*

Noël always said that song was about Cairo in summer, though I can assure you if Noël Coward found himself in

Egypt in summer, it would not have been in Cairo. Besides, Malcolm told me later that when Noël was in China, he said the song was about Pekin. I took Noël aside and told him that I wanted to know about Alice for my own sake, but also because it might be helpful in raising the girls and in caring for Malcolm. I assured him I wasn't jealous and that my interest ought to be understandable. He was dear to me about my Alice questions. I told him what Malcolm had said, and he confirmed it. They had been great friends and in fact he had visited Alice's grave in Hong Kong just last year. I'm sure he wrote to Malcolm about it at the time, though it was never mentioned. Noël told me that he thought as Alice got older she and Malcolm had grown similar. He was certain that they believed they loved one another, but he was not sure that it held much meaning. 'They had been married a long while,' he said as we were taking tea. 'If they could have taken separate holidays from time to time, I believe it would have invigorated the marriage.' It was difficult for him to tell me that. He didn't want to be disloyal to Malcolm or to Alice's memory, but he knew it would give me comfort. It also gave me courage to ask for his counsel in the matter of the Chinese carpets. 'They're quite beautiful, I'm sure, but when Malcolm sees them, he gets a far-away look and I know he's with Alice.' It was just the sort of problem Noël liked, as it concerned friends, love, and furniture. He got up straight away and insisted that we go directly to the ball-room.

He smiled when he saw the carpets. 'Oh, my dear, my dear,' Noël said. 'Those are Alice's imperial pillar rugs.'

'And what may I ask might that be?'

'They're from various palaces. They're not meant for the floor at all. They were specially made to be wrapped about pillars in grand houses. They're loosely woven, don't you see?' He picked up the corner of one and crushed it between his fingers. 'You can't do that to a carpet meant for a floor. They are much too valuable to be left underfoot.'

'What should I do?' I said, sounding, I am sure, even younger than my years.

'Give them to a museum, of course. Select one with a furniture collection.'

'Would the British Museum be interested, do you think?'

'Not there. Malcolm will want to go see them, then the whole business will start up again.'

'Where then?' I asked, starting to treat him like my father who was meant to sort out all my problems.

'The Liverpool Museum has a furniture department. They'd be pleased to get them, I'm sure. Do it in Alice's name and the world will marvel at your selfless generosity.'

'Do you think it will make Malcolm uneasy?'

'Say the girls will appreciate it in future. That is your trump card.'

'Yes. I see. Thank you.'

'I can't bear the thought of you being unhappy over such a trivial matter. Malcolm would certainly not want that. He does love you. I have never seen him happier.'

He had solved it and without much effort on his part. The Liverpool Museum was thrilled to get them and put several on permanent exhibit. Once, after the war, Malcolm and I were in Liverpool, but by then he had forgotten all about it.

The business with the carpets made me confident that I could manage the Residency's affairs. I was more concerned for Sarah and Elizabeth. Malcolm never said so directly, but I knew he was depending on me to keep them content. He didn't have the faintest idea how I might go about that, but as I had been their age far more recently than Malcolm, I knew how delicate a matter it could be. I did not wish to replace Alice in their affections, only in their father's. I didn't often raise their mother's name, but if Alice were to be mentioned, I made a point of how much I admired her.

I took another opportunity to move closer to the girls when they mentioned that they had taken an interest in the souk. I arranged for us to spend an afternoon observing this ancient way of buying and selling. The idea of bargaining, which is of course the principle upon which the bazaar has been based for a thousand years, made the girls uneasy. They preferred things be settled, and it's little wonder considering all they'd been through. There were similar markets in China, I am sure, though Sarah and Elizabeth's standard of comparison was England, where shops keep regular hours and prices are posted and known to all. What the girls liked about the souk was the great abundance of merchandise. The whole lot was set out in the road for all to see or touch in a way that had no rhyme or reason. There was a long tin roof that covered much of it. Only a little sliver of the sky could be seen.

It felt as if we had landed in the attic of a madwoman, or as Elizabeth remarked, 'A great, huge jumble sale.' We drifted through a world of ironmongers, carpet-sellers, and jewellery makers who sat cross-legged in front of their wares, in an attitude of religious contemplation. It was a sham, as they had their eye out for any passing European.

We developed a particular fondness for the spice market where there were lovely little hills of intensely coloured spices spilling over the top of wicker baskets. There would be a concentrated yellow – saffron most

likely – and next to it, an equal mound of the richest
green peppercorns, then coriander, frankincense, cinna-
mon and whatever else it all was. 'Special price. For you,
special price,' the man said. I bought a pinch of the ones
of the richest colour and the man wrapped each sample
in a tiny parcel and tied it with string. Elizabeth kept
them in her rooms at the Residency, spread out next to
her bed, her own little spice market, until it drew insects
and she had to have the servants take it away.

They had heard of the tent-maker's bazaar, and the
idea held great interest. Sarah had assumed that the tents
were of the sort that were put up at the Residency for outdoor luncheons. It turned out that those were entirely
bespoke and not on display. The tents we liked the most
were called sewans and they were of the sort that had
been used as the royal enclosure at Montazeh on the
evening the girls and I were presented to the old King.
That particular sewan, made of coloured, quilted fabric,
was far more grand than the ones on offer in the souk. We
went inside the largest and found brass lanterns and carpets. Sarah asked, 'Do you suppose Rudolph Valentino
was a customer?' It was quite droll of her and though I
can't say who began it, once Rudolph Valentino had been
mentioned, we began to sing. It was quite spontaneous,
and if I do say, perfectly in key:

I'm the Sheikh of Araby
Your love belongs to me.
At night when you're asleep,
Into your tent I'll creep.

The fellow in charge was amused for a moment, but
soon saw we weren't quite cash customers. He went all

fidgety, which meant we should move on. I believe recognising the sewan, and knowing its name, all from their own Egyptian experience, and then singing that silly song made a turning point for us. It meant they were comfortable and behaving as they no doubt would do had I not been there. I didn't forget that I was their step-mother and not their sister, though given our ages it would have been unlikely that I could have pretended to be a stern grey elder.

We wandered a bit, until we heard the musical clinking of brass castanets that announced the presence of the liquorice-water man. When Elizabeth saw him, with his brass tank strung across his shoulder and his basket of sweets, she wouldn't be content without a taste. Malcolm had been abundantly clear before we had set out. We weren't to eat anything in the souk. 'Liquorice-water is quite out of the question,' I said, as firmly as I was able.

'P'pa didn't say anything about sweets.'

'Darling, I promised your father we wouldn't eat anything,' I said, feeling awfully strict and a bit foolish.

'Only a tiny bit. Oh, please, Vera, please,' Elizabeth said.

'P'pa wouldn't mind,' Sarah said. 'He meant we shouldn't have our luncheon here.'

It was a child's argument. Malcolm was quite plain. He didn't want us eating anything because not even Allah knew where it had been. They so wanted to taste it, and if the truth be known, so did I. The fellow was so appealing, all bent over from the tank and the basket of the sticky liquorice he used for flavour. I gave him a few piastres and asked for a small sample. He was so pleased that he had European customers, that he tore off three great strips and wrapped them in butcher's paper. Sarah stared suspiciously, then said, 'On count of three, we'll all take a bite.' We counted aloud and then attacked the liquorice. It was lovely and chewy and all sugary. We laughed and began pushing it into our mouths. It made our lips and tongues go black, so after a short while we gave what we hadn't eaten to the urchins who followed us everywhere, begging for baksheesh. The liquorice did not make us ill but it did make us quite thirsty. We bought a bottle of fizzy water, which was thought quite safe, though there were no drinking glasses. I realised that more experienced mothers brought such items with them. I'm sure Alice would have been properly equipped. The fellow offered the use of his tin cup, but that's where I drew the line, not that the girls were about to accept such an offer. Instead, we drank directly from the bottle, a ghastly habit. 'Better to tell your father we ate liquorice than tell him we drank water in this manner,' I said as I gulped it down, shame-lessly. They agreed it was much the wisest course that it be our secret.

We had one more bit of adventure when we came upon a bird-seller with a remarkably vigorous song-bird, a little yellow thing with a wide fan-tail, a canary of some sort I should think. It lived in a wire cage that had been mirrored. It was Sarah who realised that the crea-ture was singing to its reflection in the belief that it had company. It was hardly a new technique for producing music from song-birds, but it was new to Sarah and she was so happy to have sorted it out without any help from me. It made her feel mature and I know she was pleased to have her sister's admiration for explaining it. There was a different sort of reward for me. I believe I came to know one of the joys of children. I observed the moment when Sarah felt a bit older, and a bit more confident of herself. That I was able to play a small part in that was my pleasure.

As we rode back to the Residency, the girls leaned against me and were soon asleep, comforted in the soft cocoon of the Rolls's leather and my arms. They were my little chicks and I was moved that they were coming to depend on me. As I watched over them, I knew their happy presence in my life made my connexion with Malcolm ever deeper. The girls depended on me, certainly, but in another way I depended on them. I held them close, all the way home.

I believe the entire city was excited at the prospect of Farouk's investiture, I know I certainly was. The ceremony was to be at Parliament. The Prince made the journey from Abdin in a golden coach surrounded by the royal guard in their red tarbooshes. Barefoot Sudanese boys in white robes ran alongside. The coach was preceded by the Egyptian Cavalry. Malcolm looked at those horse soldiers and said to me, 'Soon his to command.' It gave us both pause. They were followed by Nazli and the Princesses. The Queen, about to become Queen Mother, was unveiled, which was a shock to some, but a message that she wasn't going to stay in the harem any longer. I only got a glimpse because Malcolm and I had to be in our places at Parliament, in the Hall of Deputies.

In the first rows, among the British generals and diplomats, were the Arab Sheikhs in their robes and the European dignitaries. Malcolm, in full dress, towered over them all. As Farouk passed by on his march to the platform, I saw Fafette Zulficar smile radiantly. Farouk looked right through her and turned to me. My dear husband thought it was he who was being acknowledged.

In his last moments as Prince, Farouk climbed the stairs to the platform and knelt before the Imam who had been his theology tutor and was also rector of Al-Azhar University. He held the gold crown of Egypt's earlier boy-king. He spoke in Arabic, but Mazhar Pasha had supplied English translations. There was a long bit about Allah's greatness, and then about the Night of Power when the Koran came down from heaven. Finally, the rector said, 'Wear the gold crown that sat upon the head of Tutankhamen. Commander of sea, land and air, in Allah's name: Farouk, King of Egypt.' He placed the crown on the King's head and himself kneeled as Farouk rose. It was all graceful, but the crown looked precarious. Tutankhamen had been ten years old. Farouk was now six feet tall with a man's head. Everyone was watching the crown rather than its latest custodian, wondering what would happen should it fall off.

There was a great round of parties and celebrations and Malcolm and I were expected to drop in at many of them. Over the next days, Farouk gave several grand balls at Abdin, each for one thousand guests. On this evening, his first as King, he travelled about the city, making appearances at several of the embassy parties and greeting crowds of his subjects. There was no advance notice of which party he might favour. He just popped up, sending ambassadors and their wives into complete dithering confusion.

As we were driving from the Dutch Embassy to the French, Malcolm made a detour into the centre of the city and had the Rolls stop near the Ezbekiya Gardens, where it seemed the entire city was out to celebrate. There were pictures of Farouk in windows, in trees, and on lorries. Green Crescent banners flew and there was random gunfire in the air. The fellahin were dizzy with pleasure. Fires with long spits had been started in the road. Mutton was cooked and handed out along with milk pudding and baklava. The people were eating and dancing into a delirium. It was the moment I became fully aware of the dimension of what was occurring. Malcolm said, 'No monarch ever had a better start.'

'Is he up to it?'

'That is no longer a question we need concern ourselves with. The fact is, for better or worse, that boy is the King of Egypt. I shall do what I can, offer what counsel he'll take, but in truth, I have come to agree with the Egyptians: It is in Allah's hands.'

Despite Malcolm's fatalistic comment, he was in rather a dark mood after all the parties. At home that night, he'd gone into his dressing room and gave no sign of emerging. I wondered if it was something I had said or perhaps done, but Malcolm was hardly one to pout. I knocked, and when he escorted me in, I realised I hadn't ever been in this room before. It was lined with his cupboards and served as a little hideaway for him. 'Whatever do you do in here?' I asked.

'Well, I don't know, really.'

I could see his gloom had little to do with me. I should have guessed. Malcolm took political issues personally. This had to do with the coronation. I sat next to him on a tatty little divan that looked as if it had come from the souk. 'I'm losing him,' he said. 'He patronises me.'

'You mustn't take it so hard.'

'What matters is, if there's a war it will come to Egypt. Of that you may be certain.'

'I see.'

'Do you?'

'Give me some credit. Obviously we must see they abide by the treaty.'

'I give you great credit, my dear.' As he said that, he began to stroke my hair. It was a loving gesture and a signal that his mood was lifting, though he continued to examine the question. 'He'll pay no attention to the treaty. I didn't have long enough with him. Next he'll choose a bride, you know. He'll want to put her off in a harem along with our treaty.'

'Would you fancy that? Your wife in a gilded cage?'

'Only if I could be there with her.' Then he kissed me and we discovered a purpose for that silly little divan.

Malcolm and I went to many parties and receptions, though we had less glamourous duties as well. After the son of one of the PM's deputies died unexpectedly, Malcolm felt he should pay tribute at a ceremony marking forty days of mourning. The young man was about my age, though we had never met him. The father was a Mr Afifi who served as go-between for Malcolm in dealings with the PM. For me, it was an opportunity to visit the City of the Dead, which is where the younger Afifi was buried. As I understood it, it was a village of houses that also served as tombs. As unlikely as that seemed to a European, I reminded myself that in Egypt death has a sanctity that can be quite dear and yet at the same time it is an industry. Still, I was a trifle nervous as we set out because I was never certain if I'd be admitted to any Moslem institution with a religious aspect, which is most all of them. It is a rich culture in so many ways, though the Moslem view of my sex is positively Neanderthal.

Malcolm thought we should take Jimmy Peel as he knew a bit about all the praying. He had made a study of it. Mazhar Pasha was the best one for that sort of thing, but Malcolm never completely trusted him.

'I'm always interested in these events,' Jimmy said, 'though I must say I'm at a loss to understand why you feel you should attend.'

'Simple Christian decency, Mr Peel,' Malcolm said.

'Yes, of course. It's that Europeans are rarely in attendance.'

'Then it will be an adventure.'

'Yes,' Jimmy said, extending the word a bit and suggesting that he thought the whole business was for political advantage. Perhaps it was, but it was also the right thing to do and that is why we were going.

There was some confusion in getting there. The graveyard, as I kept thinking of it, is to the southeast of the city near the quarries in the Mokattam Hills – the source of limestone for the building of Cairo houses since the time of the Sphinx. We arrived rather later than we had intended, which made Malcolm cross. Jimmy had explained what we could expect, but nonetheless I was not prepared for the enormity of the place. It was at least the size of Hyde Park. We found what appeared to be the start of a thoroughfare. A porter was loitering there and we had our driver ask where the Afifi family might be found. The fellow was of no help even after Malcolm gave him baksheesh. If a plan for the City of the Dead existed, it was not offered to us. I often think Egyptians have an aversion to maps, probably because maps are information and not to be given out lightly.

Lacking a guide or a plan, we simply began walking about. As Jimmy explained, the mausoleums are built like Cairo houses, set out in streets, pressed together, one on top of the next. Perhaps because it was so still, and of course because the mausoleums had such an odd double purpose, sheltering both the living and the dead, I was uneasy. The strangeness, what I once heard someone (a European, of course) call 'the otherness' of Egypt seemed embodied in a city that made little distinction between life and death. I don't mean I had those thoughts at the time – then it just seemed macabre. The place put me in mind of the seashore out of season, when the cottages and the hôtels sit empty. I kept expecting to see vultures flying about, like the gulls at Brighton, but there was only the dusty quiet.

Jimmy, bless him, really was the best guide because he knew what would interest us. The Egyptian guides always told too much, as if they were being paid by the word. 'The ceremony we've come for is the arba'in,' Jimmy told us. 'It marks the end of the mourning period.'

'Will I be permitted to go inside?' I asked.

'Certainly,' Jimmy said. 'People live here year-round. I suspect the Afifi family uses it more in the traditional way. For burial, that is.'

'Anything more we ought to bear in mind, in the event we discover the correct house?' Malcolm asked.

'We shall improvise,' Jimmy said, with a mischievous look that had little to do with Christian decency.

I was still trying to understand that these houses were indeed houses but also tombs. It was quite complicated, as there were mosques scattered about and one small café though it was shuttered. I suppose in that regard it was no different from more traditional streets. The houses were rather low, two storeys at the highest. Some had square harem windows with lattice shutters, but most were modest.

As we were taking it all in, looking for someone who might be able to direct us, Jimmy said, 'A Moslem burial is rather less complicated than I once thought. I believe it is because the living feel directly connected to the dead.'

'I am sure you're right,' Malcolm said. 'Still, there is an element of the surreal here and it cannot be denied.'

I suppose the presence of English people had raised some sort of alarm, because a bare-footed and veiled Egyptian woman carrying a palm branch saw us and ran ahead, no doubt to report our arrival. Soon enough, an Egyptian gentleman in Western clothes came hurrying toward us, waving his arms.

'Sir Malcolm, Sir Malcolm,' the fellow said. 'I am here. We are so very honoured. Welcome, indeed. Merci beaucoup. Thank you.'

This was Mr Afifi himself. If Jimmy had thought Malcolm had some political purpose in our coming, it was nothing compared to Mr Afifi who was quite an excitable fellow, though whether that was due to our presence or the death of his son, I didn't know. He was making salaam upon salaam and it wouldn't have surprised me if he had suggested we pose for photographs. He had the grey look government functionaries of all nations take on after a few years. He was dressed in a brown tweed suit that seemed right for neither a funeral nor a day at home. I suppose he was about Malcolm's age.

He planted himself at my husband's side and said, 'You know, I hope, Sir Malcolm, that we are not among the residents of the Qarafa.' When he could get a word in, Jimmy told us that was the Egyptian name for this place. 'We bury here,' Mr Afifi said, 'though our home, which I hope you will someday do us the additional honour of visiting, is in the Quartier Al-Roun by the Syrian church.'

It all came tumbling out of him, a bit of an apology, though also a boast and in a mix of languages. When Jimmy caught my eye, I thought we both might laugh.

Mr Afifi took us to his family's house which was larger than those nearby, a point he did not comment upon. The entry-way was strewn with fragrant flowers which didn't quite mask an elusive musty odour. We stepped into a modest whitewashed drawing-room crowded with family members who seemed as taken with our arrival as Mr Afifi. There was a low ceiling and Malcolm all but filled the room. It was quite warm, though the family did not look at all uncomfortable. Several of the women were holding palm branches of the sort the veiled woman carried. Mr Afifi introduced Malcolm as if he were not the King's plenipot, but the King himself. He gave no sign of bothering about Jimmy or me, so Malcolm nodded to the family members and said, 'May I present Lady Cheyne and Mr James Peel, tutor to King Farouk.' That brought an appreciative bit of cooing from the relatives. Malcolm might be an English grandee, but Jimmy's was the name to conjure with in this household or whatever it was. They knew Malcolm had dealings with the English King, but that was a faraway business. Jimmy had, or so they thought, traffic with the only monarch who mattered.

A buffet of salt fish, bread, and sweet cakes had been set out, though I couldn't imagine eating, as flies buzzed about the table, unimpeded. A servant brought Turkish coffee, which we accepted, though I did not drink it. Malcolm could always take food to his mouth without consuming any of it, a diplomatic skill I have yet to master. When the coffee had been poured, two elderly religious men who looked quite alike, brothers certainly, possibly twins, each with wrinkled skin and thick eye-glasses, who Jimmy explained were called fikees, began reciting verses from the Koran. Jimmy told me, quietly, 'The boy is buried here.'

'Yes,' Mr Afifi murmured. 'Asaad is here, but soon he will go on his journey. He is Hadji. He will be protected.'

I did not require Jimmy to explain that what was meant was that the deceased had made a pilgrimage to Mecca. Mr Afifi may have been foolish in some ways, but he was bereaved and I felt we should honour that.

'I'm sure it gives you great comfort,' Malcolm said. He called Mr Afifi 'Abu Asaad' which Jimmy told me later meant Father of Asaad, and though not strictly Egyptian, the respect in it, which Malcolm intended, was clear enough.

'Yes, yes. Thank you,' Mr Afifi said. The elderly fikees were directing their recitation to what I now realised was Asaad's tomb. It had been built of bricks in a corner of what I had thought of as a library adjacent to the drawing-room. It was recently made and did not appear quite completed as there was a gap in the bricks near the top. Whether there was a religious aspect in that or simply unfinished construction, Jimmy didn't know. The women had broken the palm branches into pieces and laid the bits at the tomb, along with sweet basil, both of which were traditional offerings. Whatever the sacred nature of the arba'in, all the fussing stirred up the flies. They came swarming out of the not quite walled-up tomb as if they had been shot out of a gun, most of them going straight away for the food. Malcolm was able to ignore them, save those that went to his face. I slapped them all away. It was an involuntary reaction and I hope not offensive. Malcolm's expression was the usual mask, though he could not be unaffected by the discomfort.

I so wanted to feel at least a part of the family's religious awe, though all I could really see were the wretched
flies with their tiny green eyes and incessant drone. Over
it all, the fikees kept up their recitation, each one speaking his verses in turn. Once the flies were out, despite
Egyptian burial techniques, I knew we were smelling the
rank odour of putrefying flesh. The stench was beginning
to fill my head. I began to perspire, and not from the
heat. It was hardly my first experience of Egyptian flies,
though until now I had not been under siege by any
which had issued directly from a corpse. I felt that a
swarm of the ghastly things had been draped over my
back, like a cape, as if they were linked one to the next,
making a chain of their beating wings. I soon had the
unsettling sensation that the surge was coming not from
the tomb, but rather from my arms and face. I saw in my
mind's eye, that my cape of flies had emerged from my
person, not from any particular orifice, but rather as if by
unnatural magic directly from my flesh. I was in a cocoon
of my own making. It was terrifying and though a part of
me – the part that was clinging to mental stability – knew
it was not so, it did not seem any the less real. The horror of it wasn't simply that these hideous little creatures
were coming out of me, but that I could see them doing
so as if I were standing outside myself watching as my
hair turned entirely to a swirl of flies, buzzing about my
skull like the devil's halo. I was both source and victim of
these furies. I went all wobbly. Malcolm saw it and he
held me by my arm. Jimmy took the other. I kept thinking, Oh, God or Allah or whichever, please don't let me
faint.

'Can you stand?' Malcolm asked, meaning, You must
stand.

'Yes,' I said, hoping it was so. I was reacting like a child, when what was required was that I be a diplomat's wife. I held myself upright and determined to ignore the insects. As the old fikees continued their recitation, Malcolm nodded to Mr Afifi in respect, thanked him for his hospitality, and we were able to take an early leave.

On the return journey, Jimmy told us that the buffet the flies were feasting upon was not for the family at all – but would later be given to the poor in tribute to Asaad.

'Well, that's a relief,' I said. It made both Malcolm and Jimmy laugh, though not unkindly.

'Should we ever need an example of the divide between us and the Egyptians, the arba'in is certainly it,' Jimmy said.

'It's not the religious aspect though, is it,' Malcolm said.

'No,' I said. 'It's not Allah that divides us. It's hygiene.' We rode in silence after that. I tried to push the memory of my hallucination out of my mind. I felt perfectly normal again, though there was little question that for a few recent moments all my doubts about this difficult country and my place in it had descended upon me. A number of fleeting fragments of thought raced through me. I couldn't get a proper handle on most of it save one question: Had this been an isolated incident or would something like it come again? I didn't tell Malcolm about my little break as it would only upset him. For now I contented myself with looking back at the red sun over the chalky quarries of the Mokattam Hills.

3

The King had invited us to go with him on a celebratory cruise on the river. His Nile yacht, the Kassed Kheir, was a gorgeous vessel made of polished teak. We sailed from Alexandria, out of the Yacht Club harbour. The cruise would last a week, perhaps longer, depending on how much the King was enjoying it. The Queen Mother would be in the party, accompanied by Madame Zulficar and Fafette, along with Mazhar Pasha who was acting as escort to the Queen Mother, and most happily for Malcolm and me, Sarah and Elizabeth were invited.

I don't know if the Nile is the oldest river, I don't know how anyone would determine such a thing, but to Egyptians, it is the mother of all rivers. It flows through the desert and seems like a god to the people who live along it. They depend on it for so much and suffer so when it is not good to them. Malcolm said, 'The desert is time, but the river is life.' As for royal yachts, this was my first. I admit to feeling a thrill at the very idea of it.

As we sailed out of the harbour, we were preceded by

the royal guard in sleek racing boats, meant to protect us from any white-sailed felucca foolish enough to come near. I believe the feluccas tacked back and forth hoping for a view of the King. If one sailed close, the guard set them straight. We required the guard because in Cairo the river is quite active, crowded with commercial boats with sailors with long poles on deck. Their task was to prod any other boat that came too near. Those sailors looked quite serious, though I kept thinking they were all about to begin sword fighting with their poles, like schoolboys. They didn't seem to notice, or perhaps simply weren't interested in a royal yacht. The public ferry, however, waited until we were underway. I could see the fellahin on deck, trying to see their new King. There were so many of them, and what with their children and animals, the poor, rickety ferry began to list to starboard. An official in a white uniform was flapping his arms, trying to get them to move back so the boat might again be steady.

Our cabin was adequate, though there was little doubt it had been decorated by one of Fouad's favourites. There seemed to be gold in everything and colours in combinations that I had learned to identify as Egyptian royal – a great deal of red. Malcolm couldn't understand why the cabin made him slightly uneasy. I explained that the décor was unusual. 'Oh, I see,' he said, looking round. 'I'm sure that's the reason. Very clever of you to see it.'

That first afternoon, we had tea on the aft deck, under a striped awning. The Queen Mother wasn't paying the slightest attention to me. I could see that she and Mazhar Pasha were more than close. I think it's that she had been locked up for so long, that she was now going to cut loose. I never thought of Mazhar Pasha as anyone's lover.

I had heard he was married, though I had never seen his wife. I told Malcolm to watch the way they stood, leaning toward one another.

'That is hardly reason to assume there is more to it. He is an adviser to the family.'

'Well, the nature of the advice has changed.'

As we were having our tea, Madame Zulficar kept pushing Fafette forward. It was comical. The King was holding forth about Woolwich. 'In Our school-days we were taught the meaning of discipline. Cold showers in the morning. Barely time to towel off, then onto the Parade Ground for morning drill. That was life at Woolwich. The Shop.'

As he talked, Madame Zulficar shoved that child into his line of vision. Fafette grinned at him as if she was a monkey in the zoo. It occurred to me that her pet name had been chosen because of its initial letter. Her forename was Safinaz, not that the King cared. He just kept going on about Woolwich-the-Shop. Finally, Malcolm, bless him, found a little opening and said, 'Woolwich's loss is the country's gain. May I salute you on the occasion of your accession. Long live the King! Long may he reign!' I thought that might be that, but Malcolm kept moving ahead, conducting business. 'And if I may, Your Majesty, to the Anglo-Egyptian Friendship Treaty. May it bring grace to the Dynasty.'

'The treaty, indeed. And to your marriage. And Lady Cheyne,' the King said, raising his tea cup to me. He had to peer round Fafette to do it. I may have blushed.

A little later, Malcolm asked Sarah if she had spoken with the King. 'Not since Cairo, P'pa,' she said.

At her very next opportunity, Sarah summoned her courage and spoke to Farouk. She was young, but she was doing what she knew was right and what would please her father. I admired her for it. She didn't sound at all awkward as she spoke to the King. 'I'm sure you are up to your duties, sir, but it's hard not to think you could be overwhelmed.' I could see Malcolm was a tiny bit nervous, though Sarah was self-assured, her father's daughter. The King said, 'Not at all, Miss Cheyne. We are not afraid.'

'I so admire that,' Sarah said, sounding as if she meant it.

'How very charming,' the King said. Malcolm had such a calm look on his face, that I knew there was more to it.

When we were dressing for dinner, I asked, 'What was that business with Sarah?'

'What do you mean?'

'Jane Austen comes to mind.'

'Jane Austen?'

'"It is a truth universally acknowledged that a single man in possession of a good fortune . . ."'

'". . . must be in want of a wife."'

'I think you fancy a royal son-in-law.' I now understood better just what he had meant in his dressing room when he was concerned with Farouk's naming of a Queen.

'English blood would benefit the Dynasty.'

'What if he doesn't want an English wife?'

'What man wouldn't want an English wife?' Malcolm could be very romantic. As our wedding trip had been interrupted, we both saw this expedition as a honeymoon.

We weren't the only ones. As the voyage continued, it became obvious that Nazli and Mazhar Pasha were

lovers. They were inseparable. She was glowing. There was
something faintly ridiculous about them, though
Malcolm and I agreed that people should take happiness
where they can. Our lives were testament to that. I think
the only person on board who didn't notice was the King
of Egypt. Even Sarah, who rarely confided in me, asked
about it. Sarah was still confused by my marriage to her
father. My step-daughter was only a few years younger
than I. Sarah was a great, strapping girl, her father's daughter in a physical sense. Her figure was ample, and that was
a problem for her, and an unspoken issue for the two of
us. A mother and daughter are likely to be constructed
along the same lines. Sarah and I could not possibly have
been blood relations. I tried to be as understanding as possible, to make myself available to her and to give her all the
time she needed. This notion that had come into
Malcolm's head to put her in front of Farouk seemed
wrong to me in the light of all the scheming about Fafette
Zulficar. I determined not to interfere if I thought it
might make matters harder for Sarah. I could hear
Malcolm and Sarah at morning tea. I almost interfered,
but then just listened.

'Invite him, that's all,' Malcolm was saying.

'He's the King. He should invite me.'

'You were charming with him. If you don't want to,
that's another matter.'

'P'pa, please. It's too horrible.'

'Darling, you must lead the conversation. It's one of
life's duties. You'll never make a marriage without it.'

'A marriage? Oh, P'pa.'

'Invite him to join us. Perhaps a swim. You'll be the
hostess.'

'But I'm not,' she said, with her wound showing so

very clearly. It was painful to hear that. She was quite right. I was now the hostess in our family. She shouldn't have to be available for duty only when it suited her father's diplomatic purposes. Malcolm must have heard the anxiety in her voice, because he softened a bit. 'Yes, I see. Perhaps the King will invite you to something.'

'Don't go putting him up to anything. I couldn't bear it,' she said.

After luncheon, when several of us joined the King and Mazhar Pasha on the sun deck, Sarah once again summoned her courage and said, 'This is such a marvellous cruise. Thank you so much for inviting us.' She really had absorbed a good deal from her father. She was taking the best of him and putting it to her advantage. I loved her for it. 'I was going to organise a bathing party,' she said, as if she were chatting with her schoolmates. 'Will you join us?'

'We would be delighted,' the King said. I could feel Malcolm's relief.

I arose quite early on the day of Sarah's bathing party. Perhaps I was a bit nervous, though at the time I didn't know that. I simply enjoyed seeing mornings on the Nile. As the sun rises over the mud villages and the fields of cane and sweet clover, it burns off the river mist so that from early in the day the only shade comes from the all too few palms. The fellahin in the fields looked up at the Kassed Kheir as she passed, but unlike their city cousins, the fellahin of the Nile Valley did not realise that their King was on board.

The Kassed Kheir was moored in a lagoon at the river's edge for the bathing party. The brown water of the river near Cairo had changed to a deep blue. We were several days out, not quite half way to Aswan. There were lovely stone formations where a flock of egrets were sunning themselves. Before we could start splashing, men from the boat beat the waters for crocodiles. They would wade about with sticks making a fuss. They didn't find any, but there were some hideous looking Nile catfish, huge whiskered things that looked older than the Sphinx.

Unfortunately, the party divided along generational lines. Sarah, Elizabeth, His Majesty, Fafette, and I went in the water. All the others, including Malcolm, stayed on board and watched. Several of the royal bodyguard waded in as well, fussing about and keeping an eye on the King.

From the moment he was in the water, the King began swimming round me. At first he was kicking up surf and splashing in my direction. It seemed no more than playful and perhaps I splashed back a bit. It was harmlessly amusing. When Sarah saw the fuss, she began floating on her back as if she were unaware. Fafette, who had been done up in a fetching bathing costume that showed her figure to advantage, began flailing her arms, complaining of a cramp, trying to attract the King's attention. A guard swam to her to help. I turned to watch and Farouk swam in a circle round me, moving close. Fafette was shouting in Arabic at the guard. He gathered her up, despite her protests, and was removing her from the water when Farouk went below the surface and swam between my legs, like a darting fish. I was confused for a moment. Then he popped up again, grinned, and then went under once more. This time he pulled on my leg until we were both beneath the surface. The water was wonderfully clear, and I could see him, but I was concerned with holding my breath until he might release me. He pulled me to him, pressed his face to mine and ran his hands over me. There were bubbles coming from his nose, and his cheeks were filled with air. The look on his face said: You are mine to do with as I wish. I was too shocked to know what to do. When he released me, I shot up to the surface. He came up too, but in no hurry and with a mocking smile. 'Come sit with Us,' he said, taking my wrist and moving toward the shallow water. I shook free, refusing and treading water like a fool. I felt pique, but I fear looked more as if I were merely pouting.

'We apologise. Come over here now,' he said as he climbed up onto the rocks.

I should have just gone back to the Kassed Kheir, but he seemed genuinely sorry. He offered his hand and helped me climb up beside him. As he made no attempt to do anything untoward, I sat beside him, hoping to enjoy the sun. One of the wretched guards, a horrible fellow with mats of hair growing from his shoulders, came wading over to us with towels and a thermos. The King waved him off and then held out his fist to me, as if he were making an offering. 'We have found something for you,' he said, making a show of slowly opening his fist, uncurling one finger at a time until I saw what I took to be a pretty pebble.

'Rather a nice one, don't you think?'

It took me another moment to realise that what I was looking at was no pebble, but rather a black pearl, a perfect sphere, the size of a grape and the colour of ebony. It absorbed the sunlight, taking the very air itself. 'It's a pearl,' I announced, a remark that made me feel even more foolish than when I was pouting in the water. Farouk's beau geste which was meant to delight me, seemed to be turning me into a girl, younger still than I actually was.

'We discovered it in the oysters, down in the rocks.'

That was clearly nonsense. He must have brought it

from Cairo. 'I can't possibly accept such a thing,' I said, unable to take my eyes from it.

'It would please Us so much if you would.'

'It is very beautiful and I'm flattered, but I cannot and you know why.'

'It can be our secret if you like.'

'Certainly not.'

'Then it is of no value,' he said and tossed the most beautiful jewel I had ever seen into the sea.

I do hope that my jaw didn't drop. I wanted to think that it was all a sort of joke, and that my ebony pearl was not lost at all. That the King would now plunge into the water, dive down among the imaginary oysters and retrieve it for me.

'Shall we go back?' he asked as if nothing of any consequence at all had occurred. Still feeling stunned and certainly confused – which of course was exactly what he wanted – I managed to nod. He rose, helped me to my feet, and said, 'Perhaps We'll find another,' and he stepped back down into the water and swam toward his yacht. I followed after him, as if I were on a lead.

That evening I refused dinner and stayed in the cabin. A tray was sent in, but I couldn't eat. I just lay in bed thinking. Later that night, after Malcolm had returned and gone to sleep, I slipped out to go up on deck to clear my head. I was at the rail, looking up at the stars, when Farouk appeared. I didn't hear him approach. It startled me. 'We were told a beautiful woman is on deck all by herself,' he said in a courtly way.

'I wanted some air.'

'We have been looking at the stars. Now We shall look at you. Far more beautiful.'

'Thank you. You really mustn't say things like that.'

'We have met many beautiful English ladies. We love to hear the accent.'

'Please, sir.'

'English ladies, they are all so pink. Your colouring is wonderful.'

'I have Italian blood, on my mother's side.'

'That's it, then! So exciting! English accent, Italian blood. Quite astonishing. It is Our pleasure to gaze at you.'

'You're a flirt, aren't you? A royal flirt.' When I saw that's what the King was, I felt easier. I understood the little game he wanted to play. I was aware that it could get out of hand, but I was sure I could control matters.

'If you say it offends, We will stop.'

'You embarrass me.'

'So deliciously charming. Do you know why it is dangerous to play cards in the jungle?'

'I haven't the faintest idea.'

'It has so many cheetahs in it.' I tried not to laugh, it was such a ridiculous joke, but I couldn't help myself. The King of Egypt, after all, and here he was with this schoolboy riddle. He told his riddles as if they had never been told before. He was quite pleased whenever anyone didn't know the answer because then he could explain it. 'Thank you,' he said, perhaps because I had laughed. 'You like Us. We could tell, in the water.'

'You were very naughty in the water. You upset Sarah.'

'Who is Sarah?'

'My husband's daughter. You were quite nice to her earlier.'

'We couldn't stop looking at you.'

'You were doing more than looking.'

'Just a little.'

'You make me confused.'

'Let Us make love to you.'

'I'm going to leave now.' When I turned to go, he touched me. Patted me. Actually, he kept his hand there. Hands, I should say. It startled me. I think I must have glanced back at him. That same look, the royal proprietary look, was on his face.

Later that night, Malcolm found me quite ardent. As he held me, he repeated, 'Verita, Verita.'

The next day, I felt uneasy. It might have been better if I had simply told Malcolm that the King had acted inappropriately toward me. Or, possibly if Sarah had said to her father, 'You are not to try to make this ludicrous match.' She couldn't speak like that to Malcolm. I couldn't either, because I wasn't sure if I had encouraged the King. I knew I hadn't meant to, but I also knew that I hadn't ended the flirtation immediately.

Malcolm was spending a great deal of time with the King. I was always afraid they were talking about me. I made a point to listen to them, to eavesdrop, and I heard some of it. I made Malcolm tell me the rest. The two of them were on the aft deck where we often took tea.

'Do you know, sir, about Queen Victoria and Lord Melbourne?' Malcolm asked.

'Of course,' the King answered as if everyone knew all about that.

Malcolm assumed he was bluffing, so he said, 'She inherited the throne when she was not much older than you. He was her political councillor.'

'He had a young wife, didn't he?'

'The situations are entirely different.'

'You shall be Our Melbourne,' Farouk said, without

any thought at all. Malcolm was wary, but he had the King's ear and he was not about to lose the opportunity. 'If my experience might be useful, it would be my honour.'

'Done! Lady Cheyne is entirely charming. We congratulate you on your marriage.'

'A man needs a wife, sir.'

'So We are often told.'

'Oh?' Malcolm must have thought he had a fish on the line and was now about to reel it in.

'We must name a Queen, you know.'

'I'm sure there are no lack of candidates.'

'What does Lord Melbourne say?'

'I mean no disservice to Egypt when I point to the particular capability of Englishwomen.'

'We've met Englishwomen. Charming.'

'The burdens require a young woman of some substance.'

'We would like an English wife.'

'I shall bear that in mind, sir.'

Malcolm was coming to believe that the English wife might well be Sarah. To her great distress, Malcolm continued to press her on the King. Madame Zulficar kept shoving that pathetic little Fafette at him as well. Nazli and Mazhar Pasha were skulking about doing Lord only knows what. The King was oblivious of it. He pursued me for the rest of the voyage. At dinner, he would have me seated next to him and do frighteningly intimate things under the table. I tried to avoid it, but sometimes at night I would need air because our cabin was so close. I would go up on deck and the King would be there, assuming it was an assignation. We were his guests, I had to be nice to him. He kept manoeuvring me into dark corners. I wouldn't have thought that such an airy boat had so many hidden places. He was astonishingly persistent. I may have returned a light kiss or two, but it was only playful. I don't know quite how, but one evening we wound up in one of the lifeboats. It got a bit out of hand and by the time I got back to the cabin I think my woolly was on backwards. Malcolm didn't notice. It was difficult for me, and I was glad to see our Nile cruise come to an end, with a version of my honour if not my dignity still intact.

I assumed that once we were back in Cairo, the King would forget his infatuation. I certainly intended to do just that. About a week after the royal sailing expedition, an invitation from the Palace arrived at the Residency. It was quite an elegant thing, on creamy paper, done out with exquisite calligraphy. It was for tea with the Queen Mother and it was for me alone. Malcolm said, 'It's an honour, my dear.' Perhaps it was, but the envelope also contained a pair of diamond earrings. I didn't think they were from the Queen Mother.

When I arrived at Abdin for my audience of Nazli, the King greeted me and proposed a walk about the Palace, until his mother was available. Tea-time is a lovely part of the day at Abdin. There are European gardens with streams stocked with exotic fish. The scent of jasmine was in the air. The King was unfailingly polite and there were royal guards stationed everywhere. I returned the earrings and told him I couldn't possibly accept them.

'Won't you wear them for Us?'

'I will not.' Despite that, he slipped one of them onto my ear. They really were lovely, but I said, 'You're going to make me late for tea.'

'Tea it is,' he said, and guided me into the Palace. We were in a drawing-room that I hadn't seen before. The King backed me up against a wall and began to kiss me. I struggled and turned my face away. I pleaded with him to stop, which he did. I hurried out, but in my state I must have gone through a door other to the one we had entered. He permitted it and I found myself in a corridor facing a Sudanese giant, dressed as if he were in Parliament. 'Who is that?' I blurted, turning back to the King, thinking he was surely safer than this fellow.

'That is Murgan, the keeper of the harem,' Farouk answered, as if he were pointing out a tourist attraction.

'Harem!' I now felt it urgent to get away. The King guided me, and it seemed in just a few steps, I found myself facing the most extraordinary mural. It was enormous and I can say I had never seen anything remotely like it. It featured a royal personage and a number of what I assume were concubines. The behaviour shown didn't shock me, but that it was depicted so, shall we say, vividly. I couldn't take it in.

'Does it amuse?' the King asked.

'I would like to leave now.'

'Have We upset you? Forgive Us.' Then he knelt before me, as if I were the sovereign and he the supplicant. I was wearing a frock with a full skirt, the hem at the ankle, quite demure, in deference to the Queen Mother. His Majesty lifted the skirt and crawled beneath. There is no other way to put it. His entire person was under my skirt, only the royal boots were poking out, waggling unrestrained. He had launched an intimate activity not unfamiliar to me, and quite clear in its intent, though not what I had imagined when I set out from the Residency to have tea with the Queen Mother. I protested, begged him to stop. There is a point in such an escapade when clear thought is unlikely. If I looked up, I saw the mural. If I looked down, I saw my skirt billowing and His Majesty busy beneath. I was not controlling matters, that is clear. When my face was flushed and my protests grown feeble, His Majesty removed himself from his station on the floor and said, 'Now you may have tea.'

'You are the naughtiest man,' was all I managed, but at least we were soon back in an area of the Palace where sufragis and guards were stationed.

'Do you know how to make a Venetian blind?' he asked, taking my hand as we walked.

'Not another one,' I protested.

'Poke him in the eyes.' With all that had gone on, this was mercifully harmless. I laughed and pushed him playfully about. As I look back on it, I now believe that I heard Malcolm's voice at that time. I claimed, later, that I certainly did know that he was at Abdin that day to see the King. It was a white lie of marriage. In any case, Malcolm, in his morning coat, accompanied by Dugdale, Forbes, and Mazhar Pasha came striding round the corner talking about their endless schedules and plans. There I was, playing about and holding hands with the King. It wasn't the least pleasant at the time, but as I look back on it, considering what had been going on a moment earlier, I do find it amusing. Malcolm was flabbergasted. He didn't lose control, he never did that, but he was upset.

'Ah, Excellency,' the King said, as if he were greeting him at a diplomatic reception, 'We have been showing Abdin's collections to Lady Cheyne.'

'I see.' Malcolm took my hand and pulled me toward him. When he spoke, the words were terse as if he were biting off each syllable. 'Mr Dugdale will see you out. You seem to have lost an earring. I am ready for our discussions, sir.'

'Jolly good, Excellency. What's on the agenda?'

As Dugdale took me out, I could see the tension in Malcolm's face. Even such an old hand at palace intrigue as my husband couldn't hide his feelings.

That night, in our bedroom, we had the first serious argument of our marriage. 'Your invitation was for tea with the Queen Mother!'

'She was indisposed. The King wanted to walk about the Palace with me. I could hardly say no.'

'The two of you? No one else at all?'

'Malcolm, please. It was a stroll, not an assignation.'

'He wants an English wife all right. He wants mine!'

I laughed at that, as if it were preposterous and I was exasperated with him. But it was true. And I wasn't at all sure what I would do about it.

JIMMY:

A Curious Empire

When Sir Malcolm invited me to return to Cairo and resume my duties as Farouk's tutor, I admit to being pleased but also to some trepidation. Surely a sitting monarch will decide if he wants to receive instruction. Farouk hadn't paid any attention to me when he was Prince. I shouldn't think the crown of Tutankhamen would have developed in him a new interest in history. Sir Malcolm was so vague about the situation, I knew something was up. The man I remembered spoke clearly and concisely. One might not have liked what he said, but there was never much mystery about what he meant. I asked a few people associated with the Residency, and though they were circumspect, I gathered there had been a problem with Lady Cheyne and the King. As one who had known Vera Napier since she was a girl, which was not so long ago, I wasn't surprised. I did, however, doubt that if there was a problem of that nature I could do much about it.

While the King was at Woolwich, I had written to him

wishing him well. Mazhar Pasha had replied, offering me a position as academic tutor while the Prince, as he then was, studied in England. That time was of course cut short by the death of Fouad, which among the many other things it did, made moot the question of my employment, or so I thought. I went to Woolwich a few times, at Mazhar Pasha's invitation, and saw His Royal Highness in action as a GC. I never did accomplish much tutoring there. One of the problems was that the Prince already had an Arabic tutor and a military tutor who were usually wrangling for his attention. The winner was always Luigi Catania, who took the Prince into Mayfair most nights. On an evening when I was at Kenry House, the Prince invited Mazhar Pasha and me to go with him. I didn't know exactly where they were going. I do not mean to speak as if I were Vera Napier pretending to be unaware of her effect on men. I knew full well that Catania was not taking the Prince to the proms at the Albert Hall. Mazhar Pasha declined, but I said I would be delighted. I assumed we would go to a louche night-club or two. Catania was less than pleased that I was along.

Farouk referred to our destination as Mae's. I later learned that more worldly people knew what that was. I had never heard of Mae's and couldn't have afforded it if I had. My experience of this sort exclusively Alexandrian. What I discovered there, about myself, was best left unmentioned in England. Mae's was a private house in the old Shepherd's Market. We were ushered into a drawing-room that looked as if it had been fur-nished by someone attempting to evoke a country house. It was far more comfortable than its models. All the fur-niture was recent, and it was quite cushy.

We were offered drinks, for which I certainly felt a need. The Prince took fruit juice in London or anywhere else. He was still a Moslem. If there were other clients of Mae's, they were not in evidence. We seemed to be the only men involved. Mae herself, a handsome, slightly mannish woman with a Midlands accent, came in to greet Farouk. She kissed him on each cheek and told him it was wonderful to see him. Mae wore a black turban and powder was lodged in the creases of her face. It gave her a theatrical air. Farouk rose to greet her, saying, 'Ah, Miss Mae, delighted.' Catania offered him a leather carrier bag that he had been dragging along, and Farouk poked inside and withdrew a wrapped gift. Mae fussed a bit but didn't open it. Soon enough, beautiful young women were drifting past, each smiling at the Prince, and to a lesser degree at me and Catania. It might have been a drinks party of some sort. The girls were wearing expensive, revealing frocks, so that one couldn't have mistaken them for shop assistants. When Farouk saw one who appealed, he nodded and she stopped in front of him. She was a stunning fair-haired thing, not unlike the Circassians that his father had favoured. She was plump in a way that both Fouad and Farouk seemed to fancy, and she had lively blue eyes. Her frock provided a view of Olympian breasts. She said her name was Sally.

'Silly?' Farouk asked.

'If you like.' She certainly wasn't pushing anything.

'Will you join us? I don't take alcohol, you know. I'm sure you like champagne.'

'I do. Yes.'

Catania seemed to think that was a bit forward. Ever the arbiter of manners, he said, 'You know who this is?'

'Yes, of course,' she said.

'All right, then.' Catania snapped his fingers and ordered champagne.

'Answer a question, Silly,' Farouk said. 'Why are parrots always rich?'

'I don't know.'

'Because they suc-ceed.'

She laughed and said, 'I didn't know princes told jokes. I don't think English princes do.' As the champagne was opened, Farouk called for the carrier bag again and presented Sally with a gift. She unwrapped it immediately, and found a gold necklace from Asprey. It astonished her. 'It's beautiful,' was all she could manage. I could see on her face that she thought it was a charade of some sort and she wouldn't be allowed to keep it. Farouk slipped it round her neck and she said, 'For me? Really?'

'If you fancy it.'

'I do. I do.'

'Then it's yours.'

The poor girl grew short of breath, repeating, 'Oh, Oh' until she managed to say, 'I want to thank you. May I?'

'You may,' he said, and they retired to a place more private. Catania left as well, going off to his own adventures. For a moment, I was quite alone and feeling rather foolish. Mae soon returned and said, 'We can't have this now, can we?' I thought she was about to tell me to leave, but she called for a young woman who turned out to be French and called, wonderfully, Zazi. Mae's wasn't quite Sister Street, still it struck me as rather a different matter in England. In my mind it was as if I had brought Zazi into my family's house in Hampshire while they were away. My doubts soon passed as Zazi had a compliant nature and no trouble at all coming up with a few dis-

tractions that even dear Miriam Rolo hadn't thought of.
I was always curious about the cost of Zazi's attention,
but as the whole lot was put on Farouk's bill, I never
learned.

On the occasion of the Prince's sixteenth birthday I
went to Kenry House to wish him well. Mazhar Pasha
had invited me, saying not to bring gifts which was a
relief, as I couldn't imagine what one would buy for
Farouk. Catania, as usual, was trying to drag the Prince
into town for the evening. The others were trying to
think of reasons for Farouk to stay. It was marvellously
empty-headed of them to think that if Farouk had a
choice of staying at Kenry House working on his lessons
or going into town, that there would be any question of
what he would do. Once again, he invited Mazhar Pasha
and me to join him.

'The King has made enquiries,' Mazhar Pasha said.
'I've had to tell him that Woolwich has refused to give
you any marks at all.'

'You're absolutely right,' Farouk said, as if he had just
seen the light. 'Mr Peel and I have been working out a
plan of study to remedy that.' That was the first I'd heard
of it, but I had been so drawn into the charade of Farouk's
education that the Prince may well have believed what he
was saying. I left with them and we went to the only destination that held any interest for Farouk.

Mae had hung streamers and a paper sign, no doubt
prepared by her employees, wishing the Prince, A Happy
16th! Mae called for her girls, there were six of them that
evening, and they gathered round the Prince, a circle of
excited pulchritude. Each one hugged and kissed him and
said it was wonderful that he was having a birthday and
that they were thrilled to be with him. The Prince smiled

benignly as Mae led a few choruses of 'Happy Birthday'.
Then Farouk handed out gifts.

Now here I was in Cairo with him once more. I found
myself again living at the Residency, in daily contact with
Sir Malcolm and Lady Cheyne. The King kept putting
me off, but that was just as well as it allowed me time to
settle in and sort out what had been going on.

The only significant difference I saw at first was that
Old Chu was no longer in service. Sir Malcolm had
received several letters from China begging for his return.
It seemed the old boy had a wife and family in Pekin. He
hadn't seen them since '33. There was some question as
to whether Old Chu wanted to see them at all, but Sir
Malcolm felt the Embassy was being drawn into a pro-
tracted family incident of a peculiarly Chinese nature. So
Old Chu was sacked. Sir Malcolm found one Fawcett,
who been valet to General Ravensdale of the Grenadiers.
Fawcett became the second non-Egyptian servant to Sir
Malcolm and surely one of the very few native-born
Englishmen in service in Egypt. He was an elfin fellow,
perfectly formed but hardly more than five feet in stature.
He had thick sandy hair and always put me in mind of a
Shetland pony. He had the born servant's ability to be
everywhere yet always unobtrusive. Unlike Old Chu,
who I sometimes believed must have slept in Sir
Malcolm's dressing room, Fawcett was out and about,
often seen in the house, supervising the kitchen in the
mornings, making certain the sufragis knew to serve
English visitors cucumber sandwiches along with humus
at tea. Fawcett turned out to be a superb appointment, a
great help really. He was called a valet, but in fact served
more as a de facto butler, which the Residency certainly

required. There had always been a cahir, a head house-keeper, a man called Mutum, but he was a sullen fellow, barely competent to give orders, and rarely seen. No one had been effectively in charge of the lot of them till Fawcett arrived. The sufragis, who were wary of Old Chu, were terrified of Fawcett. They never quite knew what a Chinaman was. They had no doubt what an Englishman was, and though they recognised a difference between the High Commissioner and his valet, they kept their distance.

It was Fawcett who came into the breakfast room not long after I had arrived, with a card on a silver tray. Sir Malcolm looked at the card and blanched. I could see Vera's features tighten. Sir Malcolm glanced out the window at the main entrance to the Residency and then left the breakfast room, followed by Vera. It was an exit as abrupt as any of Farouk's. I went to the window to see what had drawn them. There was an enormous heap of white flowers – a lorry-full, surely. The petals appeared soft as pillows from Harrod's, and a few of them, nearly as large. The bright morning sun seemed like a spotlight, piercing through them. Only one man in the country had the wherewithal and the foolishness to send such a gift. 'Return these to Abdin,' Sir Malcolm said, his voice suggesting that the flowers were contaminated.

'Yes sir,' Fawcett answered, crisp and certain.

I backed away from the window, though I could still hear their voices. I should have removed myself, but I could not and did not.

In a tone I had heard him use on junior ministers, Sir Malcolm said, 'You will accept nothing. No messages, no gifts. You will not go there without me.'

'Oh, Malcolm, don't be tiresome. Are you going to

keep me in a harem?' This was a different Vera than I remembered. The girl I had last seen fawned on her husband and hung on his every word. This was a woman who would not so easily be pushed about.

'I'm going to keep you away from that boy before he provokes an international incident.'

'Do you think I'll seduce him?'

'I think no such thing. I believe all that you tell me without reservation.'

'I should hope so.'

'The boy will do whatever comes into his head, including attempting to compromise you.'

'You would have been an ideal Edwardian.'

'I am an Edwardian!' He went directly to his office, where he busied himself doing oddments and fussing with cable traffic.

I was certainly back in Cairo. I dropped a note to Miriam Rolo at the Palace. She took several days to reply, which was answer enough. We met for luncheon once, but she no longer invited me to visit her when I was at the Palace. It made it easier for me actually. Miriam knew, and I came to see, that our time together was the result of an interesting confluence of events. That time had now passed and with it whatever passion we had once had. This was not Emma Lyttelton, for whom one was either an ardent swain or a villain. Miriam and I had had one thing earlier, now if I cared to, we could be friends.

In the time since I was last in this country, I found that I had been contemplating two things about my Egyptian sojourn: Farouk's character and Alexandria. As for the latter, I think part of the appeal, that is beyond the sensual, is that I am from a country that has only one capital. There is no English rival to London. Other countries have contrasting cities. In Italy, Rome and Florence. In China, Pekin and Shanghai, and in Egypt, Cairo, the powerful counting-house, and Alexandria, the cerebral and libidinal city of excess. As for the King, I don't know that I had seen him for what he was when I had been in his presence. In England, where I could reflect on him without being so much in his orbit, I came to see him differently. A king is unlike anyone else and Farouk is unlike any other king. If his country had no more strategic value than its neighbours, say Libya to the west or the Sudan to the south, then the King's self absorption wouldn't matter much to the rest of the world. But Egypt, like England, is a small country that has greatly affected the world. It is the oldest continuously existing nation and it sits atop Suez, property that grows more valuable every day, certainly to Europeans. There are so many 'ifs' in Farouk's life. If he had been born to a younger father, perhaps he would have had a better emotional model for himself. If he hadn't been the only boy among all those sisters, and if they hadn't fussed over him endlessly, hadn't worshipped him, perhaps he wouldn't have come to believe he could do no wrong. If you add to that the particularly Arab version of divine right, the boy seemed doomed to stay an adolescent all his life. By Arab divine right, I should explain that the fellahin did not regard Farouk as a deity. The Moslems have one god, and the King prayed to Allah just as the peasants did. It was that no one ever corrected the King.

The closest Farouk ever came to an adult who acted in a European way toward him was his English governess, Mrs Parsons, who was very much of the elbows-off-the-table school. When Nazli became Queen Mother, one of her first acts was to sack Mrs Parsons. She wanted no one

in the Palace with any semblance of authority over the
King. His teachers taught him nothing. He learned to
bluff and that's what he did. An adult sensibility never
took shape. That's what those ghastly riddles were. A little boy's idea of humour, residing not only in an adult,
but in a royal personage.

Farouk had always been the mocking boy, but what in
a prince might have been taken for high-spirited, in a
king was seen as wisdom. With his accession, his face
took on a glow. As all his surface emotions were a con-
trivance, I assumed this new countenance was false, too.
His features had always been changeable, often a step
behind what he was actually feeling. Now, with what I
assume he thought of as a king's mask, I was not certain
that I would be able to read his intentions at all.

The great tragedy of the entire business was that Sir
Malcolm was not more effective at shaping Farouk. He
tried, not for Farouk's sake certainly, but still he tried. Sir
Malcolm never quite understood that he was patronising
Farouk when he called him the boy. He continued to do
that even after Farouk was King. The boy. There was no
one to tell Sir Malcolm he was in error, either. Could his
wife have done it? Perhaps, but then she had her own
problems with Farouk that affected her marriage. Could I
have done it? I have thought about that question and perhaps I could have done something more. I did not, in part
due to my own limitations, though in my defence I must
say that at least while he was plenipot no one save the
Foreign Secretary, the PM or the King of England could
tell him what to do. It wasn't the force of his personality,
it was the law. After his title was reduced to Ambassador
he was subject to certain strictures, though none was ever
applied, out of habit I suppose, and also because like roy-

alty, Sir Malcolm was his own country, no matter his title. Farouk was easy to misunderstand. He was by no means dull. His mind was quick and he saw problems whole. What he wasn't able to do was see beyond his own immediate needs. His father was a libertine, and he became one too. Even his weight, which at the time I knew him was not an issue at all, became an aspect of indulgence. By the end of his life, as the world well knew, he was grotesque. In his exile, which was still years away, he satisfied every animal longing that he had, certainly not limited to eating, without any thought of consequence.

When I returned to Egypt for my latest attempt to instruct the King, I had assumed that the subject matter would be the same. I would try to talk about history and politics and His Majesty would turn to riddles or games. Sir Malcolm's instruction to me suggested that something else was at hand. I told him that I felt some trepidation about instructing a sitting monarch. It was difficult enough when he was Crown Prince, but this was unprecedented. After Sir Malcolm reiterated that I was not expected to turn the King into a scholar, he said, 'It would be to everyone's advantage if you could teach him a bit about civil behaviour.' The irritation in his voice was quite enough for me to understand just what he meant.

As we had earlier, Farouk and I met in the Abdin library. The leather volumes were still on the shelves, and I am sure, the pages still uncut. For this lesson, I had mounted a map of the Middle East and put it on an easel. When I had reviewed the business about Egypt's strategic importance, the King replied, 'Yes. Everyone wants Our Canal.'

'Egypt has two important things – one tangible, one less so. Can you tell me what they are?'

'It is for you to tell Us.'

'Very well. Egypt has its history embodied in the pyramids, the Sphinx, and in you, sir. That is the intangible. Now tell me the other.'

His response was Faroukian. He simply read back all that I had told him a few minutes earlier. He did it in a way that was world-weary and quite aware, as if he had known it for years. 'The Canal, the Canal, always Our Canal, isn't it? We control the shipping lanes, access to the oil fields and of course the northern route to India.'

'Quite so. Very good, sir.'

'Indeed. Now you may be excused.'

'There is one thing more. It's not so much factual as ethical.'

'Carry on.'

'It has to do with privilege, sir. With your position comes responsibilities. The people will take manners and morals from you.'

'Indeed,' he said, impatiently.

I found it difficult to proceed. I believe that my discomfort is all that kept his attention. It was often my duty to correct him in historical and factual matters, but I was not in the habit of instructing His Majesty in personal ethics. It took some effort, but I summoned my courage and said, 'Sir, gentlemen do not pursue other men's wives.'

'A wonderfully English idea, Mr Peel. Most amusing.' There was a flash of anger in his eye. He took my remark for impertinence.

'I do beg your pardon, sir,' was all I could manage in reply.

'That is quite enough tutoring, Mr Peel. Good day.'

The question of Farouk's marriage was the topic of the

moment at both the Residency and the Palace. Mazhar
Pasha was the only person from Abdin with whom I spoke
with any regularity. He too had wanted me to work in his
concerns in the tutorials. After my experience discussing
adultery with the King of Egypt, I demurred at the
prospect of adding more extra-academic topics. For
Mazhar Pasha, the question of an heir was paramount. He
knew that it was a danger to the Dynasty to have a
monarch without a son. Farouk was popular with the fellahin and that was a position that Egypt had not enjoyed
in years. Mazhar Pasha knew it must be protected. Also, I
suspect, it's what Nazli wanted. It was now common gossip that Nazli and Mazhar Pasha were lovers. Mazhar Pasha
sometimes told me about events in the Palace. Sir Malcolm
explained why he was confiding in me. 'If he is giving you
information it is because he assumes, correctly I trust, that
you will report it to me.'

'Does he think I'm a spy?'

'Not at all, Mr Peel. He is opening a back channel. He
judges you to be an honest messenger. He expects that
you will be used by me in the same way. When I have
something I wish to tell him, but do not feel that usual
methods are practical, I will use your good offices.'

'I see. Yes,' I said, unable to proceed. Sir Malcolm saw
that I was still concerned about being thought a messenger by Mazhar Pasha. I was, but not in quite the way Sir
Malcolm thought. Mazhar Pasha had enlisted me because
he had found my services adequate during the time of my
affair with Miriam Rolo, which he had no doubt
arranged. The message to me was, 'You can't refuse this,
because you accepted something similar at an earlier
time.' I assumed he meant that if I did not continue as
the messenger, he would find a way to inform Sir

Malcolm of my earlier relationship. I felt slightly sick but saw no alternative to acquiescence.

'I take it that what he has reported to you is of a delicate nature.'

'Yes.'

'You see, Mr Peel, if it were not, he would tell me directly. I take it then that it concerns Lady Cheyne.' This was a sensitive matter for Sir Malcolm, a man of some pride. It did not stop him for a moment. He fully expected it wouldn't stop me.

'It concerns an event at the Palace soon after I attempted to have my talk with the King.'

'Oh, yes. Moral responsibility.'

'Exactly. Apparently, later that day, His Majesty brought his horses into the Palace and drove them up the central staircase.' I was stumbling on my words. Sir Malcolm realised it and turned things to more casual conversation, to put me at ease.

'Sammy and Silvertail, I believe,' he said. 'Fine animals, aren't they?'

'He was riding one and the other was behind, on a lead.'

'Creating quite a mess, I'm sure.'

'The King was screaming, "We are Farouk of Egypt, embodiment of the Mohammed Ali Dynasty. Allah will make her mine."'

'To whom was he addressing his remarks?'

'That is unclear, however, the Queen Mother appeared at the top of the stairs. She said, "Yes, I know. Don't bother about her. I'll tell you how to be happy."'

'A mother's counsel. Always valuable.'

'Do you believe it, sir?'

'What is important is not whether those words were

spoken, or those precise events transpired. Mazhar Pasha and Nazli wish me to know that they are aware that His Majesty has shown an interest in Lady Cheyne and further, that a royal marriage will soon occur. They will name the bride and that it is in England's interest in no way to interfere.'

'Do you judge that correct?'

'I do.' Sir Malcolm meant it as a sort of pun, though an Egyptian royal wedding ceremony does not include that Western vow. It was an unusual remark for him, and I thought rather witty. Sir Malcolm certainly had a sense of humour, but he rarely made jokes and I'm sure he thought people who did were trivial. Perhaps if he felt he was among equals, he might be inclined to tell stories, though I don't know who his equal might be. With Sir Malcolm, there was rarely any of the social pleasantry marked by laughter when nothing amusing had been said – though harmless, this is usually done out of nervousness. Sir Malcolm found it excessive. He could make others feel like giggling fools in his presence. I suppose that was the intention.

Farouk's wedding day was declared a national holiday. Fellahin gathered in the streets and squares of Cairo. Food was handed out and much of the city was decorated with pictures of the King, but not yet of his bride who was of course the redoubtable Safinaz Zulficar, little Fafette. She was fifteen years old. The ceremony itself was to be in Koubbeh Palace, the third of the great Palaces owned by the King, even though Abdin featured a circular wedding hall, meant for a royal marriage. Yet Farouk chose Koubbeh and though there were public festivities and balcony speeches from the King, the event itself was small, more business-like than grand. Koubbeh is in

Heliopolis, outside the city proper. It's like a country house, surrounded by miles of walls. Farouk was comfortable there – he was comfortable everywhere; he wore his ease like a uniform. Once, when he was the Prince, he brought me out to the Koubbeh, as he alone always referred to it, for what turned out to be yet another non-tutorial. Instead of instructing, I watched him play at football. He had imported a professional team. Farouk would kick the ball, then a few sufragis would run out onto the pitch, retrieve it and under the direction of the team captain, would move the ball to an advantageous position so that Farouk might kick it again.

Koubbeh also has gaming rooms, though the marriage ceremony was held in a drawing-room and might not have included the bride, except there was no stopping Fafette. According to Mazhar Pasha, she stood behind a wooden screen, veiled, but also in a wedding gown from Worth, and watched while her father, Judge Zulficar, and the King pressed their thumbs together as the Judge asked, 'Do you agree to marry my daughter?' The King answered, 'We accept her betrothal to Myself from you, and take her under My care and bind Myself to offer her My protection, and you who are present bear witness.'

A flag was raised over Koubbeh, a hundred-and-one-cannon salute was fired, and the nation once again had a Queen. Whether Farouk took any particular interest in all that artillery is not known. Fafette, now renamed Farida, distinguished herself from her mother-in-law by breaking with tradition and having her picture reproduced all over Egypt. Gifts and tribute came from round the world. Hitler sent an armoured Mercedes-Benz. The King of England sent Purdey shotguns and a set of golf-clubs. Farouk was pleased by the Mercedes, but he already had Purdeys and golf was a game he didn't care for and never played. It was the only sign that Sir Malcolm had any trouble at all with the wedding. In every other royal circumstance where a gift was required, Sir Malcolm advised the Foreign Office with a kind of perfect pitch for what was appropriate. Not this time.

The various family dances in which I found myself enmeshed were suited to my affinity for the sidelines. Since the death of my own father, I hadn't been able to make domestic arrangements. I lived in college and then hôtels. My home was what I carried and what I made. Language, that vault of dreams, was my permanent address. Lacking a mother, I wrapped myself in the mother tongue and wore it sometimes like a nursery blanket and other times like a suit from Huntsman. I was in my twenties. I should have been able to settle on some goal. I had a start in my father's profession and when the opportunity arose, I fled. Here I was now, an occasional chum to the King of Egypt, and a sort of unofficial deputy to a man who had enough ambition for two nations. I had the pleasure of knowing that, if nothing else, I had a front row seat at an intriguing play.

By the end of the decade the war had finally started, but not yet for us. There was little doubt that the war would come to North Africa. The question was when? The reaction to the dilemma was different in the two cities that occupied me, emphasising their distinctive characteristics. Alex looked north to the sea, to Greece and the continent. Cairo faced east toward Arabia and south to black Africa. It was hard to believe the cities were only hours apart. In Alex there was such deep soul-weariness that war might have been a relief. The religious sects

argued only among themselves, splitting hairs about the-
ological questions that even they couldn't care about. The
voluptuaries of the city – and I was once one – pursued
flesh with a determination that was meant to blot out
feeling and the inevitability of history. When I was there,
I no longer felt the need to visit Sister Street. I stayed at
the Cecil, which was more European than Egyptian. The
staff understood that English guests considered hot water
and the sanctity of their mail to be next to Godliness.
There were certainly Germans in Alexandria, but somehow they seemed to be on holiday from the Nazi party.

In Cairo, the Residency was on a war footing despite
the fact that there was no one yet to fight. Sir Malcolm
resented that terribly. He was not a warmonger, but now
that there was a war, he didn't want to miss it. The
Germans were sending men into the western desert on
reconnaissance. It was a source of enormous frustration
for Sir Malcolm that for many months, only he and the
German High Command were concerned about the
desert. The FO certainly knew it was significant, but their
attentions were otherwise engaged. I believed that if Sir
Malcolm could have armed himself and the Residency
staff, including me, he would have personally marched us
toward Libya to begin the battle.

There was no longer any question of even the charade
of an English tutor at the Palace. I was put on the
Residency payroll because Sir Malcolm needed all the
help he could get. I was not certain how valuable I would
be, but there was no question as to what I would try to
do. I had Egyptian contacts, spoke some Arabic, and so I
carried on as Honorary Attaché, an operative without
portfolio, reporting directly to the Ambassador. When I
received my first cheque from the Bursar, I was surprised

at the sum – an increase over my Palace salary. I was also aware of just how far I had travelled since my early days of not quite tutoring the Prince.

The treaty of '36, on which Sir Malcolm had staked everything, was clear about what would happen if war came. Egypt was on the English side and troops were to be stationed throughout the country and at the Canal. If England declared war on a hostile nation, that declaration spoke for Egypt as well. As Sir Malcolm said, it is one thing to get the Egyptians to affix their signatures to a treaty, and quite another to make them abide by it. The Germans wanted for themselves exactly what Sir Malcolm had negotiated for England. The Nazis may not have had a treaty, but they had no hesitation about bribing the government. Sir Malcolm believed they were sending gold bullion to Farouk. The King would do as he pleased, with the likelihood of changing his mind back and forth between the Allies and the Axis until he had made us all dizzy.

For all that, a version of Cairo life continued. We went to clubs and to dinner as we always had. Lady Cheyne stayed clear of the King, so far as I knew, and devoted herself to Embassy duties. She poured tea, entertained visitors and she and Sir Malcolm swanned about in the evenings. Sir Malcolm had a great taste for nightlife. If there was a singer in town or some theatrical celebrity passing through, he would want to have the fellow to dinner. I still went out with the Cheynes in the evening, though Vera no longer made a sisterly point of introducing me to likely women. At first I thought it was because she believed I had dealt badly with Emma Lyttelton. I asked about it as delicately as I could, stressing that I still considered Emma a friend, but we had mutually agreed to end our romance.

Vera insisted she understood. Perhaps she did. I came to believe that the King told her I had once had the temerity to instruct him in moral matters, apparently concerning her. The King eventually forgot about it, but Vera never quite forgave me. She must have known that what little I did was at her husband's request, but then she would have to blame him when it was so much easier to blame me. Later, Vera had additional reasons, in her view, to be angry with me. For now, we assumed a détente because it was easier for all concerned.

I was with Sir Malcolm in his study, examining maps of the desert, marking places where our intelligence had told us that an army might store matériel in advance of an invasion, when Elizabeth and Vera, both in a state, came to announce that a number of fellahin had gathered at the rear of the Residency. As we approached, they parted for Sir Malcolm, and a few of them, who couldn't contain themselves, repeated, 'Shufti, shufti.' They meant for us to look, and when we did, we saw that a serpent charmer, known to the fellahin as Siddiq, had arrived. He wore only a loin cloth and was himself as thin as a snake. His daughter, a haunting child of about twelve, was his assistant. Serpent charmers were not uncommon. In Alex I had seen them working in the fields. Those fellows reached into bushes or high grass and pulled out whatever garden snakes were lurking and stuffed them in the pouches that hung from their waists. This promised to be a bit more theatrical. I thought of Rafik, the royal falconer, who could communicate with birds in a way that had nothing to do with language, and everything to do with the ancient, animist ways of his country.

Siddiq bowed slightly to Sir Malcolm, in greeting and deference.

'A charmer of serpents, are you?' Sir Malcolm asked.

'They thrive in the dark, Excellency.' Siddiq opened the hatch to the cellar. A sufragi with an electric torch flashed his light down into the darkness. I could see nothing. Siddiq rapped on the wall and under the eaves with a stick. He dislodged a great array of insects, but no serpents.

'Who is this?' Sir Malcolm asked, looking at the child.

'My daughter, Excellency. Amina.' She smiled at us and I found it difficult to look away from her powerful eyes. I saw Sir Malcolm also had to make an effort.

Siddiq put down his stick and sat cross-legged at the cellar hatch. Amina gave him a reed instrument, a sort of flute. He played a vigorous Eastern melody. I almost laughed at the enthusiastic music. I suppose I was expecting something more traditionally mysterious. In a Cairo club, this might have been dance music, though it had only one theme which Siddiq repeated until it seemed like a religious chant. We saw it all as a lark. The fellahin and the sufragis were taking it more seriously. As Siddiq's melody turned darker, the fellahin grew still. We felt it too. As the music began to take my mood, I saw Vera and Sir Malcolm look at one another. Their faces seemed to say, Here is Egypt: hypnotic and utterly opaque. Diamond-back cobras with fangs to fill a man's dreams, slithered up from the cellar, tongues darting. Everyone knew there were few cobras left in this part of the country, but that made it all the better. The snakes were real, certainly, but also a display of opulence.

There was an erotic air to the whole business. I could feel it sneak through me. The fellahin began to swoon. There was little doubt what they were feeling. At the time, psychiatry was in the air in London and New York,

though not much of it had yet reached Egypt. Those
snakes rising to the music seemed driven by little Amina.
She had a glow about her that made more than snakes
rise.

Amina held a wicker basket with tethered mice inside.
As the cobras approached, they hesitated, then lifted their
heads, tongues darting, locked to Amina's eyes. Then, in
deference to her power, they lowered themselves and
wriggled into her basket. There were six snakes, and when
they were all eating mice, Amina closed the lid. She
touched her father tenderly, breaking the spell. As he lowered his flute, she kissed him on the mouth. There was
silence for a moment, then Sir Malcolm, in a soft voice,
unusually gentle, asked, 'All gone now, are they?'

'They are never gone, Excellency. They have moved
on.'

Elizabeth whispered to her father, asking, 'What does
he do with them?'

'Probably puts them in another cellar. It was a good
show.' Sir Malcolm told Dugdale to give them money
and then they were gone. The fellahin dispersed and the
cellar hatch was locked again. I had no occasion to visit
the cellar, though I doubt that I would have gone. It was
a fortnight before any of the sufragis would go down
there.

A few nights later, when a group of us were going to
the Scarabée Club for dinner, the Rolls was stopped at
Opera Square, in the centre of the city. We saw six
German soldiers come out of Kasra al Nil Street and cut
across the Square. There were Germans in Cairo, some of
them no doubt Nazi soldiers, but until now they had
always worn civilian clothes. These men were in uniform.
We went on to the club, though Sir Malcolm seemed dis-

tracted. The Scarabée was one of my favourites. It had a smallish dance floor, a little bandstand and tables crowded together. The American singer Cab Calloway was there. He wore a costume that appeared a theatrical version, or perhaps an unwitting parody, of Sir Malcolm's own morning coat. Mr Calloway's ensemble was as white as a devout Moslem's robes: swallow-tail coat, trousers, shirt, waistcoat, tie, boots, and even the silk topper. It all flowed as he pranced about. He looked like a cartoon of an American Negro and had a big voice that filled the little room. He had been here a few nights, and everyone in Cairo wanted to hear him. He sang:

Let me tell you bout Minnie the moocher.
She was a red hot hootchie kootcher.
High-dee, High-dee, High-dee-High . . .

Then he would put an enormous hand to his ear and the crowd would sing back to him:

Ho-dee, ho-dee, ho-dee-ho.

His performance evoked America for us, a place far away that seemed untouched by our troubles, where everyone shot tommy guns and ate fried chicken and danced in the streets to hot music. Sir Malcolm was trying to enjoy it, but seeing the Nazis had put a crimp in his evening. He saw in their attire a serious breach of the treaty. He said to Dugdale, 'I want to see the Prime Minister as soon as possible.'

'Shall I go now? Start arranging it?'

'Yes. We'll cable the FO. Tell them what we've seen.'

As Dugdale was about to leave, he was stopped by the

entrance of Farouk. He was with Catania, a few others, and several bodyguards. Mr Cab Calloway stopped singing while the King and his entourage were seated. I involuntarily glanced over at Vera to see how she was reacting. Her face was impassive but unfortunately she saw me looking at her – one more thing she found hard to forgive. Farouk sent a bottle of champagne and then came to our table, insisting Lady Cheyne dance with him. As if that weren't enough, when the King was twirling her about, all the other couples left the dance floor. Sir Malcolm accepted it stoically, though he didn't drink any of the King's champagne.

The next day I accompanied Sir Malcolm and Forbes to the office of the PM, Ali Maher Pasha, so Sir Malcolm might lodge a protest. We were met by Mr Afifi, the chap from the City of the Dead. He was a different man to the obsequious fellow I remembered. There were no salaams today. 'Good afternoon, Excellency. The Prime Minister will see you now.' He nodded to me saying only, 'Good afternoon, Mr Peel.' He did not acknowledge Forbes at all. Sir Malcolm did not have to point out that it was no longer in Afifi's interest to be thought on a friendly footing with the English Ambassador. He ushered us into the PM's office.

I believe that in Sir Malcolm's heart he was protesting the King's insistence on dancing with Lady Cheyne, but he limited his argument to the Nazi soldiers. 'At Shepherd's were you?' the PM asked. Ali Maher had been one of Farouk's regents. He had a fondness for the Nazis and if Farouk was receiving gold then Ali Maher Pasha was surely accepting something similar. He hated Sir Malcolm, and often called him Colonel Blimp. Like Sir Malcolm, he was from a family with a history of government service. He affected an amused attitude toward the English, the way one might regard circus performers encountered outside the tent.

'As it happens, we were going to the Scarabée. I saw six of them.'

'Is that American singer still there? "Minnie the Moocher",' he sang, in a low-keyed imitation of Cab Calloway.

'Prime Minister, the treaty to which your country is signatory precludes their presence.'

'Were they shooting anyone? Smashing windows? Rounding up Jews perhaps? Or was it that they put a damper on your evening? No matter. I have started proceedings. We will see that the treaty is observed.'

'Thank you. I will so inform my government.'

'Yes. Do.'

When we left the PM's offices, Sir Malcolm began to flush red. In the meeting with the PM he betrayed little emotion, though now he couldn't contain it. Forbes stayed on at Government House to conduct other business. Sir Malcolm and I returned to the Residency in the Rolls. Not far from the PM's office, we saw a picture of Hitler hanging in a shop window. 'They call him Mohammed Haidar,' Sir Malcolm said. I must have looked surprised at that, so he added, 'The Germans have persuaded the fellahin that Hitler is a Moslem. The Mahdi, actually.'

'The Redeemer?'

'Yes. He who will restore justice before the Day of Judgement. Ought to keep him busy, don't you think?'

'That has the PM's fingerprints on it,' I said.

'It's the King. By default,' Sir Malcolm said. 'He has no feeling for the Germans. He has no real feeling for anything.' He thought about that, and I can only conclude that what then entered his mind had also entered mine. 'Well, perhaps one thing,' he said. We were quiet for a moment, until he completed his thought. 'I tried to shape that boy, make him into something worthwhile.'

'Is there no claiming him at all?'

'We'll soon see if between the two of us, we've taught him anything.' He didn't sound optimistic, and when I remained quiet he said, 'Buck up, Mr Peel. We're not out yet. When I first came to Egypt, the King was fourteen years old and the only thing he wanted was to drive this Rolls.'

Ali Maher's patronising attitude wasn't the problem, any more than was Afifi's coolness or a handful of soldiers. Sir Malcolm knew that no country sends only six soldiers anywhere, certainly not Germany, in 1940. There had to be more of them and he was sure they were in the desert. Though Sir Malcolm held only the rank of Ambassador, he continued to think and operate as a plenipot. A more cautious man might have asked the FO to send out agents to assess the matter. He sent his own men into the desert. They reported that a German reconnaissance unit (for what would later become an armoured division, the 15th Panzers,) was already in Libya.

This marked a change in Sir Malcolm's attitude. Thereafter he conducted very little business that wasn't directly related to the war effort and went to no more night-clubs. Though there was still activity at Gezira, the Cheynes did not attend.

Sir Malcolm requested an interview with the King which was ignored. He then notified Abdin of when he would arrive, making it clear he expected an audience. If one were not forthcoming, Sir Malcolm intended to stay at the Palace until it was granted. As one who had often anticipated audiences of the King, I thought it a dubious plan. Sir Malcolm asked me to accompany him. Of late, I'd had no dealings with the King and Sir Malcolm had only humiliation from him. I wasn't sure what I could add to this confrontation, should it take place, but it was not a time when one argued with the government. Sir Malcolm put on his morning coat and we went to Abdin, to call on Farouk.

The King received us in the library, the site of my tutorials. 'I had hoped that by giving you England, you might have come to hold us in higher regard, that you would have seen the wisdom of aligning yourself with us,' Sir Malcolm said.

'We are most grateful for Our time in England.'

'I am not here for gratitude, sir.'

'We rule, but We cannot make people be what they are not. The people do not care for the English.'

'The English have given them what it is they have.'

'They believe the Germans will give them more. It is a dilemma. What do you say, Mr Peel?'

I knew I would not be asked to say much on this occasion. I wanted to make it count. What I managed was, 'I believe with Sir Malcolm that a ruler leads by example. To the degree that you embrace the English, the people will follow.'

Farouk considered that at some length. In part, he was taking a poke at Sir Malcolm by reflecting longer on what I said than on what the Ambassador had said. It meant nothing to Sir Malcolm. He waited until Farouk spoke. 'You thought We could be what We are and also an Englishman. "The modern way."'

Sir Malcolm nodded, the soul of reason, and said, 'A modern sovereign is necessarily a man of the world.'

'It is like all of your curious Empire,' Farouk said. 'Other people dressed up as you. And after they have run about playing at sport and having tea-time and all the rest, you tell them they are inadequate as Englishmen.'

'I believe the crown came to you too soon, sir.'

'Perhaps it did. Ali Maher Pasha says, "Open Cairo to the Germans. Throw the English out. Accept what cannot be changed and side with the Axis."'

'Does our treaty mean nothing?'

'What will We do with your treaty when the German army comes marching? General Rommel is coming to the desert. Have you met him?'

'I have not.'

'Quite a gentleman. He knows all your English manners. We don't think he's been to Eton though.'

'I will not be compared to a Nazi.' For a moment he almost let Farouk get his goat, which is of course exactly what the King was trying to do. Farouk didn't care any more about Rommel than he did about Eton. Sir Malcolm could see that tact would get him nowhere. 'I will speak bluntly, sir. If war comes to North Africa, we are prepared to lose a half million men. We will not hesitate to remove the sovereign.'

'Will you?' the King asked, as if Sir Malcolm had told him the price of biscuits would have to be raised.

'We will make our stand in the desert.'

'If that fails, no matter who is the sovereign, what then? Fight them in Cairo, We suppose. In Opera Square, perhaps?'

'Building by building, brick by brick,' Sir Malcolm answered.

'If you do,' the King asked, 'who will suffer?'

'If we do not, Egypt will be lost.'

'No, Excellency. Egypt will be changed. She will not be lost, except perhaps to the British.'

As we left Abdin, on the way back to the Residency, Sir Malcolm asked if I would look into finding precedent for removing a sitting monarch. The emotion I had witnessed with the King was gone and in its place was the more usual cool consideration of a problem. I started to protest that I knew little of the law, but he just looked at me. The look said, You will do what you must.

'Will it come to that?' I asked. 'Removing him?'

'If it does, I want as much law on my side as possible.'

'What if there isn't any?'

'There's always something useful lurking about in the law. Tell me, Mr Peel. My niece. Do you still see her?'

'I do not, sir.'

'I am sorry to hear it. May I ask if my marriage played a part in that?'

'I doubt that, sir.'

'My wife seems to feel it did. If my happiness in any way blocked yours, I am deeply sorry.'

'I think it's best if Emma and I remain friends but no more than that. With conditions as they are, there's not really much choice in the matter, is there?'

I thought Vera would have told him all about my position with Emma Lyttelton. She certainly took an interest in it. She may well have, and his asking in this way was his method of testing the veracity of what she had said. Perhaps he was giving me an opportunity to tell him from my point of view what had occurred between his niece and me. One never knew exactly what he was up to. Before he was done, he was sure to have accumulated any information he wanted. I'm sure other diplomats have this ability, they probably instruct them in techniques of this sort at the FO. Still, I can't think there are many like Sir Malcolm who could make his informants believe that the interrogation was done out of generosity of feeling, and entirely for their benefit.

VERA:

At the Palace

Jimmy Peel had Egyptian fever. He all but went native. He was useful around the Residency because the people at Abdin trusted him. Anyway, Malcolm thought they did. Jimmy stayed with us after he was no longer tutoring Farouk. He had developed new tastes when he was with the King at Woolwich. They used to go into Mayfair together. That's also what Jimmy liked about Alex. The girls. There were worse Englishmen in Egypt. Anyone of a mind to go brothel-hopping in Alexandria and pursue females past the age of reason, was an upstanding citizen in those circles.

Malcolm and I have long since made our peace about Farouk. It's so many years ago and almost everyone who was there is gone. Malcolm kept the most elaborate diplomatic diaries. They're all at Oxford now. I looked through them once. I'm first mentioned when I come out with Emma Lyttelton. I'm Miss Napier. Then before long he's referring to me as Vera, then it's V. It was very romantic to read those pages so many years later. I could see our whole early life together in that. The truth of it is, the King never stopped trying to see me. He would send notes and little gifts or telephone. Somehow he would know if I was going to be out, and then he'd manage to be where I was going. One couldn't just drop into a tea-shop with the King, but sometimes he'd whisk me off somewhere, or try to. The little game we played was always the same. He would be ardent, I would refuse him. The King did not lack for female company. He had more mistresses than anyone I had ever heard of. The thought of being in a parade of that sort put me off. Also, I loved my husband. I didn't chase after men. Except for Farouk, men didn't chase after me. Oh, there were little flirtations at diplomatic gatherings or sporting events, but they led nowhere. My behaviour was above reproach. Only the King kept up his pursuit.

We had been at the Scarabée when he asked me to dance. It was a famous incident. He made all the other couples leave the floor. Farouk was a wonderful dancer. He just seemed to float and carry me along. We did the Hi-Lo, a silky two-step that included a Latin dip. It was the dance of the hour in Cairo. I couldn't look at Malcolm. 'You're making my husband cross,' I said.

'Your husband? Now which of those young men is he? Oh, the old one.' I almost laughed. It's what he wanted me to do. I took some comfort in knowing that if Malcolm saw me laughing, he wouldn't imagine it was at his expense. 'We want some time alone with you,' the King said. 'We'll send for you tomorrow.'

'You know I can't. Now you're embarrassing me, terri-bly. Please let the other people dance.'

'Agree to see Us.'

I would have agreed to anything just to get the other

people back on the floor. The moment was wildly romantic of course, and Farouk knew what I was feeling. He
couldn't read my mind about anything remotely political,
though he could read my emotions. He had made a study
of them, I think. I agreed to come to Abdin. I kept my
promise, but not for the purpose Farouk had in mind.

The next day, at the Palace, we sat in the flower garden,
breathing in the lightest, most delicate perfume from the
white roses that seemed to grow at Abdin year-round.
There were guards nearby, so it really was innocent.
Whenever I expected the King to make a pass, and was
ready to fend it off, he was unfailingly polite. He had
been telling me more wretched jokes. I always determined not to laugh, but then I did. It was just so amusing to have the King of Egypt tell me riddles. He told me
he was a connoisseur of them, and while I was feeling
heady from the fragrant roses, he added, 'Also a connoisseur of feminine beauty.'

'That's the biggest joke of all.'

'We'll tell you more if you like.'

'No, no. Quite enough.' He could sense that I wanted
to bring up something else.

'Whatever you want,' the King said, waiting for me to
find the words.

'The whole of the government is upset with you.'

'The German soldiers, We are sure.'

'And the Treaty.'

'We are not ready to throw anyone out of the country
who might win the war.'

'They won't win.'

'We will not be hasty. Sir Malcolm would behave no
differently. You know that is so.' I had no answer to that.
He was right. 'We want to give you something,' he said,

raising a finger to a sufragi who was waiting with a parcel. 'Don't say no. It is of no monetary value.' I removed the tissue and found a small picture of the Palace in a simple gold frame. 'Surely even so firm a husband as yours could not object.'

It was quiet and elegant and utterly right. 'It's a lovely thing,' was all I could manage to say.

'When you look at it, perhaps you will think kindly of Abdin's tenant.' I felt rubbery. I had come with a political scheme of importance in mind, and now I was feeling like a schoolgirl. I managed to say that yes, I would think well of him.

'It might have been otherwise,' he said.

'You mean I might have been another of the King's conquests.'

'It is you who have made the conquest.'

'You do confuse me sometimes.' He leaned across the tea-table and kissed me. I permitted it for a moment, but then knew I must leave. 'I will treasure this,' I said, of the picture, perhaps unconsciously meaning more. 'On behalf of my husband and myself.'

'We will always know that when you look at it, you look at it alone.' He was quite right. That was exactly how I looked at it.

The King was so ardent that I couldn't get him out of my mind. He was frivolous, silly really. Malcolm was so serious. I wanted to play, I suppose. I was young and the King was younger still. My longing confused me. I believe I preferred yearning for him in secret to his actual presence. A better person, I am sure, might have felt badly, but I did not. The flirtation, which had never really been put to a test (well, perhaps a bit on the river cruise), made me feel strong. My private feelings for the King gave me secret power over my husband. I don't mean I intended to use it, but it was nice to have, rather like what one of our housemaids when I was a girl called her bolt money.

The King was one sort of problem for me. Quite another came from an unexpected quarter. My father was passing through Cairo. I hadn't seen him in some time and I was thrilled. I had assumed he would stay at the Residency. Instead he booked himself into Shepheard's. The story of that is difficult for me even now. Over tea at the hôtel, I told him about my days at the Residency. He said, 'I can't think, darling, that I ever quite imagined you in such circumstances so soon.'

'Well, neither had I. It's a very active life. The Palace. So many people.' He seemed to sense a discomfort in me. It was at a time when the King was very much on my mind.

'Perfectly happy, are you?' he asked.

'No one is perfectly happy, P'pa.'

'The war is going to come here, you know. It will change things.'

'What will happen?'

'That cannot yet be known.'

At that point, to my absolute astonishment, we were joined by the Very Reverend Maurice Thwaite, Dean of St Swithun's Cathedral, the man who had christened and married me. He was travelling with my father. Dean Thwaite had been in the newspapers lately and not in his clerical capacity. He had become a follower of Oswald Mosley, the leader of the British Union of Fascists. The Dean had actually preached the virtues of fascism from his pulpit. He was in all sorts of hot water with the Archbishop. It was plain why my father was not staying at the Residency.

'Hello, Vera,' the Dean said as he joined us. He was a large man, at the far edge of middle-age. He had watery blue eyes and whitish hair, parted in the centre.

'Dean Thwaite, how nice to see you, though it is a bit of a surprise. Would you mind terribly if I had just another word with my father? Then we can all have a jolly time and catch up.'

'Yes of course, but let me say, I think I understand your dilemma and I want you to know I would never cause you any difficulty.'

'That's reassuring.'

'There is one thing, however, if I may,' he said, sitting down with us even though I had all but ordered him to leave. 'Perhaps your father has already asked you this.'

'Maurice,' my father said, interrupting him. 'We have been speaking of personal matters. If you would give us a few minutes alone.'

There was something comical about it. These two men, my father who regularly put people in gaol for years and Dean Thwaite who instructed people on how they might live their lives, arguing over who should make some pathetic and unlikely plea to me. 'Of course,' Dean Thwaite said, and then just continued to prattle. 'The favour we require is an introduction to the King. I would like an audience of His Majesty as soon as possible on matters of some concern.'

The man was clearly round the bend. Did he think I would arrange such a meeting? Or that I would ask Malcolm to do it? So that he might explain the wonderful virtues of fascism? Here was my father travelling the world with him.

'Maurice, you must let me speak to Vera about this. You are rushing matters.'

'Of course, Sir Hugh. Certainly,' he said. 'I think if I could just spend an hour with His Majesty it would be beneficial to all sides.'

He began outlining a bizarre economic scheme that he hoped to present to the King. It had to do with limiting certain foreign imports and reducing the scope of chain-stores in Britain. Why he should believe that the King of Egypt would be interested, I cannot imagine, but apparently chain-stores that might replace village shops were a concern of the British Union of Fascists. Dean Thwaite also wanted to offer the King favourable terms for importing Egyptian cotton. That Dean Thwaite, let alone my father, thought Farouk would be concerned about the shopping habits of the English, or even hear it out, was quite mad. My father was plainly embarrassed by Dean Thwaite's single-mindedness in the light of my discomfort. Still, he didn't correct him or try to steer the topic to something more congenial. I could only conclude that my father agreed with Dean Thwaite and was only disturbed by his rudeness in so relentlessly presenting his case.

'You know, Vera,' Dean Thwaite said, 'the idea that I am unyielding in my views is plainly wrong. It is equally untrue of your father and of Sir Oswald. We would welcome new solutions, though as yet we are the only group of any significance so much as addressing the issue. Our economy will not get better without radical change. At a minimum, we must rid ourselves of the chain-stores.'

He was back on that. 'Chain-stores?' I asked. The very word had taken on an odd foreign sound in my mind.

'Sainsbury's is on the march. They'll soon be everywhere and no stopping them. British Home Stores as well. If they are encouraged they will create their own de facto government leaving nothing but misery and unemployment in their wake.'

'I see.'

'They are contrary to our way of life. A community is fostered by the village greengrocer, the chemist, and the fishmonger. They are here now, but if we are not strict with them, they will be merged tomorrow.'

'Dean Thwaite,' I said, trying my best to sound like a female version of my husband, 'please leave now. I wish to talk to my father in private.' It was sufficient.

When he was gone, my father said, 'He can be a trifle enthusiastic.'

'Are you a member of the Fascisti?' I asked, in what I very much hope was a calm voice.

'The Fascisti are in Italy, darling. I am a British subject.'

'P'pa, please. Are you mixed up with Mosley?'

'I listen seriously to Mosley. I am not alone.'

'Thank you then, for not staying with us. It might well have compromised Malcolm in some way.' He didn't reply, so I asked, 'Where is it you're going now?'

'The Libyan border. I'm going to have a look at the way things stand.'

'For which side?' It was one of those dreadful questions that serve to remind that in my father's presence, I will always be a small girl. He wouldn't answer, of course. I collected myself and told him, 'It is out of the question for me in any way to assist you in seeing the King.'

'It was never my intention to ask for that. I'm afraid that was Maurice's idea.'

'I am glad to hear that at least. In the circumstances, I'm afraid I must rescind our dinner invitation for this evening.'

'Perhaps you and I might go out to a restaurant. The two of us.'

'Oh, P'pa, you know I can't.' I was so firm with that wretched Dean Thwaite and now I could feel myself coming apart. My father saw it and he took my hand. He meant to comfort, but he only frightened me.

'Sir Oswald is misunderstood. I would expect you to listen to the cause before making up your mind based on what you may have read in the newspapers.'

'The cause? His cause gives comfort to the enemy.'

'I can see there's no point in arguing. I believe that you, and every other sensible person, will come round. Our goal is to avoid war. To accommodate for the larger good.'

I went light-headed and a bit dizzy. Dean Thwaite may have been a fool, but what then was my father? Had he always been like this and was I seeing it only now? 'Wars change everything, darling,' he said, then got up from the table, kissed me and left. He was gone the next day without trying to see the King.

When I told Malcolm about it, he said, 'Perhaps Sir Hugh has been in court for too long. The exposure to so many years of mischief and chicanery has affected his mind.'

'That is little comfort, Malcolm,' I said, a bit more sharply than I had intended.

'He would never do anything against England,' Malcolm said, trying to console me. 'He might sit out a war in some manner so as not to do anything against Italy, but that is the worst that might happen.' That night, I slept badly. I found myself clinging to Malcolm as much like a daughter as a wife.

Malcolm felt it was time to get the girls out of Egypt. His plan was to send them to his family's house in

Scotland, for the duration. We were in our bedroom when he told me, 'Put them on an aeroplane,' as if all one had to do was ring up and book passage.

'They won't like it,' I told him.

'It is not open to debate. My darling, we should consider whether you should be here as well.'

'That question is also closed. If you are here, I will stay.'

'It's upon us.' His voice had a mixture of dread and anticipation. I believe this reaction was at the heart of who my husband truly was. Malcolm didn't want a war, but more than that, he didn't want to miss one if it were to come. He wanted to be tested by battle.

'We'll win,' I told him, wanting to believe it.

'If we hold Egypt.'

'We will hold it if you and I have to do it alone.'

'It's in the boy's hands.'

'Then you will take it from him.' If it sounds as though I'm boasting a bit about my own performance, perhaps I am. I believe it to be an accurate picture of the events. Time may have clouded some of the details of my flirtation with the King, but time has not touched my memory of our military and political dilemmas. We had power and we used it and we did not back away from danger. I believed in my husband and I believed in my country. I do not care what is fashionable now. Late that night, he held me close and whispered my name. 'Vee,' he said. 'Vee, Vee.'

Churchill came out to Cairo to see our position. Malcolm wanted to put him with Ali Maher, the Egyptian PM and a fascist to his toes. It was quite exciting to have Churchill at the Residency. Malcolm and I went out to meet his aeroplane which arrived in the middle of the night. The time of arrival had been changed three times in the preceding forty-eight hours. I assumed this was because the PM was busy. Malcolm explained that it was a question of security. If no one knew just when Churchill would be anywhere, the chances of anyone doing him harm were lessened. By the time we were at the airstrip, I didn't know if he was coming at all. When he had landed and a staircase had been put in place, we waited and waited. Finally an officer got off, then another and then there he was, bundled in a greatcoat, wearing a little hat, like something a Greek fisherman might wear. He squinted out at us, then came down the stairs. Malcolm said, 'Welcome to Cairo, Prime Minister.'

'Hello, Malcolm,' he said, as if they had run into one another at Claridge's. He kissed my hand and said, 'Lady Cheyne, how good of you to come out.' They were taken directly to a meeting at Abdin with Ali Maher and the King. I of course did not attend, but later that night when the men returned to the Residency, I got to hear about it. They both kept telling me the story, interrupting one another like schoolboys determined to outdo one another and impress the girl. According to the PM, Ali Maher was going on about how he hoped to keep the fighting out of Cairo, as if he alone considered that a desirable end. Churchill told him, 'That will be accomplished when Cairo is protected.'

Malcolm said, 'You have handed the desert to the Axis. Alexandria will be lost.'

'It was burned once, you know,' Ali Maher said. 'The great library. All lost.'

Churchill said, 'Do me the honour of assuming we have read the history books.' At that point, according to

Malcolm, Churchill received a demonstration of Royal humour.

'I was looking in my pocket for my timepiece, about to make a point about how long we had been talking,' Churchill said. 'It was given to my father by Queen Victoria. I should have been very unhappy to have lost it. Your husband was glaring at the King. I couldn't imagine why, until Malcolm said, "Your Majesty, if you know anything of this." Then Farouk leaned over and pretended to pull my timepiece from Malcolm's pocket. "Is this it?" he said. "It must be it. How could that have happened?"'

At that point I was laughing, I couldn't help it. Not just at the absurdity of the whole thing, but at the way the PM was imitating the King. He had got Farouk's voice down. He sort of chirruped it out, as if it were all a great surprise. '"Here it is, good as new,"' he said, amusing himself now with his imitation. "No harm done."' The world thinks a great deal of Winston Churchill, but I do not believe he is generally regarded as a humorist. This was a rare demonstration. Had his life been otherwise, perhaps he could have gone on the music hall stage doing impressions. Malcolm was laughing too, which was once a commonplace, but which had not happened for some time. I was hearing all this back at the Residency, where the PM and Malcolm were drinking brandy and smoking cigars. They had told me the amusing bits and then they thought I would leave. If Churchill was cautious enough to keep altering his travel times, it wouldn't have surprised me had he said, I must now go. Perhaps it was the hour, or perhaps it was that there was no dutiful ADC about to remind him. Or perhaps he just liked having a young woman about to laugh at his impressions of the King. He told my husband, 'Follow the Alexandria situation,' by which he meant the German troops in the desert. Surely he knew that Malcolm had been going on about the significance of the desert for the longest time. Now it suited the PM's purposes, so he spoke of it as if it were a new idea.

'Shall I go and have a look?' Malcolm asked.

'Yes. You've got quite a handful here. The King and the PM.'

'The boy's unpredictable. Ali Maher is all too predictable.'

'Can the King sack him?' Churchill asked.

'Yes.'

'Who can sack the King?'

'I can,' Malcolm said.

'Does the King know that?'

'I have made grand threats.'

'I'm sure. We will back them.'

It meant that Malcolm was to go to the desert beyond Alexandria to assess the matter. He took Fawcett with him. I know that sounds unbearably grand, to go off on a military reconnaissance mission with a valet, but Fawcett was a military man. What was Malcolm to do? Take Jimmy Peel because he knew Alexandria? Fawcett was a good choice. He was loyal, not that Jimmy wasn't, but Fawcett was capable and organised and he saw to all the details. They went off in a motor-car that looked awfully small. Malcolm felt it an unnecessary advertisement to go in the Rolls. Fawcett was perfectly adequate as a driver, but it was unusual to see my husband in the front seat of a sedan, his head pressing up against the ceiling. He had to carry his hat in his lap.

The King knew Malcolm had gone to the desert to look at our position. I don't know how, but Malcolm

always said anything that goes on the servants are likely
to know about. For the duration we had to assume that
all the sufragis were reporting everything they heard.
'Perhaps we need a taster,' Malcolm said, only part in jest.
I had heard tales about Titterington, a so-called pharma-
cist who hung about the Palace checking all the food
Farouk ate. It had always seemed far-fetched. No longer.

With Malcolm gone off to the desert, the war felt more
real than at any other time, even more than when
Churchill was in the Residency talking about sacking the
King. I did not think my husband was in greater danger
than were others. Still, he was in the presence of German
troops. I could only imagine what sort of trophy he
would make as a prisoner of war. I pictured it all that
night. I can't say I dreamed it, because there was little
sleep for me. I could see him on display, in chains, an
important catch for the Nazis. I also knew what they
would do after they'd had their fun parading him about
and taking his photograph. They would stand him
against a stone wall and shoot him. I pictured that, too. I
never told him about my night-sweats, and it didn't come
to pass, but the picture came back to me from time to
time for many years.

After Malcolm left, I received a message from Abdin,
requesting my presence. Such invitations came often. If
they weren't for both Malcolm and me, I refused. This
time I accepted. I went in an Embassy motor-car. One
could hardly enter the Palace in secrecy. I suppose if I'd
thought about it, I would have asked His Majesty to meet
somewhere more neutral. As I had hoped to make him
address political matters, I went through the front door, as
it were. I met the King in a salon hung with tapestries. The

light was soft and I found him in an easy mood. If he was affected by the war, I did not see it. 'We have asked you to come many times,' he said. 'This time you say yes. Why?'

'Does it matter? I'm here.'

'Your husband is away.'

'This is not about him.'

'I am told he is in the desert counting Germans. It may take him quite a while. The Afrika Korps is there, you know. Had he asked Us, We would have told him. We have a troop count here somewhere.'

'I want you to do something.'

'You know We will.'

'For Egypt.'

'We were hoping for something more personal.'

'Stop listening to your Prime Minister.'

'Shall We listen to Lord Melbourne then, who is off on his counting expedition?'

'You know exactly what I mean.'

'Do We?'

'Support us. Join us. It's where Egypt belongs.'

'Can you name nine animals from Africa?'

'Do you care about anything?'

'That's very harsh. A giraffe and eight elephants.'

'I would almost prefer you were a Nazi and not a fool.'

'Is it so foolish to side with the winner?'

'You have chosen wrong.'

'Your husband's counting will show there is an entire army in the desert with tanks. The Germans are ready. The English are dithering.'

'Do it for me, then.' He looked at me hard, a little puzzled. I liked that. He had been the source of so much confusion in me that I rather enjoyed turning the tables. I could feel him thinking, What is on offer here? It was a good question. I had chosen my clothing with some care. I was wearing a blue silk frock that I had seen the King notice on other occasions. He would often compliment my clothing in a sort of mechanical way. But the blue silk had held his eye. It was both loose and clinging, a quality that only French dress-makers knew how to impart.

'We would do anything for you. That has been the case for some time now.'

He was a tiny bit uncertain, hardly a royal quality. I could feel it. I held the power. It was for me to say what would come next. It made me strong. It didn't hurt that he was royal, but it was equally important that he was a man. They were all royal to me in some sense, and I lived to turn the tables. My eyes went dark as I looked at him. It was a sultry quality that came quite naturally to me and that I used only when I meant it.

'Now? Finally?' I met his eyes, but said nothing. 'Not for all the presents and the playing?'

'No. Not for that,' I said and unbuttoned my blue silk. It astonished him.

Making love to him was like nothing I had known. After Malcolm and I had been married quite some time, I acknowledged that I'd had other lovers before our marriage. It was like an inoculation – enough truth that I was able to avoid the larger truth about Farouk. There was a time when I could have done something like this and then blocked out all the details. It is no doubt my relentlessly advancing age, or perhaps my years of widowhood, but I find the debauched particulars returning to me in a way that once would have been impossible. I can not only recall it, but I can conjure up the precise feelings of that time. It is one of the few advantages of age.

As the King pulled me to him, and began wrestling

with my clothing and then tearing at his own, it all seemed terribly hurried. I was regretting it even as I knew there was no retreating. Remarkably, he seemed to understand and he slowed a bit. Our fumblings went from desperate to languid, even delicate. I soon felt a swirling sensation, as if I were flowing down into a narrowing pool, until I felt myself taken over completely by the King's passion. I sat astride him, looking down into his brown eyes, and I could feel him dominating me. With just a movement of his legs, he was able to guide my trembling, to make me give what he wanted, which was what I needed to do. Perhaps because what I thought I wanted from him was political, we were less burdened by more mechanical matters. When Malcolm and I were together like that, though I tried to let myself be transported, there were too many daily concerns in the marriage bed with us. Malcolm was a man who did everything effortlessly, which in most things is an attractive quality. In bed, however, it meant that a quiet efficiency prevailed over any spirit of adventure. Farouk, who was careless and not half the man my husband was, made me delirious.

Afterward, we played about in the Palace, chasing from room to room, all inhibitions left behind with my blue silk. I can scarcely recall how many rooms we went in and out of, but after we grew tired of running, and when we were back in the salon among the tapestries, I allowed him to catch me again. He came from behind, his hands round my waist and pulled me back to him. I could feel him stirring. He bent me over the arm of a red velvet wing chair, pushed my head down into the cushion and took me from behind. I do not mean à tirgo. I mean behind. I had never experienced such a thing. I gasped for breath, but the King would not stop. He was leaning over

my back and his body within me was like the pounding
of a fierce and steady hammer. As my head began to swim
and I thought I might burst, he shouted out in his passion and then backed away triumphant, leaving the royal
essence smeared across my backside. I was shaking with a
mixture of thrill and weakness. I turned to him, so very
confused, not knowing what I felt. I had no plan, no
scheme that I knew of, but I grabbed his arms and pinned
them behind him and pushed him against an ormolu
writing desk, knocking over an ink-well and scattering
papers, till he was sprawled on his back. It was the reverse
of what he had so recently done to me. He complained
that he was spent and now must rest, but I wouldn't hear
it. I held him down, pressing my own centre against him,
then stroking him, trying to force him into reluctant life.

'My dear, We cannot,' he said, rather plaintively.

I ignored his protest and forced him to replay a version
of my earlier erotic humiliation in this Palace on the day
Malcolm found us playing in the corridor. Now I was in
control, not the King. I climbed up and upon him and
pushed into his face. I ground myself into him till his eyes
said he might be strangled. Good, I thought. Be strangled, because I am not yet concluded here. Expire and
with it the whole of the Dynasty. Let it ride out of the
world just this way. I swirled against him, till he was limp
and exhausted and I required no more. Then, lest he have
any doubt who was the triumphant one, I pushed him off
the desk and fell with him in a royal heap on the floor.
There was passion, but there was also anger, from both of
us. We had pursued one another for so long, that we were
both frustrated. It was desire, fury, and danger all jum-
bled together. He was the King and not about to leave it
at that. He found his strength again and lifted me up

from the floor and carried me into the corridor. It was only when I saw that famous mural that I realised we were in the harem. I knew instantly that I had made a serious miscalculation. There were no secrets in the harem. The King could feel the life go out of me though he didn't know why. Everyone gossiped about him all the time. What did he care? But it could mean everything to me. To his credit, when he saw I no longer wanted to play, he allowed our session to come to an end.

Later, I wasn't sure what I had done. I knew it was wrong to assume that if I gave myself to the King, he would give Egypt to the Allies. I didn't think I was Helen of Troy, nor did I think wars and nations operated in that way. Yet I believed that if I got close enough to Farouk he would do as I wanted. He was still handsome in those days, and he had pursued me since his coronation. I wanted him and I was about to lose him to the war. That he had been on my mind so vividly for so long was my true betrayal of Malcolm. It was more than my body I gave to the King. I fear it was also my heart. I dreamed that Malcolm and the Queen would fall magically away and I would become Queen of Egypt. I had spent so many years of my young life looking to make a good marriage, that simply because I had done so, was not enough to stop my imagination. It is one thing now to be able to sort all this out. I've had half a century to do it. What is it my nanny used to say? Act in haste, repent at leisure. I don't repent, though I do reconsider. It was a young woman's act, but it had a certain daring. The times were operatic and I have Italian blood.

Malcolm returned safely from the desert, though both he and Fawcett looked as if they'd had too much sun. In a tone of hush-hush, Malcolm reported that there were many German soldiers and nothing to stop them. It was serious news, but it also had an entertaining quality. I had now learned this bit of intelligence from each side. My amusement didn't last. 'It's the King,' my husband said. 'He has to go.' Malcolm saw me look up at him as he said that. Perhaps that was the sign he was looking for. My own sense of remorse came over me, and I believed my husband knew everything and this was his reaction to it. Was Malcolm going to try to throw the King out of his own country? My own reasons for my actions might be a trifle mixed, but they had at least a patriotic element. If my behaviour were to become an issue and damage my husband and my country, well, it would be more than I could bear. As I thought it could get no worse, Jimmy Peel rang up and invited me to luncheon.

JIMMY:

A Terrorist of the Heart

I had been seeing Miriam Rolo again. What with the tension between the Residency and Abdin, it might not have been the most politic thing I'd ever done, but at my age there was no stopping it. Miriam certainly understood that our romance might be in the Palace's interest, but I was the one who pursued it. Because I was so rarely assertive in these matters, I was pleased with myself for doing as I wished rather than waiting for someone else to act first. Miriam had the use of a flat in Garden City, near the Greek Embassy, not far from the Residency. It belonged to her husband who occasionally advised Farouk in financial matters, much as he had done for Fouad. His services had been passed from father to son. He was in the import and export business, which in Egypt could have meant anything from gun-runner to distributor of medicine to the poor. I believe he used the flat for assignations with his mistresses. In a marital bargain that wasn't easy for an Englishman to grasp, Miriam had the run of the flat in the afternoons. It was a lovely, sunny place but it wasn't quite as compelling for me as the rooms at Abdin.

Nonetheless, I was not about to turn down any invitation to be alone with Miriam. As we lay braided together like rope, flushed red from our exertions, I expected her to soon say, 'Je suis désolé', my old cue to leave. Instead, she let her eyes linger on the stand of banyan trees in the garden, fixed on their silvery trunks and twisted roots, then began talking about the war. I was certainly aware Miriam was a Jew, though it wasn't something I thought much about. The possibility of Farouk giving the country to the Nazis was frightening for her. 'There are some old people here, my husband's relatives. They are putting aside poison. If the Germans come, they will kill themselves.'

'Why don't they leave?'

'They are old. They have been here far longer than this Dynasty. I want you to do something.'

I had a sense of what she was going to ask. I knew I would find it distasteful, but I also knew I would do it. 'Do you have information?' I asked.

'You're becoming Egyptian. A few years ago, you would have thought I wanted help with the old relatives.'

'Do you?'

'I have documents that tell how many German units are in the desert, where they are, and how many more will be coming. I have troop counts. It's all auf Deutsch of course.' She waited to see if she had told me enough. She had, but we were now playing chess.

'What do you want me to do?' I asked.

'I want it put directly in the hands of the English Ambassador.' There may well have been some second or even third level of meaning to this, though at least one meaning was clear. Miriam's interests were not the same as Farouk's. She was operating on her own. That she wanted to make a spy of me, and further that I would have to acknowledge some portion of our relationship to Sir Malcolm, made me uneasy. 'You haven't answered,' she said. 'Will you do it?'

'Yes. I will.'

She smiled in her sibylline way, got out of bed and went to what I assume was her husband's desk to collect the papers. She was naked and as she passed the tall window, sunlight fell on her. She moved from light to shadow and back to the light. I felt an erotic charge run through me. I was about to take an enormous risk here. If the Germans learned that Miriam or her husband had these papers, they would be killed. If I were found to have them, I would probably fare no better. The papers in question were type-written lists, ten leaves, unbound. I could read a little German but I had no way of judging the authenticity of the information. It could all have been a great trap. Send me through Cairo carrying fake but authentic looking German documents right into the hands of the Nazis who would then have an English spy, a member of the legation, no less. Miriam put the documents in a briefcase, mixed in with some presumably more innocuous papers. She did not have to say 'Je suis désolé' for me to know it was time to go. In the lift going down to the road, I slipped the incriminating papers up the back of my shirt.

I hired a taxi and set out for the Residency, expecting to be intercepted at any moment. As I travelled, I could feel sweat on my back. My nervousness soon soaked my shirt clear through. Would the documents be rendered unreadable? Soon I could smell the rank odour of my

own bowels. My God, nothing had yet happened and I
seemed on the verge of shitting myself. When the taxi was
stopped in traffic, hemmed in by pedestrians and han-
tours, I was certain they were all Nazis. I knew my fears
were exaggerated but that did not make them any less
real. I swallowed my terror and told the driver to bump
up on the footpath and go round the mess. When he
refused, I did what Europeans have always done to get
our way in this part of the world. I gave him money and
told him to do as I had instructed and not stop till he got
to the Residency.

As the taxi hurried on, I contracted my stomach muscles, squeezed my bum tight, and willed my innards to be
calm. I reviewed my position. Miriam was what she said
she was: a Sephardic woman afraid for her co-religionists
and ready to accept whatever danger there was to try to
stop her King from siding with the Nazis. That was a
more reasonable motive to assume than that she was setting an elaborate trap for me. She could, however, be
using me to send false information to the Embassy, hoping thereby to smoke out our plans. The dark possibilities
multiplied in my mind, but I grabbed the interpretation
that coincided with England's needs, tried hard to believe
in it and kept telling the driver to hurry.

I found Sir Malcolm at his desk, looking drawn. His
office walls were now covered with maps, and encrypted
cables came in frequently. There had been a rumour at
the Palace and the Residency that Churchill himself had
been in Cairo and he and Sir Malcolm had been working
till all hours. I had been concerned that he would question me about the provenance of the documents. 'I have
something you should see immediately.' The sheaf of
soggy papers were still inside my shirt. I reached behind

for them and watched his face remain impassive, despite the mystery of it. I put them on his desk and said, 'I believe these to be genuine.'

He looked through them, first for content, though his German was not much better than mine. Then he held each sheet up to the light, inspecting the watermark. Then, as if to match my hugger-mugger in secreting the papers in my shirt, he produced a reading glass from his desk and examined the pages in greater detail. I do not know what he was looking for, some additional sign of authenticity certainly, but just as he did not question how I came to possess these pages, he did not offer any explanation of his own scrutiny of them. I assumed that a man of his experience knew at least the rudiments of assessing the authenticity of what appeared to be German documents. Finally, he said, 'Yes. It's quite possible they are.' He was quiet for a moment, waiting to see if I might offer any further information. When I did not, he got up and left the office, taking the documents with him. His abrupt departure reminded me of the way Farouk used to walk out of our lessons.

Very soon after that, Sir Malcolm and Fawcett left the Residency, I am sure to go to the desert to look into the information I had provided.

I reached Miriam on the telephone, an appliance she hadn't much trusted in more relaxed times and certainly doubted now. She wouldn't permit any discussion of my recent activity, but instead asked if I wouldn't like to join her at the Palace. Conditions were changed there for Miriam now that Nazli was Queen Mother. She still required her ladies-in-waiting, but Nazli was no longer restricted to the harem. She had the run of the Palace and was often with Mazhar Pasha. When they were away, Miriam and I could spend time once again in those precincts that were so charged for me. I'm sure the sufragis knew, they knew everything. I suppose I cared, but not nearly enough to deny myself such pleasure. I might now be a spy, Miriam might be a traitor, but this was Cairo and nothing stopped illicit romance. I would have expected that while we were relaxing, Miriam would want to hear about Sir Malcolm's reaction to the papers, but it didn't seem to interest her. She knew he had gone to the desert. That seemed to be common knowledge, though she and I knew a good deal more about it than most. Not a word of that.

Instead she asked me to interpret the ways of Englishwomen. Her views in this area always amused me. We were in her bentwood boat of a bed, our feet entwined, when she asked, 'Why do they wear that colour on their legs and arms?'

'Colour? Whatever do you mean?'

'They have yellow or red painted on them. Sometimes there's a white business on the nose.' Miriam always surprised. A few days earlier she was putting both our lives at risk for what she knew to be a high purpose, and which she understood with some subtlety. Now she had taken an interest in women she thought were trivial to their core. 'Is it meant to be like henna?' she asked. 'Decoration?'

'It's medicine of a sort.'

'What disease do they have?'

I explained that Europeans believed that in tropical climates the smallest nick or bite could become infected – thus they paint their limbs with iodine or Mercurochrome. 'The dabs of white on their noses are called Nivea. It's a cream to protect them from the sun.'

'Why do they go out in the sun in the first place?'

'It's one of life's mysteries.'

'They are colourful as lemon trees. Do you find that attractive?'

'It's not done for beauty. The idea is to protect one's health.'

'How marvellously English.'

'My dear, we are a people who can sleep under netting and still fret the night away about insects.'

She laughed at that and pulled me on top of her. She had a way of catching my attention whenever she chose to. She would bring her long slender legs, that never so far as I knew had ever borne iodine or Mercurochrome, up round my back and deliver her hands to the part of me that I had so foolishly thought might not stir again. She would remain beneath, open to me, making it plain that my pleasure was what mattered, and yet she was in control of all that occurred. She managed our rhythm, and yet I felt dominant. Later, when I thought about our coupling, it reminded me of England in Egypt. We thought we were in charge but the Egyptians knew so much better that we were only here on temporary sufferance.

There were often strange noises in the Palace. No matter how long I had been in Egypt, I never quite got used to the daily prayers. Even to my Anglican ears, this was no call of the muezzin. Miriam heard the sounds first and went to the door where there was a peephole that allowed for a view of the corridor. 'My God, look at this,' she said, beckoning to me to join her at the door.

I saw the King, absolutely naked, racing about like a randy goat in a state of high tumescence. Since nothing about Farouk could ever surprise me, I found it amusing. Then I saw who he was chasing. Her figure, which I knew

to be appealing, was astonishing undraped. Her slim legs
were brown from the constant sun. It looked at first as if
she were wearing lisle stockings and nothing more. It was
startling because the brown, which was also the colour of
her throat and face, gave way abruptly at the neck to her
pale white torso and full breasts. It was as if she was twice
naked. Her face was flushed and her hair swayed as she
ran. To see her there, like that, was to know all at once the
end of decorum and the birth of desire. The King cap-
tured her, pushed her against the wall and tried to take
her standing upright. She permitted his struggle for a
moment and then wriggled away, laughing, and running
off down the corridor. The King chased her like a hound
with the spoor of a fox in his nostril. I watched until
Miriam pulled me away from the door. Miriam and I
were not wearing any more than the King and Lady
Cheyne. Miriam said, 'I think your reaction is too obvious.' Miriam, ever the heart's detective, was practical in
matters of love and chose not to be hurt by what could
not be denied. She simply took full advantage.

Later, the question in my mind was had I been used in
this in some way I hadn't foreseen. Had Farouk given
Miriam the German documents to hand to me knowing
that they would get Sir Malcolm out of Cairo for a few
days? What if he had? Farouk had no political beliefs. If
he had to harm the Germans in favour of the English in
order to get at Lady Cheyne, well of course he would do
it. Miriam, as a Jew, would be the ideal person to imple-
ment his scheme because she had me. I might well have
been a pawn in this, yet, if this last reading was correct,
what did it matter? Miriam was getting what she needed,
England would benefit in a vital way and as I could plainly see, Farouk was getting what he wanted. Concern for

Sir Malcolm's sensibilities would have to be set aside. He would make the same judgement, I am sure.

I asked Miriam if the King and Lady Cheyne were regulars in this part of the Palace. 'She has been here, certainly, and the two of them cavort endlessly. But nothing so colourful, shall we say, has happened before.'

'Quite a show.'

'Would you find it amusing to look in on them?' Miriam asked. 'It can be done. They would never know.'

'Interesting perhaps, but no.'

'The King's put on a bit of weight. Still he's always looked better than his father, I think.'

I knew Miriam and Fouad had been lovers, but till now it hadn't occurred to me that she had probably slept with Farouk as well. Perhaps because I had picked up her style in these matters, I found that amusing. She refused to compare them, though. She said it was vulgar. 'I think this must confirm what all Englishmen think of Egypt, anyway.'

'What is that?' I asked.

'That the entire country is a brothel.'

I denied it, but she was more right than not. She refused any further discussion of the activities at the far end of the corridor, calling me closer, to resume our own pleasure.

I believed I had stumbled upon something of value to England in a situation that had to be more complex than I was aware. It was quite possible that Vera was being used for more than the King's amusement. I had to remind myself that at least thus far, England was ahead in part because of the risk I willingly took. I wanted to spare Vera as much as possible, but given the volatility of the circumstances I could hardly ignore it. At first I thought I might say that I had heard about the events, not witnessed them, though that seemed as if I were trying to let myself off the hook. I chose a public place for our luncheon because I was afraid she might come apart. That would be more likely to happen at the Residency than in a restaurant. We went to Groppi's, in Suleiman Pasha Square, a favourite of Vera's. It was a sort of Swiss patisserie, quite well known among the English. It wasn't much more than a café that put chocolate in most everything. One entered through a bead curtain and had a choice of staying inside in the dining room with its high ceiling, or continuing on, as we did, to a walled garden beyond. I had secured a private table shaded by a brightly coloured umbrella and had instructed the waiters to please not attend to us unless summoned. In all the time Vera and I had been in Egypt, this was the first meal we had ever had à deux. I could not run away from the difficult facts, nor could I patronise nor hide in euphemism. After we'd had a glass of a lovely white Burgundy as an apéritif, I said, 'You know about my friendship with Miriam Rolo, I'm sure.'

'I thought that was all over.'

'We still see one another. I was at Abdin with her.' It was at that point that Vera knew. I could see it in her eyes. Fear came across her face.

'With Miriam Rolo?'

'Yes.'

'Then just tell me, Jimmy. Don't make me ask questions.'

'We saw you in the corridor of the harem. With the King.'

'Perhaps it was someone else you saw.' This had to be terrible and frightening news for her, but she kept her composure. She turned icy, rather than emotional. It was as if her husband, certainly the injured party here, was coaching her, telling her to negotiate, not collapse.

'If it were only me, that would indeed be the case. Others may know.'

'Can't your Mrs Rolo see that they're kept quiet.'

'Perhaps.'

'What does she want?'

'It's not like that. She wants what we want. For the King to honour the treaty.'

'Why should she care?'

'She's Sephardic. A Jew. The last thing she wants is for Egypt to go with the Germans.'

'Does she know you're telling me all this?'

'Only you and I know that.'

Vera had kept steady till now, but her tears were not entirely in her control. Her intention to stay cool dissolved as the plain facts of the matter came over her. I gave her a table napkin and called for more of the white Burgundy.

'How could you, Jimmy? How could you look? Spying on me,' she said, exchanging tears for indignation.

As I had no answer that I could easily say, I told her I thought Egypt had affected us both. 'We say coming out here is about all the issues we learn in school. About Empire and expanding trade and furthering God's word. It's not.'

'What is it then?' she asked, regaining her self-control.

'We do things here that in England would seem mad. It's for romance. That's why we come. The Empire is about avoiding the monotony at home.'

'That might be true enough for the two of us,' she said with a rueful smile.

'May I give you some advice?' I asked, which is not the way her husband would have done it at all. It gave her an opportunity to be harsh and she took it.

'If you know, everyone will know.'

'Am I such a gossip as that?'

'Oh, everyone's a gossip.'

'People gossip, it's true. Then it's forgotten, so they can gossip about something else.'

'It was the only time, you know. I hope you believe that. It means the end of my marriage.'

'If you were caught out in these circumstances with anyone else, it would indeed be the end.'

'Just shut up, Jimmy.' She stood suddenly as if she were about to flee. Did she think she could just walk away? I took her wrist and made her sit down.

'It is unthinkable for your husband to acknowledge an involvement on your part with the King. He will deny the truth of it.'

'Perhaps no one will tell him.'

'There is only one person with the nerve to throw this in his face.'

'Oh God,' she said and I knew that she now fully understood.

'The King will do as he pleases. Your task is the most difficult of all. Do nothing. Don't ask the King for anything. Even if he has feeling for you, and I'm sure he does, if he sees an opportunity to wound your husband he will take it. You know that is true.' She had been so hard on me so many times that I'm sure I enjoyed giving some of it back. I didn't have to spell out that no matter how genuine the King's feelings for her were, His Majesty was doubtless quite happy to be cuckolding Sir Malcolm Cheyne, and would be even more pleased to let him

know all about it. I couldn't get the picture of Vera running naked in the corridor at Abdin out of my mind,
which might have made another man act more generously, but I suppose I wanted to hurt her in the name of
helping our country. I was in love with Vera and she knew
it, so she had been high-handed with me many times. She
was a terrorist of the heart and, I'm ashamed to admit,
now I was enjoying her discomfort.

She was crying again. 'Tell me Malcolm doesn't have to
know. Please tell me that. Please, Jimmy. Tell me that.'

'Don't see the King again. If your husband in any way
discovers this, deny it. Let it be the worst lie of your marriage.'

She reached across the table and took my hand. She
clutched at it, then squeezed it, gently rubbing her thumb
against my first finger. She didn't know she was flirting,
but she was. Perhaps it was more. Not an offer, but a signal that she would entertain a proposition. Sex was the
only coin she had and now she was spending it. It was the
one way she knew to plead her case. I wanted more than
for her to squeeze my hand. I didn't give my wish a voice,
even to myself, but I don't doubt that what I wanted was
to be the King of Egypt so that I might run naked in the
halls with Vera and pin her to the wall and take her standing up. As I had already learned, the world is filled with
wonderful women, creatures of my desire, who will never
be mine. I usually managed to push my desire away, but
since seeing Vera in the corridor, I had known more clearly than ever that I wanted her. I also knew that the circumstances made it impossible. The tiny signal of a
squeezed hand was a desperate act of which I could not
take advantage. I took an honest pride in that, but it left
a hole in my heart.

Vera and I never spoke of our luncheon. A few days later, I was at the Residency, in the dining room with her and Forbes when Sir Malcolm joined us to announce that London had sent out abdication papers for Farouk. 'Same as the Duke of Windsor's,' he said.

The news shocked Vera. I could see her eyes dart from her husband to me. 'Is that the only solution?' she asked. 'What if he does as you want?'

'I'll give him an option. He'll be too thick to take it.'

'Do you think you might be underestimating him?' she asked. I was afraid she was going too far and she would alert her husband to her fear.

'I have some experience of His Majesty. I want him removed.' I could hear something beyond the political in Sir Malcolm's voice. Perhaps he already knew about his wife's transgression and had chosen to deal with it by this abdication scheme. It was quite possible that I was not the only one who reported to him about activities at Abdin. He could have had an entire network of spies. I had told Vera that Farouk would use whatever he could to hurt her husband. I now realised that this was no less true of Sir Malcolm. Diplomats are gamesmen to their core and Sir Malcolm was one of the great diplomats of his time.

'Who becomes King?' I asked.

'Without a male heir, Fouad's brother. Too old to do any harm. I'll run the country from my desk. I'm going to put the pen in his hand.'

It was the season for the royal transfer from Cairo to Alex,
and I at least was anticipating it. When Abdin gave no
sign of movement, Sir Malcolm told me it was more than
casual rudeness. 'Farouk knows something we do not,' he
said as we were discussing the situation in his office at the
Residency. He made enquiries and was preparing to send
another reconnaissance unit to the desert. The effort
proved unnecessary as we, and the entire world, soon
learned that the Luftwaffe had bombed Alex. I felt sick at
the news, more so than at anything else in this war. I cannot say how it affected Sir Malcolm but I excused myself
and sat for a while in the Residency garden. I worried for
the city, of course, though in a general way and not nearly as much as I worried about the people and the places I
had known. The reports were maddeningly incomplete,
though there was no doubt that bombs had fallen. Where
they had landed was not yet known. I pictured it all hap-
pening in the streets and alleys near the Minerva. Was the
hôtel gone? What of Pastroudis? What of poor Giddoes?

I imagined him in his House of Answered Prayer, bombs falling about him, oblivious of the danger, lost in his opium haze and Sufi parables. I wondered, did Giddoes dream he was under attack while in fact he was? Could opium, the ancient soother of souls, subdue the Luftwaffe, the very definition of modernity? Sad old Giddoes and his soiled suit. If he was dead, I hope it was quick and that he had the pipe in his mouth. And the girls in Sister Street, what of them? The ones I knew, or didn't, are surely long gone. When I try to conjure their dark faces, I see the strands of beads wrapped round their bodies, the badge of their office, or sometimes I see the coloured glass that hung from their ears and was meant to keep the evil eye away. I wonder how effective it was with the Luftwaffe.

Under such circumstances I would have thought everything in Cairo would change, but of course it did not. We waited for news as we went about our business. I had planned to go to the souk to find a gift for Miriam. When I first arrived in Egypt, the souks put me off. The idea of bargaining with people who had so much less than I once seemed beneath contempt. Now it's second nature. I was in Bab al-Zuwayla, in the old city, where one could acquire anything from unmarked tablets, supposedly aspirin, and sold by the handful, to lovely hand-crafted jewellery. The merchants in the souk speak with their hands, an entire language of shrugs and palms. A European could learn to follow it, but never to speak it. When I argue with a merchant over a tiny sum, I imagine myself in London, walking into a pub and haggling over the price of a pint. 'Ten P,' the barman says. 'Five and that's my final offer,' I answer.

I was looking at a faience scarab pin. It was late

Victorian and there was an image of Khepera, the sun-god, on its belly. To the ancients, the scarab was a symbol of resurrection. It seemed just right for Miriam. The pin was worth, at most, two quid in the Portobello Road, though the merchant was making a fuss about how it had been brought out of a tomb at Luxor. The fellow started at fifty Egyptian pounds. I said three was my last offer. As he was considering his next move, there was a disturbance in another part of the souk. I paid no attention, but my man began to speed up our negotiation. Nothing short of death could entirely interrupt a sale, but imminent calamity might hurry it along. An unruly pack of political demonstrators were moving through the souk, calling for Mohammed Haidar. Given the events in Alex, I should have just packed it in, but I wanted the scarab and the merchant wanted to sell it. He said, seven, I said four. We agreed on five, and he all but shoved the pin at me and began shuttering his stall. When I looked round, I saw the whole lot of them were doing the same. He told me that a fuss had started in the Ezbekiya Gardens, which was often the site of political demonstrations, none of them pro-English, had reached Abdin, and now seemed to be coming here. The Gardens were the informal divide between European Cairo and the native quarter beyond. I should have realised that if trouble had started in the Ezbekiya and had managed to get to Bab al-Zuwayla, then it was trouble indeed. It was so sudden that I didn't think it through. My scarab seller's parting words were, 'Fery bad. Go home.' There's no V in Arabic. It comes out F. The meaning was clear enough.

When I got out to the road, the sun was masked by a gauzy haze of smoke. There was neither cab nor coach, not a hantour to be had. I was at most a thirty minute walk from the Residency. It was a matter of going west to the river. If I could get to Abdin, which was mid-way, I ought to be able to find a taxi.

The demonstrations were erupting into a riot. Houses and shops were torched by young men who dragged shopkeepers into the road and beat them. I recognised some of the factions: Blue Shirts, the Moslem Brotherhood, the Wafd, Misr al-Fatat, but also many unaligned fellahin, which meant the potential numbers could not be counted. Some doused trees with petrol and set them afire. A bird, trying to escape, caught fire and came hurtling to ground. Though I could not know the extent of the damage, I could see that Cairo had exploded. It was chaotic in a deep sense because the rioters couldn't have known who was who. They didn't have as much as an insignia let alone uniforms that might identify them.

Street urchins ran past me, exhilarated by the anarchy. I decided it best to leave the thoroughfare and make my way through back streets. The riot, or whatever it was, seemed to be everywhere and without a centre. I hadn't seen that the disturbance was specifically anti-English, but surely the bombing in Alex must have given these people the courage to turn on us. The government was making no attempt that I could see to keep order. I might well have been better off in the main road where I had started, rather than the narrow and nameless street I now found myself in. The smoke was so dense that breathing had become difficult and I could hardly see. The usual odours of onions and kebabs, of spices and cooking fat, of dry sweat and piss, were smothered by the smoke. Even the scents of over-ripe fruit and sweet jasmine that in normal times were my escape, were lost in the smoke. It was not my Cairo now, perhaps it never had been, but till today I had allowed myself to think so.

I stumbled on a donkey that lay dying in a doorway, still tethered to a burning cart, as if someone had tried to force it into the building. The creature's hind legs were broken and its breath came in slow heaves. Flowers and a charred bow had been hung round its neck. Flies, the furies of Egypt, had descended in such numbers that the poor beast was covered in humming black patches. Two pariah dogs sniffed and circled. A vulture, not often seen in the city, was waiting in a banyan tree. Vultures, like rioters and soldiers, do not travel alone, though in the haze I didn't see others.

I no longer knew what direction I was taking, until by chance, I wandered into a midan not far from Sharia Mohammed Ali, which meant the restaurants and night-clubs of Cairo, potent symbols of the European presence here. It didn't require much cleverness to know to avoid such places.

There was certainly plenty of fire, though there were no fire-starters that I could see. Did that mean I was fol-lowing them, or that they were going in the other direc-tion? Whichever, I continued in what I dearly hoped was west, looking for the Palace. The Arab names of the streets were evidence of the growing nationalism. Street signs often had the English or French name painted over and an Egyptian one in its place. It was already mid-day and hazy smoke or not, I could see that the sun had peaked, which confirmed that I was indeed going west.

When I arrived at the Palace, the landmark I needed to feel confident of finding the Residency, it appeared safe enough, at least the part of it I could see, though it was eerily quiet. There is usually activity around Abdin, but today the guards seemed to have gone to ground. I wondered if Farouk was there. I pictured him in the library playing chess, or more likely, running about with his latest mistress, hardly aware that his capital was burning. Perhaps Miriam was there too. She would help me, certainly, but was I to knock on the door and ask for Mrs Rolo? The entire riot and fire could well have originated in the Palace, though now it was surely out of any semblance of control. I would have to take my chances on foot. I skirted the Midan Abdin and wound up in a mixture of shops and slum dwellings, that I believed to be west of the Palace. Thieves were rampant, breaking windows and looting shops, taking what they didn't want and couldn't sell. I saw people running with all manner of goods: tinned food, cakes, shoes, hats, tools. They were on holiday from constraint, and it seemed from reason. I was grateful that they didn't seem at all interested in me.

My complacency ended when I heard chanting, growing louder. I couldn't see anyone, nor could I make out the words, though the meaning was clear enough. The voices were praising Allah and dedicating themselves to destroying heathens. I went into an alley in the hope that it might be safer. It was strangely silent. No noisy rabble, no crying children, no one trying to sell me anything. I do not know if anyone was watching me, though I felt quite exposed. The chanting came nearer until the rioters materialised out of the haze, like a Biblical apparition of destruction. There were about thirty of them in robes that were once as white as pure faith, and now were smeared with ash and blood. They were running hard, looking for prey. They were in a glazed-eye trance that I knew would not lift until they had killed and burned to their fill.

In this alley, I was little more than a target for enemies unseen. My clothes were sooty and my face and hair heavy with ash. If I were to perish here, a place I could not name, surely my white body would be consigned to the fire by the faceless mob. The fellahin would say that live or die, I was in Allah's hands. I moved on, knowing only that I must keep going west, toward the sun, until I found the river. I passed nothing that I recognised until I saw the Hôtel Ezbekiah, named of course for the Gardens, which meant I was farther north than I intended, and too near the native quarter on a day such as this. The hôtel was a favourite of English travellers who either couldn't afford Shepheard's or who simply preferred less formality. A portion of the facade was on fire and a mob swarmed about, stealing furniture and the like. Two men came running out of the main entrance carrying off a portrait of Lord Cromer, one of Sir Malcolm's distinguished predecessors. It must have hung in the lobby or perhaps the bar. Its captors couldn't possibly know who Lord Cromer was or anyone in Cairo who would want the picture. Surely they were more scavengers than thieves. Then, rather suddenly, they threw Cromer into the fire, making their point plain enough, I suppose. Whoever they were, they surely weren't fellahin, a group unlikely to destroy anything that might prove of value. As I was considering the worth of Lord Cromer as metaphor or property, I realised that something more compelling than this old picture had now taken their attention. A woman, surely a European and most likely a guest, was standing in a third-storey window, shouting in Italian about the fire which had apparently reached her room. As I was taking in her predicament, she jumped. Or perhaps in her terror, she fell. It was all so fast and there was too much smoke for me to be certain of anything. For the few seconds it took for her to hit the ground, my eye was drawn to her billowing frock and her exposed legs. They were slender and as she plummeted, they twitched like scissors. It was horrible and yet my eye was drawn to the white of her knickers. I watched her arms wave about too, as she shouted for the help I could not give her. I didn't see her hit the ground, but I could tell that it was a bloody collision from the mob's collective swoon. I meant to go to see if I could help, but the crowd was nearer. I don't know if she was alive, I hope not, because once that lot got to her, she had no chance. Some simply kicked at her, while others beat her and ripped off her clothing. It made me ill, dizzy.

They carried her off, running with her nearly naked corpse held aloft like a laurel wreath, retreating from the Ezbekiah into the smoke. As she was beyond all mortal help, and I did not wish to be next, I moved on, feeling weak and in a state that was past fright. My mind was drained, and as Europeans were falling from windows, I began preparing myself for the possibility of my own end. I walked in what I'm sure was fast becoming a somnam-bulistic state, until I landed in a little square that was burning. People were weeping and keening, beseeching Allah. If He intended to answer their entreaties, He had better be quick.

I saw a child, her clothes on fire, running and scream-ing in a voice that pierced the smoke. As she came near-er, I saw that more than her clothes were on fire. An arm and part of her upper body was burning. Her skin was bubbling and popping, making a hissing sound that, like the image of the Italian woman in the window, I knew I would not get out of my head. A woman, the child's mother perhaps, caught her and threw her down to smother the fire with her own body. I went to them to try to help, though in truth there was little I could do. I couldn't bear the thought of failing to give help to another person. As I approached, the mother, if that's who she was, threw a stone which opened a nasty cut on my forehead. I was nauseous, and not from the smoke which had grown so dense that I couldn't make out my direction. I stumbled forward, hoping I could find the water. The Bulaq Bridge, the northern route to Gezira, should be somewhere hereabouts. If I were to find it, I would just stay by the river, walking against the current, which flowed north. I would have to take as an article of faith that the Residency would be standing.

As I looked for a road I recognised, or perhaps a sign pointing to the bridge, I saw a religious fanatic of a sort more common in Alexandria. His nearly naked body was smeared with ash and he was praying: 'God is great. Praise God. There is no God but God.' He was also mumbling about Al-Nil, so I followed him through a bewildering maze of back streets, some burning, others not. Had it come to this, that I was following a babbling madman through a fire? I tried to banish despair, but I could not. At that black moment, I smelled the pungent odour that even in this fire could mean one thing only: the River Nile. I followed my nose down to the embankment till I saw the lapping waters that might deliver me. I did not believe that God – Christian or Moslem – had saved me. I could offer neither praise nor thanks, though there was relief. I did not feel blessed, only sick at heart.

Before I could determine the most efficient way to follow the river, I saw huddled in a green patch, under a sycamore that had been spared, a small boy, perhaps ten years of age. He had delicate features and yet the stoic look of one who expected little from the world. My Arabic was sufficient to learn he was called Zayed, and he was hungry. I had no food and though I gave him a bit of the cash left in my pocket from the souk, I knew he would not be able to buy anything with it. I couldn't help this boy. I had no business here and he knew it. He stayed because there was nowhere else for him to go. In his view, I could leave when I chose to. That I did not, but rather wandered in the road like a tourist who had lost his reason, only made me seem baffling, I am sure.

I offered my hand to help him to his feet. I don't know where I thought I might take him, but the question proved moot. As he arose, his hand darted up to my jacket pocket. He stole my spectacles and ran away, disappearing into the haze. As I had another pair, it wasn't a great loss. I'd have given him the scarab pin if I'd thought of it. Perhaps he hoped to sell my spectacles to a nearsighted Egyptian. As I had seen beggars, in less desperate hours, trying to sell a single shoe, or a broken bottle, he might well be successful. Perhaps Zayed would wear them himself and try to see the world through the eyes of an Englishman.

I couldn't have been more than twenty minutes walk from the Residency. I determined to avoid more streets and went down to the Nile's edge to make my way. The cool smell of green growth was there. It was a merciful respite. The River Nile which offered everything to the fellahin now offered salvation to me. For the first time, I saw the point of river worship. As none of the other Embassies along the river seemed in danger, I began to feel more optimistic, allowing myself to imagine the bath in my rooms, a porcelain behemoth on lion's paw feet.

The thought made me hurry and stumble on the rocks. I got quite wet in addition to being filthy. When I finally saw that good white building untouched by fire, I hoisted myself over the wall that divides the Residency's garden from the river itself. I made my way through the grove of scarlet flame trees that were meant to provide a bit of privacy and now seemed to offer asylum. I had to force myself not to run and shout, 'I'm safe, I'm safe.' I simply walked up from the river and across the lawn. A pair of hoopoes were feeding from water that had collected in puddles in the grass. It occurred to me that the sufragis must have been out watering the garden. The birds fluttered away as I hurried past, stirring up the dragon-flies that buzzed about them.

Fawcett, who opened the door for me, said, 'Good afternoon, Mr Peel. Sir Malcolm has been asking for you.' Seeing the gash in my forehead and my dishevelled appearance, he suggested a wash and a whisky. I accepted, though asked for them in the reverse order.

The whisky was delivered to my rooms by Ibrahim, an old sufragi who had been in the Residency for years. Apparently, Fawcett had instructed him in my care. I was enjoying the warmth of the whisky, while Ibrahim set about dressing my wound, then drawing my bath, adding salts and aromatic oils to the hot water. As I had quite recently seen the darker side of turning a portion of the population into servants, I wasn't at all certain I wanted Ibrahim's assistance, but aching muscles will allow one to justify most anything. As he fussed about, heating towels and bringing my dressing gown, I tried to see what manner of man was there. He was small, quite lean with thinning grey hair. I judged him to be about sixty, but his was not a face I could read. His dark skin suggested he might be Sudanese. He could anticipate what I was likely to need, and yet, at the same time, look through me. He must have understood some English, though all I ever heard him say was a murmured, 'Yes sir.' With the fires now raging, did he regard me differently? Did he see his masters as newly vulnerable? He was a Moslem of course, though I had never seen him at prayer. Perhaps he had three wives and a flock of children stashed somewhere. As I lay soaking and ruminating, Ibrahim collected my soiled things and laid out fresh clothing. He poured another whisky and then was gone.

The hot water relaxed my body, if not my mind. I should have been relieved, but my churning thoughts would not let me rest. I saw the Italian woman, as I thought of her, falling from the window. I saw – more than once – those twitching legs and the desperate flail-ing. I knew that if I were fortunate, I might someday for-get the picture of the child and her burning skin, but I would never free myself of the Italian woman.

Perhaps the situation in the streets resembled what London was like during the Great Fire which was caused by citizens attempting to purify the city of the Black Death. What was this present fire but a Cairene attempt to purify their city of us? I thought of my own youthful escapades with matches from my mother's pantry. What had I been trying to rid myself of? Was it simply the unhappy impotence of childhood? Did I too, even at that tender age, wish to rid myself of an oppressor? There was no Black Death in Hampshire and the closest to an oppressor was my dear father. Was I trying to destroy him, using the baffling and obscure symbolism of the very young? And why was I so drawn to the nihilism of fire? When I set out from the souk, had I believed that my

Englishness would protect me? The hubris of that appalled me. A Freudian interpretation of my mischief was once offered to me. In that construction, the matches represented my father's penis and the hills and ditches I set ablaze were my dear mother. It was laughable, but that did not make it untrue. The men who were burning Cairo, whether or not they knew it, were trying to appropriate England's power and potency. To get it, they were willing to destroy mother Egypt.

When I was finally clean, though still restless, it was about four o'clock and the light had faded a bit. Fawcett would have reported my arrival, so before I presented myself to Sir Malcolm, I went out on the upper balcony, for a proper view of the difficulties. Andrew Coats, a junior on the commercial desk, was leaning on the balustrade, smoking a cigarette. Coats was a roundish man who was balding, though he couldn't have been much older than I. We watched the fires in Sharia al-Waldah, the little street beyond our gates, companionably enough. 'Has the fire brigade made any headway, do you suppose?' he asked.

'I doubt that,' I said. 'Far too widespread.' I didn't mention that two hours earlier I had been walking in the midst of it.

'Caught a bit of it yourself, I understand.'

So much for my discretion. Were my trials the subject of gossip? Before I had to manufacture a reply, we were joined by Sarah Cheyne and Dugdale, followed by a sufragi pushing a tea trolley with cucumber sandwiches. Sarah and Dugdale were too absorbed in one another to pay much heed to the fire. When Coats pointed out the burning tenement houses, Dugdale asked, 'Can you see well enough, Miss Cheyne?' as if they were taking seats in the stalls in the West End. He offered his hand to help her onto a footstool.

'Yes, thank you so much, Mr Dugdale,' she answered, stepping up as daintily as she could. She was gazing at him, as if to say, A footstool! How clever you are. Sarah was imitating Vera's technique with Sir Malcolm, though I doubt she was aware of it. Dugdale had long since forgotten his crush on Vera, and had not been aware of Sir Malcolm's attempt to make a match for his daughter with Farouk. When Coats realised he might be intruding, he moved farther down the balustrade. As I watched the budding romance in front of me and the firestorm beyond, others arrived, most of them up from the chancery in the west wing. I recognised Samuel Grigg-Pierce, a fellow Wykehamist, who was a councillor on the political desk. He was followed by Major Thomas Rand, a windy old fellow who had a parrot on his shoulder. The Major had been in the Great War and was said to have been at Gallipoli. With his white handlebar moustaches, he seemed a version of the portrait of Cromer that I had so recently watched go up in flames as a prelude to the death that I was struggling to rid from my mind. As the Major stepped out onto the balcony, he announced, 'All safe. Charger, too.'

'I am happy to see it,' I said.

'I've seen it before, you know. Nothing new in Gyppy mischief,' he said. 'What do you think, Charger?' The parrot offered no opinion, so the Major began berating the Residency staff, perhaps believing they had some control over the fire-starters. 'You should send out troops and you should have done it by now,' he declared.

'I might point out, Major Rand, that it is their country.'

'It is not theirs to burn,' he said.

'Theirs to burn,' the parrot repeated, finding his voice,

to the delight of the others. It was my opportunity to move away. While I had been engaged with the Major, something like a dozen more people had arrived, including Forbes and his family. He had gone round for them with two guards. Forbes held his wife and little boys close, a sign that he was more frightened than his cool demeanour might suggest. Mrs Forbes, who was quite handsome, though after three births had grown stout, was listening to an older woman, who I believe was a colonel's wife. The whole business seemed like an ad hoc diplomatic reception, except of course there were no Egyptians present. The guests were talking shop or of houses and children, reassuring one another with optimistic analyses of the situation. The colonel's lady who had button-holed Mrs Forbes was going on about, I believe, the servant problem.

'Our Omar would not do anything of this sort,' she said. 'He has no politics at all, don't you see. I mean really now, what would he do with politics?'

'I'm sure,' Mrs Forbes said, looking for her husband to rescue her.

When a sufragi came out onto the balcony with a fire hose and an axe, followed by another with more tea and a tray of cakes, I thought, What next, a string quartet? I was about to accept the tea, when I realised that a fine layer of ash had settled in my cup. Most of the guests were no longer paying any attention to the fire, except for a group that included Coats, at the balustrade, their eyes hazy from staring out at the trouble in Sharia al-Waldah. If I turned toward them, I found myself drawn back to the fire. If I looked the other way, toward the tea party, I thought, surely I was hallucinating, except I could smell the smoke.

I believed that the balcony could not hold one more Englishman when Sir Malcolm and Vera came strolling out. Their presence brought a halt to the chattering. Dugdale stood a little taller and moved away from Sarah a bit. I could see that Vera knew something was up with her step-daughter. Sir Malcolm was preoccupied and not aware of the romance. No doubt, Vera would tell him of that adventure later.

They were walking about the balcony, greeting some, looking straight through others, depending on who was in favour at the moment. A few of the women, who moments ago were nattering, managed to strike attitudes of fortitude. When the Cheynes approached me, Sir Malcolm said, 'Well, Mr Peel, at last. Caught in it, were you?'

'Just a bit.'

'Oh, I suspect it was more than that,' he said.

Vera smiled at my discomfort and said, 'We were told you were rather in a state when you turned up.'

'So I owe this to Fawcett, do I?'

'You mustn't blame him,' Sir Malcolm said. 'My wife drew it out of him.'

'I can see that I've been the topic of the day,' I said, trying to sound amused.

'A word with you, please, Mr Peel,' Sir Malcolm said, changing his tone as well as the subject.

I followed him into a drawing-room off the balcony, where there were silk curtains and shelves of books and framed photographs of earlier Embassy personnel, several of whom were on camels. As Sir Malcolm dismissed the sufragis who had followed us and were attempting to serve yet more tea, I glanced back out to the balcony, and saw Coats and the chancery men at the balustrade, regarding our little tête-à-tête with interest.

'I am happy that you were unharmed in your misadventure. It is a comfort to my wife as well,' he said. I knew full well that our subject would be neither my health, nor Vera's sensibilities. I nodded my thanks, ready to hear him out, though I could already tell this interview was in the nature of a rap on the knuckles.

'I can only assume you are not aware that your recklessness might have been costly indeed.' His voice was not raised, but there was anger in it.

'I believe I acted as prudently as possible in the circumstances.'

'You had no business out there.'

'It was not my choice, I assure you.'

'If you had been injured, or worse, we would have had to send troops to rescue you.'

'I'm glad that was not required. May I ask why you did not send troops – not for me, certainly, but to put down the riot?'

'We are not a police force. It is an internal matter for the Egyptians.'

'It's just that the question has been raised,' I said, not mentioning that the only person who had raised it was that old fool with the parrot. Sir Malcolm did not look pleased, but as I had so recently been through hell, I decided that if I was about to be criticised for it, I'd have my say. 'It is quite difficult out there. People are suffering terribly. I should think, if I may say so, that Christian decency requires reasonable action.'

'You must understand the larger issue here. We do not condone the destruction of property or the loss of life.'

'I'm sure you do not.'

'Cairo has always been burning,' he said. 'Dividing, reforming, remaking itself. Fire always wins.' Then he was silent, gone inside himself, terra incognita. Finally, in a voice hardly more than a whisper, he said, 'It got out of hand.' It seemed an admission of some sort on his part. He didn't confide, still he was telling me something.

'If the fire wins now, who will have the victory?' I asked.

'I intend to take full advantage of the opportunity that has been presented.'

Now I understood. He saw the knowledge come over me, I'm sure. He wanted the fire to burn freely so he could hold the King responsible for the catastrophe. Sending out a military rescue party for one hapless Englishman would put into question why he hadn't done anything for the many others in similar straits. The Italian woman could hardly have been the only European death. Nonetheless, he would let the city burn. I couldn't help wondering if he would be quite so harsh if he didn't have particular reason to be angry with the King.

'We must always think of our country's needs above all else,' he said. 'Don't you agree?'

I didn't agree at all, though all I said was, 'I apologise for causing concern.'

'It would be best if you do not speak of this further. Do not make any remarks about the tragedy of it all, no matter what anyone on the balcony might say. Such comments are emotional, made without benefit of full knowledge. Do we understand one another?'

'I think we do.'

'Shall we go back outside then?'

When we returned to the balcony, darkness had fallen and the fires had abated a bit. Vera took her husband's arm and they made a last easy circle, dispensing noblesse oblige, and then they were gone. It meant that the tea party was now concluded. People took their leave, some to stay the night, others to be driven home. Dugdale and Sarah were among the last to depart, wandering off to be by themselves.

I was left alone, standing at the balustrade, thinking it was fortunate I hadn't attempted to stop at Abdin. God knows what he would have said about that. As I looked out at the ruins in Sharia al-Waldah, I began to wonder if Sir Malcolm hadn't done more than take advantage of the King's lax treatment of the rioting. Could Sir Malcolm have started the fires? Not with a torch, but could he have incited this horror in some way, perhaps using the bombing of Alex as a pretence and causing what will surely amount to many deaths, putting the entire city in grave danger? Of course he could. He had the means, certainly. He controlled significant sums of money for which he was not required to make an accounting. A large bribe and a promise of future favours to a member of the Moslem Brotherhood, and almost anything in the line of trouble could be achieved. That's what all that talk was about letting the fire take Cairo. He had the motive, and he could wrap his actions in Realpolitik. If he also knew about his wife and Farouk, his anger would be great enough to burn more than one city. He was explaining himself to me and, I believe, to himself. He felt his actions were justified, but he also felt guilty – an unusual emotion for him – not at the prospect of many Egyptian deaths, but at the possibility of mine. I did not regard it as a personal compliment. He would have seen the value in causing riot and fire before anyone else. He could always see several moves ahead. If my surmise is correct, and I believe it to be so, I'm sure his tracks are well hidden. If accusations were ever to arise, he would

profess shock that anyone could think such a thing. I
have watched him now for going on seven years. He
would be King of the ashes before he would let Farouk
continue as King of Egypt. It was at once both appalling
and thrilling. Well, I mused, at least I had my spectacles
back.

Sir Malcolm used the bombing of Alex and the Cairo fire
as a wedge to force Farouk's abdication. The Egyptians
had so clearly violated the treaty that no one could deny
it. Sir Malcolm sent Forbes to Abdin to meet with
Mazhar Pasha to begin negotiations. Forbes read out a
letter saying that if a new government wasn't formed and
the treaty adhered to, the British Embassy will, 'by whatever means it finds appropriate, force the abdication of
the King and will form its own government under martial law'.

Mazhar Pasha heard him out, unfailingly polite of
course, then asked, 'Will Sir Malcolm declare himself
King?'

Forbes told him that the Ambassador had the complete
support of our government in this. As always, as Sir
Malcolm expected, the Egyptians did nothing.

Because of my past relationship with the King, Sir
Malcolm had me with him when he and General
Hobson, who was Chief of British Troops in Egypt and a
man almost as large as Sir Malcolm, went to Abdin to
confront the King. Hobson had political ambitions. I
think he might have wanted to have been an ambassador,
just as part of Sir Malcolm would have preferred to have
been a general. If Hobson thought being Chief of BTE
would give him authority over Sir Malcolm, he was dis-
appointed. Hobson operated out of a block of flats in

Garden City, which meant, in effect, under the Residency's supervision. It was the morning of 4th February 1942, a date for which Egyptians still curse my country. We were in a military motor-car, unable to proceed through central Cairo because of the crowds. The rioting had cooled, but the people were still angry and there were flare-ups and pockets of trouble. General Hobson told his driver, a young lieutenant very likely out of Leeds or somewhere for the first time, to go round the mess.

'I'm afraid we can't, sir,' the Lieutenant said. 'There's no way round it.'

'Then go through it,' Sir Malcolm said.

The driver accelerated and we ploughed directly into the crowd. That tended to get their attention. I do not know if we ran over anyone, but I do know that Sir Malcolm was not interested in the question. I wanted to glance back, to see if there were bodies in the road, but the set look on Sir Malcolm's face told me not to.

As we approached Abdin, I heard a great thumping and clanking coming from the direction of the Palace, as if steel bars or perhaps boulders were being dragged through the streets. My initial thought was that a pack of rioters, cut off from all reason, was attacking Abdin. The source of the noise soon became clear: British tanks were rolling into place, ringing the Palace. It may have surprised me, but not Sir Malcolm as he was the only man in Egypt with authority and motive to have ordered this display. The clatter came from all the desert vehicles scraping across the pavement. Such machines, not unlike the army itself, went where they were required, no matter the terrain. It was an astounding show of strength, and the fellahin who had gathered to observe, from a prudent distance, seemed to recognise that the Palace, a building that to them was as durable and unyielding as Islam itself, was now threatened.

I do not recall ever before using the main entrance to the Palace. The doors were great bronze things, used only for ceremonial occasions, probably because they were so heavy it would have been a bother to open and shut them. Sir Malcolm was not about to use a side entrance. He was taking a great risk here. He had once again assumed the rôle of the King of England's plenipotentiary. The Foreign Secretary and the Prime Minister both had sufficient opportunity to rein him in. They had not done so. It was not an oversight. On Sir Malcolm's order, these tanks, perhaps three hundred of what Churchill called his Tiger Cubs, surely every English tank in North Africa, was now pointing its turret gun at the Palace.

Sir Malcolm, General Hobson, the young Lieutenant, and I approached those huge doors. Sir Malcolm was wearing his morning coat. He always wore it when he appeared at Abdin, so it hadn't seemed unusual. The fact that he was also directing an attack, did not in his mind outweigh protocol.

The Lieutenant pushed on the doors which were of course locked. The man seemed to be looking for a door knocker or perhaps a bell, which was entirely too polite for Sir Malcolm. He reached over, unsnapped the fellow's holster and took his sidearm. It shocked the Lieutenant more than the sight of the tanks. Sir Malcolm shot the locks off and pushed the doors open. They creaked loudly. There was so much noise, we might as well have been announced by the King's protocol master. As we went down the corridor I knew there were royal bodyguards in hiding. I had spent enough time here to have a sense of their tactics. I told Sir Malcolm that we were being observed. 'I expect so,' he said, as if I had pointed out that there were pigeons in the park.

At Farouk's study, the door was open. The King and Mazhar Pasha were having tea. 'Excellency,' Farouk said. 'How good to see you. And Mr Peel. Have you come to give me a lesson?' He said nothing to the General, perhaps expecting Sir Malcolm to make introductions.

'Sir, the country is dissolving into anarchy,' Sir Malcolm said.

Farouk nodded slightly, as if to say, Thank you for reminding me. He was quiet for a moment, then asked in a casual voice, 'How is Lady Cheyne? Is she well?'

I thought, Surely this is it. The King will now use his own heavy artillery. Sir Malcolm tried to stare him down. Farouk was royal. He wasn't about to be intimidated by Sir Malcolm's harsh look or his three hundred tanks.

'My wife is well, sir.'

'We are glad to hear it.'

I, alone in that room, could see they both knew. Sir Malcolm would deny it to himself as much as to the world, in part for his wife's sensibilities but surely because the political issues were so great. Farouk didn't elaborate. He didn't have to. They spoke in a code that was Etonian old boy by way of the Valley of the Kings. His Majesty was confirming what Sir Malcolm had either surmised or had been told. By going no further, Farouk was saying, 'I will not sacrifice Lady Cheyne, no matter the cost.' Farouk could have learned behaviour of that sort from only one source.

Sir Malcolm began his prepared remarks. It was a speech, actually, and plenipot or not, I suspect he had cleared it with London: 'It has for long past been evident

that Your Majesty has been influenced by advisers who
were not only unfaithful to the Alliance but were working against it, assisting the enemy. Such recklessness on
the part of the sovereign endangers the security of Egypt
and of the Allied Forces. They make it clear that Your
Majesty is no longer fit to occupy the Throne.'

The King watched Sir Malcolm as he spoke, as if he
were watching a performance, a play perhaps. Mazhar
Pasha spoke first. 'Sir Malcolm, I would like to know if
you are prepared to discuss, or simply to –'

'Thank you, Mazhar Pasha,' the King said, cutting him
off. 'We will speak now. All that you say, you believe to
be true. We see no likely purpose in debating these asser-
tions.'

'Sir, I offer only incontrovertible facts.'

'Ali Maher Pasha says the English are a losing horse,
not to be backed. Of course, he is one of the "unfaithful
advisers."'

Sir Malcolm drew out the abdication paper. It was
hand-written, in calligraphy. In that regard, the House of
Windsor and the Mohammed Ali Dynasty were similar.
Neither believed in typewriters for momentous documents. Every English person knew the substance of it
from the days of our own abdication, in the Year of
Three Kings. Certainly Mazhar Pasha knew and if
Farouk didn't know the precise words, he knew enough.
Sir Malcolm read it out anyway: 'We, King Farouk of
Egypt, mindful as ever of the interests of our country,
hereby renounce and abandon for ourselves and the heirs
of our body the throne of the Kingdom of Egypt and all
sovereign rights, privileges and powers in and over the
said Kingdom and the subjects thereof, and we release
our said subjects from the allegiance to our person.' Sir

Malcolm put the document in front of the King and said, 'The Crown is ready to transport you and your household to the Seychelles.'

'Seychelles,' Farouk said, enjoying the word. 'Nice touch that.' Then he began to negotiate. 'We are prepared to declare martial law and We will sever diplomatic relations with the Axis.'

'Sir, those things will be done with or without your help. Sign it.'

'Just today, Excellency, you suggested We dissolve the government and appoint one more congenial to English interests. We are ready to do so.'

'It is too little and it is too late. Sign it.'

'Is it? You mean an offer made at one hour is withdrawn at another? Are you buying and selling eggs?' That stopped Sir Malcolm for a moment. My loyalties here were without question with my country, though it was also clear that Sir Malcolm was negotiating for his own satisfaction. The others in the room, however, did not know the exact nature of his distaste for the King. Farouk was giving in. He could count the tanks. What else could he do? Sir Malcolm wanted him out, but that Farouk was not prepared to give. The King's ability to negotiate his position came from watching Sir Malcolm Cheyne in action for all these years. He had become one of us, though hardly the sort that Sir Malcolm once had in mind.

Sir Malcolm was a far greater chess-player than Farouk. I had played with them both. But in this instance, both men saw the endgame. 'What do you propose,' Sir Malcolm said.

'Exactly what you wanted. You have decided that your interests will be better served under another party. Then choose someone else to be Prime Minister. Let him form a government.'

'His Majesty is agreeing to your requests,' Mazhar Pasha said. 'He is doing it a few hours after your deadline. The world will not look kindly on a nation that sends a king into exile over a few hours.'

Sir Malcolm knew that he now had, in hand, victories on the strategic issues. The personal aspect, throwing Farouk out of the country, was not to be. Farouk had lost a great deal, certainly including control of Egypt, but he was still on the throne and for him that was sweet. 'There. You see?' he said. 'Not so difficult. We rather enjoy diplomatic negotiation. After all, look who Our teacher was. "Under pressure, compromise but do not collapse," wasn't it?' Then Farouk tore the abdication letter in half and tossed it at Sir Malcolm's feet.

As we came out of Abdin, through the bronze doors, now under our guard, Sir Malcolm instructed General Hobson to remove the tanks and order the Eighth Army to Cairo and the Canal. Sir Malcolm took me aside, away from the others, to watch the tanks pull out. Those great green beasts, each with a crew of young Englishmen a moment ago prepared to fire on the Palace, now looked less menacing somehow. It was hardly a retreat, and an army that can win a battle without firing a shot is great indeed, still there was an awkward quality to it. We watched in silence. I knew Sir Malcolm was thinking about Farouk. 'Did he win, sir?' I asked.

'England will win, Mr Peel.'

'Yes. Of course.'

'I would have preferred him gone.'

'It would have been better.'

'Mr Peel, do you believe sons always come into conflict with their fathers?'

'I have heard that said. I am unmarried and my father died young. I am no judge.' I was sorry I had brought up my own situation. I knew full well what he was thinking. He was not deterred by an inadvertent change of subject.

'There was a time when I would have made that boy a son.' I suppose by Sir Malcolm's lights that was true more than merely self-serving. It was not a time for argument, though I might have said that if he believed that entirely, then he was the only one.

'I've spent these years trying to form him. Now that it's come to it, the effort has meant very little.' He looked again at the tanks and the soldiers, now absorbed in the details of removing themselves. 'In the end, I just used a bigger stick. I have persuaded no one.'

I was about to point out that whatever his methods, the victory was his, and in an undertaking as practical as a war, winning was the only issue that mattered. Happily, I had enough sense to say nothing. Sir Malcolm knew all that, just as he knew that the son business was a diversion from the real issue. We continued to watch the tanks in silence. Finally, he said, 'We do what we feel we must. All of us. My own preference is unimportant.'

I believe with those words he was saying that whatever it was his wife might have done, he knew her to be loyal to him and to her country. He forgave any action on her part that might be construed otherwise. He also meant that he would not consider the question again. His mind really was a wonder. He simply moved to the next compartment. Now that Maher Pasha was out, it was time for another PM. 'Have Forbes call Nahas. Wake him up. If he's going to form a government, we'd best get him started.' Mustafa al-Nahas Pasha, stalwart of the Wafd, was to be the next Prime Minister. Sir Malcolm had negotiated

the treaty of 1936 in London with him. He was a patriot, but chiefly a man Sir Malcolm felt he could talk to,
which really meant order about. He was a bulky man, an
orator of some power who was quite popular with the
Egyptian people, even if he did tend to change his mind a
bit as to just which people he meant to serve. He would
be in office as long as he stayed loyal to the Allies and he
surely knew it. Farouk was gone from Sir Malcolm's
thoughts. 'I want General Hobson at the Residency. We
must get started in the desert. Rommel will try to move
east. If we cripple him now, we will save Cairo from
bombing. Let's go. Let's begin.'

That night as I was reflecting on the events of 4th
February 1942, what history now calls 'The Abdin
Incident', I wondered if the King had outfoxed the
Ambassador. Farouk had cast his lot with us even while
Rommel was about to take Alexandria. It was a momentous decision, a question that a King either gets right or
he perishes. Though Farouk and Sir Malcolm hated one
another, they were actually at their best when each was
goading the other. It would be difficult to say if the
results would have been any different if they had felt
mutual respect rather than contempt.

With Hobson and Wavell deploying thousands of
khaki-clad English soldiers, I was confident we would not
be defeated. When the Eighth Army, Alamein's sand still
on their boots, entered the city, a last straggling rabble
determined to die in their holy cause, fired on the troops.
General Wavell couldn't tell a Blue Shirt from a Moslem
Brother any more than the Egyptians could, but he was
not about to allow anyone to shoot at English soldiers
unimpeded. He ended the rioting with extraordinary dis-
patch, leaving the dead where they fell.

Later, perhaps it was that day, perhaps the next, I stood outside the Residency watching the RAF overhead. The blue-and-white Egyptian sky seemed filled first by supply planes and then squadrons of Hurricanes, then Spitfires, all heading for the Canal. They seemed to block out the sun. They took up the light, even as they gave it. It was a sight to quicken the pulse, not easily forgotten.

VERA:

The Blue Train

I am no expert on the details of the war. By now, I think every bullet fired has been the subject of a book or a BBC programme. For years historians came trooping up to Broughton to talk to Malcolm and occasionally to me. His memory for that sort of thing was better, but those interviews showed how uncertain what we call history really is. One young man, writing a book about the Foreign Office, referred to Malcolm as a primary source. He was generous with his time to the fellow, but he said the whole business made him feel stuffed and on display in the British Museum. Malcolm tried to be accurate with the historians or whatever they were, but he always shaded things in our direction. How could it have been otherwise? By the time they got round to interviewing whichever old Nazis were still creeping about, they did the same I am sure. My historical concern is more personal, it lies with recalling what was once pain and memory and now, burnished by time, is memory alone. With Malcolm gone, no one cares to interview me, but still, the past keeps me strong. My old soul restores itself and protects me from time's depredations by reconstructing what once was. Let the experts quibble, to me it is all true in a way that is more important than facts.

In the early years of the fighting, I recall generals that I now know were Archie Wavell and Claude Auchinleck (who was divine) coming and going and then, finally, Montgomery. He was an odd man who could be dynamic and wonderfully confident, then silent and taciturn. He was not nearly so dramatic-looking as The Hawk, as the men called Claude, nor so distinguished as Wavell. Monty looked like a greengrocer at one of the better stalls in Covent Garden. What he might have lacked in personal élan, he more than made up for on the field. He was without fear and he assumed the same in his men. In his very first battle as a general, he retook Alamein and pushed the Panzers back, whereupon he pursued them until they were scrap metal and their officers were left to rot in the desert. I am sure that the bitterness I held then and do not reject now is an example of how the war coarsened my sensibilities. That is what war does. It is for those yet unborn to forgive. I cannot. My husband once said, 'Anyone who was there and says otherwise is a saint or suffers from amnesia.'

When we learned what Monty had accomplished in the desert, Malcolm saw immediately what it meant. 'It will be different now,' was all he said. In his silence, there were tears. It was the only time in thirty-five years I saw him weep.

He was right, of course. After Alamein, we held Cairo and the war in North Africa went our way. During that time, Farouk chased his mistresses, gorged himself into grossness, and lost whatever political grip he had once had on the government. He launched the period of dissolution that the world now accepts as his signature. It has always been assumed that losing power to Malcolm after the Abdin Incident was the cause of the change for the worse in the King. It is certainly true that after Malcolm reduced his power, Farouk became ever more anti-English. I know in a way that no historian does, that was only one part of it.

After our day at Abdin, the King tried to reach me with notes and messages and of course gifts. As Jimmy Peel had instructed, I ignored the messages and returned the gifts, though I longed to see him again. That the King was not more insistent was a sign he understood my position. I was so relieved that my actions had not exploded that I became an obsessively good wife. I made the ballroom a military hospital and exhausted myself tending to the wounded. I do not mean to suggest that I became a latter-day Florence Nightingale, but merely that I did my duty. If Malcolm felt I was acting out of a sense of remorse, he never said so. It was during that vivid time that our first child was born. To enter the world in wartime is an especial burden. Victoria is old enough now that I hesitate to say the precise year of her birth, but she was born while the very sand of the desert was burning. I had been a step-mother for several years and Malcolm's girls had become mine, too. A baby of my own was a felicity in my life that I had not foreseen. Because Sarah and Elizabeth so completely embraced their new sister, Malcolm was able to start his second family with the same joy and enthusiasm he had known earlier.

There was little nightlife left in Cairo. We were all on constant alert. In that regard, Cairo was not unlike London. Now and again Malcolm and I got out. Jimmy had gone home and was in the RAF, acquitting himself bravely, I am glad to report. We no longer took guests with us for long evenings of carousing. One night we were at the Turf Club, which operated at a sort of half-speed. It was just the two of us. There was no entertainment and food was scarce. The Turf had a collection of wine bottles, all empty, that they filled with whatever they were able to get. It wasn't a cheat, only a sad joke. An uncorked Haut Brion bottle might be produced, but it was likely to contain Tunisian swill.

Malcolm and I were trying to laugh at our bottle when the King arrived. He was accompanied by his shadow, Luigi Catania, and two tarts dressed as nurses. Perhaps they actually were nurses, though Malcolm said, 'I do not believe they are meant to concern themselves directly with medical issues.' There were so few people in the room that of course the King saw us. He left his party and came to our table. If it bothered Malcolm, he didn't show it. He accepted the King's perfunctory greeting, which could be attributed to the political tensions of the war, except that the King almost immediately kissed my hand and said, 'Good evening, Lady Cheyne. How lovely. May We offer Our congratulations on the birth of your daughter?'

He held onto my hand for an extra moment before releasing it. I know Malcolm saw it. How could he not? When the King spoke of Victoria, I thought I heard him say, 'The birth of our daughter.' There was no doubt about Victoria's paternity. A simple look at her, even in infancy, made that quite clear. Yet, when I first learned I was pregnant, I admit to a certain irrational fear running through me. What is now called 'birth control', a horrible, anti-septic term that always makes me squeamish, was certainly in use at the time. I had hardly gone to the Palace equipped with that sort of baggage and it wouldn't have surprised me if the King had never heard of it at all. There are a few things about my life I would change if I could, and one of them is the way I felt as the King was sliding his hand slowly down my fingers, so reluctant was he to let go. I once again felt the tingling spark I had known earlier. I believe that Malcolm was distracted by the King's bloated condition. Malcolm attributed it to the war and the King's failure to play a significant rôle while we continued to control North Africa, as if Farouk had indeed been removed to the Seychelles.

Before this night I had always thought that the King cut what the Italians call 'bella figura'. He certainly didn't lack for feminine comforts – the nurses were only the present example. When he kissed my hand and held it, he also caught my eye, and sent a clear message. I knew what had upset him so. That there had not been an encore past that day at Abdin, damaged the King. I do not mean he was hopelessly in love with me, in the manner of the Duke of Windsor and Mrs Simpson. If the King could not have me, he certainly could and did have plenty of others, many far more alluring than I. Nevertheless, something changed in him. He lost a part of his royal confidence. He grew grotesque, as if he were saying, 'I will justify her rejection. I am no longer worthy.' He spent those years chasing about like a mad fool, ever more corpulent, as if there were no war at all. I know how self-absorbed and grand it must sound to attribute the changes in the King's person to myself, but consider this: If any other woman had refused to see him as I had done, in similar circumstances, he would have forgotten the incident in no time. That did not happen. I remained with him, in his mind if not in his company, for many years. I know that is so because he lingered in mine.

Though Malcolm was looking forward to bringing our Egyptian tour to a conclusion as soon after the war as possible, we were not able to leave until 1946. He had been there as High Commissioner and Ambassador for thirteen years, the longest posting of his career. He had achieved the great treaty of 1936 and stayed on to see that full advantage was had. By war's end, he was a peer, Lord Broughton, and though he still retained an interest in India, independence for that country was on the horizon. As is well known, the King's cousin, and not Malcolm, was to be the last Viceroy.

Farouk was soon deposed and he began the exile for which the world knew him best. He went from fleshpot to gaming hall, from spa to night-club, skittering across the continent. I followed his exploits in the newspapers, though I did not discuss them with Malcolm, who I assumed read them as well.

A few years after Farouk lost the throne, Malcolm and I were in Paris on holiday and to meet Sarah and her fiancé, Edward Rathbone, who was with Coutts, posted in Paris. He was the son of a Foreign Office man, though to Malcolm's disappointment, Edward showed more interest in banking than diplomacy. Elizabeth, who was at school in Switzerland, had joined us for a few days. The younger children, Victoria and her brother, my greatest gift to my husband, his son Will, were at home in Scotland. The rest of us had gone, en famille, to Fouquet for dinner. Farouk was there when we arrived. He was at a large table with a soigné group that included the ever vigilant Luigi Catania. I did not recognise anyone else in his party, a flashy and oily bunch. The one similarity that

Malcolm and Farouk had, aside from their interest in me, was a taste for good restaurants.

As was his custom, Farouk sent champagne. Everyone in the dining room recognised him. Forks and knives seemed suspended as he made his way across the floor to our table. Malcolm made the introductions and thanked him for the wine. Farouk said little more to me than, 'Lovely to see you.' He kissed my hand, but in a quite perfunctory way that did not seem to upset Malcolm, nor cause any notice among the children. Then he was gone. Except he had put a note into my hand. I squeezed my fist so tightly that I dug my nails into my palm. I was more concerned that I might drop the note onto the table's snowy linen, than with what it might contain.

The King and his party did not stay to dine. Whether our presence played a part in that, I do not know. But he was soon gone, without a good-bye. The girls remembered him of course and were quite impressed, though they too were astonished by his weight. Sarah well recalled that wretched period when her father had tried to push her onto Farouk. She said nothing, and I'm quite sure she hadn't ever told Edward about it. He was quite taken with Farouk, remarking that though he'd had the privilege of meeting royalty on other occasions, he did not recall ever meeting a deposed Monarch. I excused myself to find a private corner where I might see what Farouk had written. Sarah got up with me and asked, 'Are you well?'

'Yes, of course.'

'You look a bit pale. Shall we go out? Take some air?'

'Not at all, darling. Thank you.' Then she followed me into the lavatory, where what with her hovering and the attendants offering towels and whatnot, I had to depart for one of the stalls to achieve any privacy at all. On a little card headed 'Farouk' he had written, 'We go to Monte tomorrow, le Train Bleu. Gare de Lyon at 21 h. I would love to see you, if only for a moment.' It was signed, 'F.'

I had thought I might just ignore it, but I could not. A better woman, a stronger one, might have permitted herself some little amusement at the presumption of it, but wouldn't have considered responding. I knew I might come to regret it, but I wanted to see him more than I wanted the assurance of domestic tranquillity. I knew I would put myself at risk again. The problem was not so much ethical as practical. I could hardly say to my family, 'I'm going out now, by myself, and shall return later.' My solution wasn't terribly imaginative, but it was sufficient. The next evening, I told Malcolm that I wasn't feeling well and he should take everyone to dinner and perhaps I would join them later. I might go out if I thought the air would do me good. I believe I added something about too much Parisian food, as if at this late date I had become one of the nervous English tourists that the French were certain we all were. The other issue was the hour. Malcolm never dined before eight. I urged him to take the girls and Edward for a cocktail at the Deux Magots, as Elizabeth, who had taken an interest in the arts, would doubtless find it romantic and she could hardly go there alone. We were at the Crillon, as usual. Off they went, across the river to St Germain, while I, miraculously arisen from my frailty, took a taxi to the Gare de Lyon.

That majestic old station with its enormous steel scaffolding was like the skeleton of a great cathedral. Through it, one came and went from the city in the grand manner, like, well, a king. The Blue Train ran from

Paris to the Riviera and was something past première classe. For Farouk, it must have been a comedown. He had grown up on private trains. For him, this must have been a bit like the way Malcolm had regarded the ferry from Southampton to Le Havre: public transport. The newspapers reported that Farouk was on the Blue Train often, shuffling between Paris and Monte Carlo. He could hardly be seated in a public carriage, no matter how grand.

The train was easily found in the welter of suburban rapides. It was splendid with its shining wooden carriages, each with the name of a city where it stopped, ever so briefly, in gold leaf on the side: Dijon, Lyon, Marseilles. At the conclusion of the train, was an unmarked carriage. Standing near were a pair of large men, dark and quite serious, surely still loyal members of the royal guard. Did Farouk think I would just knock on the door? I had no intention of doing that and was feeling a bit put out that he was not there to greet me. I had gone to some length to get here and now I felt abandoned, when, in that grating Sicilian accent, I heard the one voice out of Egypt that never failed to annoy. Luigi Catania, done up in a faddish costume that featured a foppish hat he may have thought stylish, said, 'Lady Cheyne. Good evening. Please come this way.' I nodded, but did not speak. What he said was perfectly civil, but from him it made me feel cheap, like one of the so-called nurses at the Turf Club.

In the carriage, Farouk was seated in a pale yellow chair. The curtains were drawn. I can recall a marquetry of flowers in a frieze that ran round the whole of the carriage, and I remember the yellow chair. I am sure Farouk simply hired the entire carriage then had the exterior markings removed and furniture installed. The décor is hazy, but the King is not. He rose laboriously and moved toward me, filling the carriage as he came, or so it seemed. He had grown so huge. What had shocked me at Fouquet seemed more extreme now, in this closer space.

'Good evening, Vera,' he said. I realised that he had rarely used my Christian name. When he was King, I was always Lady Cheyne and I called him sir, or perhaps Your Majesty. Now I was Vera, but I couldn't quite call him Farouk, though that was how I thought of him. I managed a simple hello.

'I am so glad you came.'

I sat next to him and he took my hand. I permitted it. It was comforting to me, though it was quite close in the carriage. Farouk saw that I was not entirely at ease. 'Forgive the circumstances,' he said, meaning the luxurious carriage. 'The fans begin when we move. I have no control.' He must have seen me glance at the curtains, because he said, 'If I open them, people gather to stare. It is even less pleasant than the temperature.' He knew how to be a king and nothing else. People everywhere gawked at him, not as a royal personage, but as a supernumerary to the royal world. It was difficult, I could see that. Royalty, even deposed royalty, has a serenity that may be a lie, but that permits equanimity no matter the circumstances.

'You are looking wonderfully well,' he said. 'I am looking, how shall we say, ample.'

I laughed at that and told him, yes, there certainly was a lot of him these days.

'I don't mind it, you know. It gives the cartoonists something to do.' In the newspapers at that time there were often drawings of him, a great ballooned monarch with a tatty little crown perched on his head. 'Do you mind my size?'

I did, of course. I found it frightening. 'It's harder to get used to you using the singular pronoun.'

'Oh, yes. I have abandoned the royal We as no longer appropriate. Occasionally, I slip up.'

I was weary of the small talk, when he changed the subject to something more personal.

'I often think of our times together, do you know that?'

'I'm not surprised. I do, too.'

'That last time at Abdin is etched in my memory.'

'I haven't forgotten.'

'A part of me wants to beg you to stay on this train, to go to Monte Carlo.'

I smiled at that, though we both knew it was impossible. 'I want to thank you for something,' I said. 'I'm sure you know what.'

'It is I who should be grateful.'

'It's about all that. About what we did.' I lost my way in the words. Farouk waited until I managed to say, 'You could have used it to your advantage. It might have benefited you.'

'It would have cost you terribly, I am sure.'

'Yes.'

'So how could I?'

'It meant a great deal to me that you didn't.'

We talked without ever quite naming it. As if even to say, 'You protected me from my husband at your own expense' was in itself a transgression. Also, by talking about it, but not quite, we assumed a kind of intimacy, a connexion that we no longer in fact had. I could again see the beautiful young man that I loved. Such a picture is of

course in the mind's eye only. I was in the presence of the
corporeal Farouk who was in such a grotesque state that
it made me feel at sea, separate from my life. As I sat in
that sweltering carriage, my thoughts may have been confused, but still, I could feel the past swallowing me. I
wanted to go with him to Monte Carlo. I wanted to follow him wherever he led. He and I were once again in
Cairo and our passion, the greatest I had ever known (forgive me, Malcolm) had returned. It made me light-headed with memory and desire.

The train began to rumble and the announcement
came that the Blue Train would soon leave the station.
That too was a measure of the difference in Farouk's life.
I could recall a time when no train left until he was ready.
I, with a commoner's sense of the power of schedules,
rose to leave. Farouk embraced me and kissed me. It was
a lover's kiss, but it had a practised quality to it that I did
not find attractive. He knew it. He always knew that sort
of thing about me.

'May I try again?' he asked with a wrinkled little smile.
Silence is the only assent to such a question. He brought
me to him, though there was so much of him that I felt
pressed against a great cushion of flesh. Then the kiss
itself came and the present dissolved and I was carried
back to when he really was lean and handsome and I was
young and careless. It was my first experience with the
power of memory to create a new present. I believe that
was the moment I left my youth behind me and became
an adult in a new way. The kiss was passionate, but I felt
no need to pursue its message. That is unlikely in youth
but quite pleasurable in maturity. As I left the carriage he
said, 'Adieu, Vera. I'm happy you were here. I remember
it all.'

I stepped down, back into the bustle of the station, and the train moved on, presumably with its cooling system engaged. I returned to the Crillon and my family and our life, hard-earned and treasured, the centre of everything for me. I never saw him again.

MR JAMES PEEL:

Epilogue

I didn't stay on in Egypt after the Abdin Incident. I wouldn't have minded, as I had developed quite an attachment to that country, but I was needed elsewhere. I had a good war with the RAF, first in London and then in the air over France and Germany. That is another story, for another time. By then, it was late for Empire. Communications between London and the outposts of the world were quicker now, and the very idea of a plenipotentiary seemed out of the past. Lord Broughton, as he then was, took a less active rôle in affairs of state and he and Lady Broughton spent more time in Scotland. I didn't speak to Vera for some years. As her husband grew infirm she wanted old friends to send greetings. She told me that Farouk's European exile and his gaudy travels made her husband bitter. He was then in his eighties. Vera has long been widowed, dividing her time between Scotland and London. We became if not friends again, at least civil to one another. As we got older I think we both saw that nothing would ever be for us as Egypt had once been.

Farouk died about a year after Lord Broughton. He was forty-five, the boy-king grown middle-aged at last. He was in a Roman restaurant, dining on lobster thermidor, with the latest in a line of voluptuous young women of dubious reputation. He lighted one of his Havana cigars and as he drew in the smoke, he seemed to disappear into a sort of reverie. His young companion was able to quote his words, though she didn't understand them. He said, in what she called a far-away voice, 'What did the wall say to the floor?'

'What?' she asked, 'What do you mean?'

He didn't answer, but he came out of his trance, kissed her on the throat and then grew pale. His left arm went stiff. He dropped the cigar and gasped for breath. No more words came out. He fell face first into the creamy remains of what was his last meal. A heart attack, the newspapers declared. Perhaps, but it was whispered under the arches at the Foreign Office that operatives of the colonels who had deposed him had been seen in the restaurant earlier that day. Old Titterington was long gone. He never found any poisons anyway. Perhaps Farouk finally did need his services. The colonels hated Farouk and they hated England. They abolished the monarchy, though Farouk's heir, Fouad II, lives on, a decent chap by all accounts, a businessman in Paris with dreams perhaps, but no likely plans to seek his birthright. The colonels felt neither colonialists nor kings should run the nation, but rather the people, which is what they believed themselves to be. It is the 'modern way' as Lord Broughton once put it, describing another, earlier period of political change. Perhaps the colonels and their successors are right, but it is also true that the country has seen a precipitous decline into zealotry since the days when

King Farouk and Sir Malcolm Cheyne battled so fiercely.

A question that has remained for me is just how valuable were those documents that I so nervously carried from Miriam Rolo to Sir Malcolm? Did they in any way hasten our victory in North Africa? Did they, even in an indirect way, help save any lives among the Sephardim? I pondered that for years until with time I came to understand that it doesn't matter. Wartime demands improvisation. It gives no answers save the final one: Who is the victor and who is not. I played the hand that I was dealt by war and circumstance as well as I was able. I have heard it said that old age is a museum of regrets. If it is so, then I have my share of exhibits there. As for my time in Egypt, my great school, I regret nothing.

I am long retired from a satisfying, if late starting, career in the City as a merchant banker. My grandchildren are grown, though they once enjoyed the stories of my Egyptian years. I have a great-grandchild now, my namesake. I do not know if he has yet started lighting fires. The old, the very ones who might best understand such adventures, are never told. I believe that is because the young think such desperate information will be the end of us. James, as he is called, is of an age when I can enchant him with my tales out of Egypt. It is a distant time, even to me, and to him, my granddaughter's son, a pink-faced English boy, the stories might as easily be of pyramids or pharaohs. His world is much different to the one I recall, but I see his eyes light when I tell him about the red roans, Sammy and Silvertail, and the way the young Prince greeted them each morning, and how he went to Woolwich to be a soldier and blew up a lorry at target practice. The approaching century will belong to him, just as the one that is now receding into history was mine.

Time past can be revisited by memory, and at my stage of life I am what my children call a frequent flyer to that place, with many miles to my account. I am glad to take any of them along, should they care to go. It is the only way it can be seen, because the Egypt that I and my distant friends once struggled for and cherished is gone.